White Raven

About the Author

Maggie Ritchie's novel, *Looking for Evelyn*, was shortlisted for the Wilbur Smith Adventure Writing Prize for Best Published Novel 2018. Her debut novel, *Paris Kiss* (2015), won the Curtis Brown Prize, was runner up for the Sceptre Prize, and longlisted for the Mslexia First Novel Competition. *Daisy Chain* was published by Two Roads/Hachette in 2021 following a Society of Authors funded research trip to Shanghai. Maggie graduated with Distinction from the University of Glasgow's MLitt in Creative Writing.

A journalist, she lives in Scotland with her husband and son.

White Raven

MAGGIE RITCHIE

For Michael and Adam

All rights reserved
Copyright ©Maggie Ritchie

The author's right to be identified as the author of this book under
the Copyright, Designs and Patents Act 1988 has been asserted.
The publisher thanks Creative Scotland for their
help in the publication of this novel.

ALBA | CHRUTHACHAIL

A CIP record for this book is available from the British Library.

ISBN: 978-1-917881-02-9

Printed on responsibly sourced paper
Cover image and design by Emily Benton.

Printed and bound in Great Britain by Bell and Bain Ltd, Glasgow

Prologue

The journalist's car wound through country lanes lined with hedgerows. She'd left the city far behind, and her shoulders dropped as green hills appeared, touched with gold in the mid-morning sun. Kirsty was on her way to interview one of the last surviving Glasgow Girls, artists who had been all but forgotten until their rediscovery in a 1988 exhibition at the Glasgow School of Art, curated by a feminist art historian. A quarter of a century after the exhibition that gave the Girls their name, ninety-three-year-old Rosie Anderson would be the star turn to open the latest show to feature their work. Kirsty found it interesting enough, but it was just another assignment to add to the ragbag of stories that crowded her mind. She'd forget Rosie Anderson once she'd seen her copy in print.

The artist's house was made of honey-coloured sandstone, mellowed like the hills by the early summer sun. The day was unusually warm for Scotland and Kirsty was taking off her jacket when the front door opened. Rosie

Anderson studied her visitor, as if reluctant to let her in. Kirsty had time to register sharp blue eyes and strong bone structure framed by jaw-length silver hair.

The journalist produced her warmest smile. 'Kirsty Greenwood, from the *Sunday Courier*. I'm here about the Kirkcudbright exhibition.'

The old woman's expression softened. 'Oh, yes, of course, I've been expecting you. Come away in. We'll start in my studio and then we can have a chat over tea.'

Kirsty followed the artist down a dark corridor. Rosie Anderson was wearing what looked like the kind of white flannel trousers men used to wear to play cricket and an old fisherman's jersey that had seen better days. Kirsty had been expecting a Paisley shawl, an embroidered peasant skirt, dangling earrings and long hair as more in keeping with her idea of a bohemian lady artist. She made a mental note of the details; it would be good colour for her feature.

The studio was tiny with barely room for an easel and a small table crammed with tubes of oil paints, jam jars of paint brushes, and some rags that filled the room with the sharp smell of turps. The only canvas on display was propped on the easel and showed a scowling young girl holding out painfully red palms.

'One of my former pupils at a rural school, the last one I taught at. There was a lot of poverty. She'd been given the strap for being late and wanted to show me the marks a brute of a teacher had left. She was late because she was the one who looked after the younger children at home and had been getting her little brothers and sisters ready for school. I tore a strip off that teacher, and he never hurt her again.'

Kirsty peered more closely at the painting, at the large, round slightly asymmetrical eyes somehow denoting a life of hardship and poverty, the hands looming large in the foreground. 'It reminds me of a Joan Eardley.'

'I suppose there are similarities, I met her in my first year before I had to leave to do my bit, but Joan had left art school by the time I went back after the war. There were a few of us mature students, my friend Margot Robertson was one of them. Glasgow School of Art – the Mack as we called it – was a wonderful place, buzzing with ideas brought over by refugees from Eastern Europe. It was an exciting time to be an artist, although Britain was a rather miserable place in those days, poor, shabby and broken, the future uncertain. But we art students could forget it all. It's a miracle the Mack wasn't bombed as it's on a hill and has all Charles Rennie Mackintosh's glorious mullioned glass windows. It was kept open during the war, you know. I suppose it was a show of defiance.' She righted the canvas with a tiny adjustment. 'We used to take turns on the roof at night looking out for German bombers. So dark, but when the moon was out, we could see the sleeping city spread out below us right down to the Clyde.'

Kirsty scribbled in her notebook. She set it down next to a carton filled with sketches. 'May I?'

'Look at anything you like.'

She flipped through landscapes in pastels and watercolours, recognising the hills she'd passed earlier. The pictures were unframed but backed with cardboard and protected by plastic, like the prints she'd seen for sale in galleries and museums. Kirsty's fingers stilled and she looked into the eyes of a young man. She took the charcoal portrait out of the box and studied it. He had striking looks: the high cheekbones and wide, full mouth of a Slav and a thick head of hair, a loose curl hanging over his forehead. He stared back at her with a fierce and challenging look.

Kirsty drew in her breath. 'This looks as if it was drawn with love.' Dragging her eyes from the portrait, she glanced at the artist. 'Who is he?'

Rosie took the sketch from her and traced the outlines of the man's face. 'He was my lover, a Russian. He was an intelligence agent in the 1950s, during the Cold War, right here in Scotland. He was a spy. And so was I.'

Kirsty picked up her notebook and switched on her recorder. 'Let's have that tea.'

When they were settled in the sitting room with its picture window looking onto the hills, the journalist was left alone on a sagging sofa with a photograph album while Rosie made the tea. As cups clattered and a kettle sang, Kirsty looked at black and white images from a different age and a different world. There was Rosie as a young woman on a beach, laughing in a group. She was the only one in trousers, the other women wore printed summer frocks with wide skirts, the men wore tweed jackets over open-necked shirts. Here was Rosie at work in her studio, her short hair tied back with a scarf like a female munitions worker in an old film. There was one picture of Rosie, arm-in-arm with another young woman, taken in front of a peculiarly ugly stately home that looked as if it had been put together from a jumble of mismatched architectural styles. Rosie came in and put a tea tray down on the coffee table and joined Kirsty on the sofa.

'That's me and Margot at Bletchley Park. I was a cryptographer, and a bloody good one; I helped crack the Enigma code.'

'I want to hear all about that as well, but mostly about being a spy.'

Rosie didn't answer while she poured the tea and Kirsty surreptitiously checked her tape recorder was on. The artist took the album off her lap and handed her a thin porcelain cup and saucer.

'I'm afraid I can't tell you anything more than that. It's ultra, you see.'

'Ultra?'

'Ultra secret. I signed the Official Secrets Act when they took me on at the Park.'

'But surely, after all this time, it doesn't matter.'

'I can tell you about day-to-day things, our routines and so forth, but not about the work I did at Bletchley Park or . . . after.'

Kirsty knew there was a whole shelf of books about women who had worked at the wartime codebreaking centre. The real story, her journalist's nose told her, was about spies and the Cold War being fought not in East Berlin by Cambridge men in raincoats, but right here in Scotland, and by a woman who was a respected artist.

'Isn't there anything you can tell me? How did you meet the man in the sketch?'

'I bumped into him, or his dog I should say. On the beach at Crail in the East Neuk of Fife. Lovely corner of Scotland – marvellous for seascapes.' She gazed out of the window, smiling.

Kirsty waited. 'The Russian.'

'Oh yes, he was setting up a Russian language school for National Servicemen, the brainy ones, of course. You've heard of Alan Bennett and Michael Frayn, I take it? And, oh now, what was his name? Sorry, at my age names can be elusive. Dennis someone, the one with the singing detective.'

'Dennis Potter?'

'Yes, him. Nice lads.'

'You met them?'

'Of course – they stood out because they became famous later, but thousands of conscripts went through various JSSLs, and hundreds at Crail. I forget what the letters stood for, but the camp was just outside the town. It had been a Navy base, I think.'

'Why were they teaching these men to speak Russian?'

Rosie Anderson turned her blue stare on Kirsty. 'My dear, you're a journalist, it was the fifties, Russia was a real threat.'

'How did you become a spy?'

The artist turned away. Kirsty saw at once that she'd made a mistake and gone in too hard too soon.

'I can't talk about any of that.'

'But you've already told me about, what did you call it?' She looked at her notes. 'The JSSL.'

'That's a matter of public record. The camp is still there, although it's nothing but abandoned buildings and huts.'

'Please, I'd love to know more about your Russian, er, boyfriend.'

'My lover.'

'Yes, your lover.'

'No. I've already told you no. I thought you were here to find out about the exhibition, about women artists who came out of the Glasgow School of Art.'

'Of course, we'll get to that in a moment. But your backstory, it's fascinating, and I'm sure it would draw more people to visit the exhibition and give the Glasgow Girls a higher profile.'

But Rosie would not be persuaded to talk about anything other than the upcoming exhibition. After trying every trick in the book, Kirsty realised she was up against the steel will of an elderly woman who had nothing to prove and nothing to lose. Finally admitting defeat, Kirsty stowed away her notebook in a soft leather handbag she'd bought to reward herself for the long hours she put in at the newspaper and got up to go. The artist walked her to the door. Kirsty turned to give it one last shot, but Rosie waved a papery hand and closed the door in her face.

Rosie Anderson watched the car drive away. Once it was out of sight, she went back to her studio and picked up the sketch that had caught the journalist's eye. She'd drawn it nearly sixty years ago, but her memories were as clear as if it had been yesterday. It had been a stormy day on the beach in Crail when she met the man who would change her life.

Chapter 1

1956, Crail, East Neuk of Fife, Scotland

Rosie dipped her paintbrush into the palette, mixing a little more cobalt blue for the sea into the grey she'd used for the sky. The waves shushed over the boulders and crept up the sand at Broome Bay while seagulls cried to each other as they swooped and circled above. It was spring but the wind whipping in from the North Sea made Rosie pull her woollen hat down over her ears and tuck the ends of her scarf around her neck. She'd thought spending the two-week Easter holiday in Crail would be a pleasant break from Edinburgh, where she was an art teacher at a private girls' school, but the cold seemed even more biting in the East Neuk of Fife.

She shifted her weight on the canvas stool, stretched her stiff back and looked out over the sea again. In that brief moment, the light had changed, and the water darkened, reflecting the gathering clouds. She dabbed her paintbrush into a blob of violet and mixed it with red and blue to make deep purple. That wasn't right, she needed a dark, brooding green. Rosie was searching in her battered leather satchel for the right tube of paint when a bundle of black fur seemed to come out of nowhere, knocked her off the stool and pinned her into the sand. Big brown eyes stared into hers and a wide, grinning mouth panted into her face.

'Boris! Get away from there, you idiot.' The sound of running was followed by the dog being yanked off Rosie by its collar. She squinted up at the man who stood over her. The sun was behind him, and his features were in shadow. He extended a hand and helped her to her feet. 'I'm terribly sorry. Are you hurt?'

She brushed the sand off the seat of her Oxford bags and pushed her hair out of her eyes. 'No, I'm all right. You might think about keeping your dog on a leash, though.' Standing, she was nearly as tall as he was. Rosie had been told her height, fair hair, blue eyes and rosy colouring had been inherited from her father. The man in front of her was her opposite, a photographic negative of dark hair, a deep tan that any sailor or fisherman would have been proud of, but she couldn't see his eyes in the shadow of the sailor's cap he wore. There was something familiar about him, but she couldn't place him.

He shrugged. 'It would be a shame to tie him up. Boris loves running free on the beach.' The man's stare was too bold, his features cat-like with high cheekbones and a wide, almost feminine mouth. Despite the apology, he didn't look or sound remotely abashed. A foreigner, then, but with no trace of an accent: pure BBC English. He glanced down at the dog, now sitting demurely at his feet gazing up in adoration, its tail leaving semi-circles in the sand. He grinned at the animal and ruffled its head. 'All the same, Boris, that was very ungentlemanly behaviour.'

A gust of wind made Rosie cross her arms. She was wearing an old army greatcoat over a thick Guernsey jumper and woollen trousers, but the snell wind cut through it all. The more he talked, the more convinced she became that she knew him from somewhere. But where? The stranger glanced up at the black clouds and back at Rosie. 'A storm's coming. You're going to get soaked if you stay out here.' He picked up her camp stool and put it under his arm. 'Pack up your things. One of the hotels in Crail has a semi-respectable lounge bar. You look frozen, a nip of whisky will warm you up.'

'I'm not in the habit of going for drinks with strange men I've just met on the beach, but I'm sure I recognise you. What's your name?'

'Forgive me,' he said, removing his cap to reveal a thick head of dark hair peppered with grey, and once again looking far from repentant. 'Aleksander Kuznetsov. Or Alex for those who can't get their tongue around the consonants.'

Now she remembered. Seeing him so out of context had thrown her. He was older now, but he looked much the same as he had then. Colonel Kuznetsov had cut quite the figure at Bletchley Park and had an impressive reputation, having single-handedly set up the anti-Soviet intelligence unit and convinced Churchill that Stalin, for all that he was their ally against the Germans, could not be trusted. Margot and Rosie, only eighteen and barely out of school, had developed a silly crush on Colonel Kuznetsov and had even learned the Cyrillic alphabet to write down idiotic romantic scenarios starring the dashing Russian in the privacy of the attic room they shared in their digs in town. She couldn't wait to tell Margot she'd met the object of their girlish fantasies more than a decade after they'd left Bletchley Park.

'We've never been introduced, but I know who you are.'

'And I know who you are, Rosie Anderson. You were at the Park.'

'I don't think we ever talked.'

'No, but I heard about your work – you cracked a German code that had defeated Alan Turing's hut.'

Rosie glanced at her feet, embarrassed by the compliment, but pleased. It had been her finest hour during a time that had been the best in her life so far, even better than her art school days. She looked up. 'You're Russian, obviously, with a name like that, and given the work you did at the Park.'

'Yes, but I pass as English as long as I don't tell anyone my surname. I was sent to boarding school when I was eight and soon had the Russian beaten out of me. Cambridge smoothed out any rough edges. Now, how about that nip of whisky?'

Another gust of wind threw a smattering of icy rain into Rosie's face, making her wince. 'A dram, you mean. You're not in Cambridge now.'

He scowled at the expanse of the North Sea, churning up under the vast grey sky. 'Don't I know it.'

Rosie's teeth had begun to chatter, and a warm pub and a drink sounded inviting. She shut the portable easel into its wooden case and picked up her bag of materials to follow him up the dunes. Alex strode ahead with the dog leaping beside him, careless of the wind and rain, while Rosie hunched her shoulders and walked behind him to get some shelter. Inside, the pub was warm from a peat fire and her wet coat steamed as she took it off and hung it on a hook. Alex dropped her camp stool at a table near the fire and went to the bar. Rosie sank gratefully into an armchair and warmed her hands on the glowing peat. The dog settled down next to her with a sigh and put its head on its paws.

The Russian came back with two whiskies and raised his glass. 'What brings you to this Godforsaken part of the world? I take it you don't live here.'

'Why? I could be a local.'

He looked at her thick jumper and man's trousers and she tried not to shift uncomfortably under his scrutiny. 'Not dressed like that you're not. And you don't sound like you were brought up in a fishing village clinging to the edge of the North Sea.' He leaned his head on one side as if listening. 'Scottish but with only a slight accent. You have clear, anglicised diction although with fewer diphthongs than an English person would, and there's a slight roll to your Rs. A city girl, I'd say, private school. Edinburgh?'

'Leave my Rs out of it, thank you very much.' She snorted at her own joke, emboldened by the whisky. He raised an eyebrow, and she straightened her face. 'You're half right, Henry Higgins, I'm Edinburgh by way of Glasgow. I moved east a few years ago to live with my mother.'

A memory of her tiny Garnethill flat near Glasgow School of Art came to mind and she tried to push it away before others followed, but it was too late. There was Frank pulling her back into bed and his arms as she tried to get ready to go to her studio in the Mack. But the affair had turned sour, and she had worked hard to put it behind her, moving back in with Mother in Edinburgh and taking a teaching job that kept her too busy to dwell on the past. Rosie glanced at her ringless finger. She didn't believe in conventional ideas about marriage, but now she was in her mid-thirties and childless, she knew some people considered her an old maid and looked on her with pity. Rosie told herself she didn't care. Still, she made herself look away from women pushing prams or trailing small children. At St Leo's, the girls were older, and it was easier not to think that her childbearing years had been taken from her. The depths of pain and humiliation that followed her affair with Frank had dwindled over time, but the exhilarating highs had gone too, and she had been bored and restless for a while now. Teaching should have been enough, even though the headmistress and the board of governors had placed art lessons at the bottom of the pile. The occasional bright spark of a pupil would illuminate Rosie's days, but she was tired and ground down by the demands and routine of teaching, the hours marked by jarring bells. Preparing lessons and marking work took up so much time and energy that she spent less and less time on her own painting. She'd booked this fortnight in Crail in the hope of reigniting the fire that had once burned inside her. Perhaps another type of fire was being relit. She'd more or less given up on men – there had been a few who had been interested but they were usually married, or she wasn't interested in them. Maybe this strange encounter would lead to something different, and she had been fated to meet Alex all these years later, on a beach in Fife. Rosie looked up from her drink and saw he was studying her and she blushed, even though there was no way he could have read her thoughts.

'What about your father?' he said. Rosie frowned, having lost the thread of their conversation. 'You said that you live with your mother in Edinburgh. What about your father?'

'Oh.' She swirled her whisky in its glass, glowing amber in the reflected flames. 'He died when I was little, a boating accident in Shanghai. I was born there, moved back to Scotland when I was five.'

'Yes, I remember reading your file. I was on one of the panels that vetted you for the Park.'

'My uncle Ned took us in, my mother and me. He's not really my uncle, not by blood anyway.'

Alex frowned. 'How did you become an artist?'

'My mother's an artist. Perhaps you've heard of her? Lily Crawford? She's quite well known.'

'No, but I know your uncle Ned, or Sir Edward Raeside as he is now.'

Rosie gave him a sharp look. 'Really, I know Scotland is a small country, but how could you possibly know Ned?'

'We worked closely together during the war; he was a bit of a mentor to me in those days.'

It made sense, Rosie thought: Ned had worked at Bletchley Park in a senior position, and it was he who had put her name forward as a decoder, said her artistic eye was good at discerning patterns. He worked mostly in Whitehall, but the top people at the Park would have reported to him, and Alex was highly regarded, heading up his own unit. Rosie was gratified that he had remembered her – and how she'd broken a code that had foxed even the great Alan Turing's hut. Rosie took another sip of her whisky and felt it warming her. She had never talked to Alex at the Park, but that wasn't unusual as more than ten thousand people worked there throughout the war and they were under strict orders not to talk about their work and huts usually kept to themselves at meal times. But Alex was a well-known figure and held in high esteem by the top brass – and by many of the women at the Park. His good looks hadn't done him any harm, and his aloofness gave him an enticing air of mystery. Rosie felt an affinity towards this man, who reminded her of those heady days when she was part of something bigger, the race to defeat the Nazis. He didn't seem at all like a stranger, and he knew her teasing, affectionate uncle, was perhaps even a close friend of his. The thought of Ned made her smile. A former High Court judge, he had worked for the government since the war.

'That's better, the whisky has put some colour into your cheeks,' Alex said. 'You could almost pass as attractive. A pearl amongst the fishwives of Crail.'

'I'm not sure if there's a compliment in there.'

'I don't approve of flattery, empty words to charm fools. It's not in the Russian nature. We are a simple lot and say what we mean, from the heart.' He pounded his chest and Rosie tried not to roll her eyes. 'We're not mealy-mouthed like the British.'

'What you call mealy-mouthed we call good manners. Are you quite sure all your rough edges were smoothed off?'

'Perhaps not, but I don't much care what impression I make.'

'Well, that's obvious.' Rosie leaned forward. 'Why don't you stop asking me so many questions and tell me what a Cambridge-educated Russian is doing in this out of the way corner of Scotland and why it's no coincidence that you happened to bump into Ned Raeside's niece?'

Alex swallowed the rest of his drink and stood up. 'Come with me and I'll show you.' He held out his hand and she found herself taking it and following him. Boris scrambled to his feet and trotted after them.

Outside, a jeep was waiting for them, the driver a man dressed in an approximation of an RAF uniform with a woollen scarf knotted around his neck and a cricket jumper worn under his leather aviator jacket. He jumped out of the jeep and stowed Rosie's things in the back.

Taking off his cap to reveal a mess of tow-coloured hair, he smiled at Rosie. 'I see Alex found you.' He put out his hand and Rosie took it, bewildered. 'Cosmo Montgomery, at your service, but everyone calls me Monty.'

'Like the Field Marshal?'

He grinned. 'Yes, but without the Desert Rats.'

'Not Russian, then?'

'Well, only half. My dear old mama is from St Petersburg.'

'You mean Leningrad.'

'I most certainly do not.' He helped her into the jeep. 'Sit up front with me and bugger-lugs can sit in the back with the Hound of the Baskervilles. All right, Alex? Cheer up, old thing, I know you'll miss the bright lights of Crail but duty calls.'

They roared out of the fishing village, leaving behind the slate houses, some of them bare stone, others painted cottage-white, but all with the distinctive red pantile roofs and gables of east coast harbour towns. The jeep raced into the open countryside and Rosie hugged herself, wishing she hadn't left her jacket back at her digs. Monty, like Alex, didn't seem to feel the cold. He kept up a steady flow of cheerful nonsense, most of which was lost in the wind that howled about the jeep. They rattled at full speed towards big steel gates and a weathered sign reading 'Naval Air Station HMS Jackdaw', but it was a soldier in army-issue khaki who leaped out of the sentry box and let them in. Monty gave him a cheery wave instead of a salute and they barrelled on past an airfield, control tower, huts and barracks, before screeching to a halt before a long, low building with rows of windows. Rosie jumped down before Monty could come round to help her. Alex climbed out more slowly and leaned against the bonnet, with Boris landing with a thump at his feet. Rosie came to stand beside Alex, and he nodded at the rather ugly building.

'There it is, not much to look at,' he said when she joined him. 'No graceful quads and dreaming spires, but the JSSL offers a finer education than you'd get at any university. Just like at Bletchley Park, we have some of the brightest minds here from all walks of life and from all over the country. An agile mind is valued over brute strength or your background. Everyone is bent to one task. A true meritocracy.'

'What does JSSL stand for?'

'Sorry, force of habit. You'd think we'd all be sick of acronyms since the war. It's the Joint Services School for Linguists. We've just moved lock, stock and barrel from Bodmin, from one bleak end of this damp island to the other. Didn't think we could get any more remote than Cornwall, but here we are.'

'And what happens here? Or is that Need to Know?'

'We teach Russian to clever young men, National Service conscripts.'

Through an open window, Rosie could hear a bad-tempered voice, a woman with a heavy accent shouting: 'You are murdering my mother tongue, you fools! Gogol would strangle you with his bare hands if he could hear you. Again, all of you, but this time I want to hear the dark L and no gargling your Rs, we're not speaking French.' A chorus of male voices boomed in Russian.

Rosie turned to Alex. 'This whole base, it's a Russian language school?' He nodded. 'Interesting, but why have you brought me here?'

He ignored her question and held open the door. 'Come into the teachers' mess and meet Valentina. She's the one you've just heard berating those poor chaps.' He looked at his watch. 'Class should be nearly over.'

Chapter 2

Valentina Nazarova knew how to make an entrance. In faded black velvet and trailing a silk scarf, she collapsed into a worn armchair in the teachers' mess and put a weary hand over her eyes. With the other she waved towards the samovar on a table in the corner.

'Someone get me glass of tea before I kill myself.' Unlike the two men, she had a thick, guttural accent that seemed to come straight out of the Urals, and it soon became clear that she had been unable – or disinclined – to master the English definite and indefinite articles. Rosie's fingers itched for a piece of charcoal to capture the other woman's striking looks, her deathly pale skin, high cheekbones, bee-stung lips and dark eyes that seemed to be filled with centuries of sadness. Monty leaped up and Valentina called after him. 'Don't be stingy with the jam, Kusima, rationing is over.' She reached into a threadbare embroidered evening bag for a cigarette holder, extracted a cigarette from a gold case, broke it in two and inserted one half into the tortoiseshell holder and stowed the other back in its case. Monty handed her a glass of black tea in a silver holder. He looked inquiringly at Rosie and mouthed 'Tea?' but before she had a chance to reply, Valentina tapped him on the back of his hand with a long, painted nail and he lit her cigarette. The Russian woman inhaled deeply, closed her eyes and coughed. 'Stinking Craven A! How I long for smooth, rich Sobranie.' She settled back in the chair and studied Rosie through a cloud of smoke.

'So, you're artist? Good to have another woman in this den of wolves and pigs. But with this haircut and clothes,' she gestured at Rosie with a languid hand, taking in her short hair, trousers and fisherman's jersey, 'they will leave you alone.'

'Valentina, play nice,' Alex said.

She ignored him and beckoned Rosie over, who was irritated and intrigued in equal measures, before deciding she was amused rather than offended by Valentina's sharp eyes and sharper tongue. After going through the war and working among so many eccentric characters at Bletchley Park, she was unfazed by this creature's rudeness. Rosie took the cigarette holder from her hand and inhaled. Valentina wasn't to know she didn't smoke. She breathed out a plume of the acrid smoke and handed back the cigarette to Valentina, who shifted her eyes to Alex. Satisfied she had discomfited the other woman, Rosie sat down across the room from her and spread her arms along the back of the tatty sofa and looked at each of the three Russians in turn.

'Tell me what I'm doing here and why you all seem to know who I am.'

Valentina let a long end of ash drop onto the floor. 'It's small town and not much gets past Sasha,' she said, using the Russian pet name for Alex. 'He is always skulking in the shadows and turning up unexpectedly. You're like vampire, aren't you, darling? Very handsome vampire.' She smirked at Rosie. 'Dream boat – that's what girls in village call him.'

Alex ignored her. 'We need an art teacher for the summer to give the troops a break. The language classes are intense with long hours of grammar, spoken Russian, listening and reading comprehension, and learning reams of fiendishly technical vocabulary. The conscripts are a clever lot and studious with it, but they can only take so much military jargon and dense Russian literature. They've set up a musical group and a theatre company under their own steam, as well as the usual chess club and card schools, but they need to do something physical, with their hands and eyes, to give their overheated brains a rest. I'm afraid our intellectuals aren't too keen on square bashing and not one of them can change a plug, so metal and woodwork are out of the question. Art classes would take the men out of themselves, stop them thinking so much.'

Rosie was reminded of the plays and concerts that had been put on at Bletchley Park, and how spirits had been lifted out of the fug of anxiety over the war for those few hours, so she understood what Alex was driving at. She'd set up a small art school with the director of the Courtauld and overseen classes with him. The Park had been exhausting but it had been stimulating to be surrounded by some of the best analytical and creative minds in the country. And Alex was right – it didn't matter what class you were or, more importantly for her, whether you were a woman or a man – all that mattered was how quickly you could break the Germans' codes. They had been the best days of her life and nothing since had lived up to them. Perhaps here, in this strange little corner of Scotland with these odd Russians, she could recapture that sense of purpose, of making a difference and of being at the centre of a moving world. But even though Alex could vouch for Valentina and Monty, she had only just met them, and everything was happening too quickly.

'Let me get this straight. I'm to teach the language students art to give their brains a rest?' Rosie stood up. 'I should be getting back to Crail, if you wouldn't mind arranging for transport – or I can walk.'

Monty sprang away from the samovar and brought her a NAAFI-issue enamel mug of tea. 'At least stay for a cuppa – I've even put in a drop of milk and there's sugar in the spoon, not jam. Allow me to apologise for Alex. He can be rather abrupt. Poor fellow doesn't know how to talk to women, you see. All those years at a single sex school, then

Cambridge surrounded by men who are frankly terrified by the fairer sex. His doting parents spoiled the little prince, and there wasn't a sister or even an aunt or female cousin in sight to soften his rudeness, so you see, he didn't stand a chance of becoming a charmer like me.' He preened his moustache and Rosie had to laugh. 'That's better.' He led her back to her seat. 'You would be doing us – and your country – a great, great service, if you would consider sharing your considerable artistic gifts with our chaps, who are quite civilised in the main, no matter what Valentina says.' He glanced at Valentina, who turned her head away. 'What do you say? Won't you join our merry band?' Monty had struck the right chord with Rosie; a call to duty never failed to win her over. But she was puzzled by the whole set up.

'I don't understand why you're teaching all these conscripts Russian.'

'I'd think that's pretty obvious. Because of the threat of another war, of course,' Alex said.

Rosie glared at him, rankled by his gruffness. 'I'm not sure I believe all those stories about Reds under the bed, let alone that they're about to declare war so soon after the last one. Besides, a lot of my friends at art school in Glasgow were communists – they don't call it Red Clydeside for nothing. They were fighting for the rights of the workers to have better pay and safer conditions. And don't we owe the Russians? They were our allies during the war after all.'

'It's true that Russia fought bravely alongside the allies, and that we could not have defeated Hitler without them, but that alliance is gone and the balance of power teeters between the West and the Soviet Union. We need to be ready for the next war with translators and intelligence officers fluent in Russian.' Alex paused in front of the window and looked out over the barracks. 'Stalin may be gone, but Communism is more of a threat than ever.'

Monty got to his feet with a sigh and spoke to Valentina. 'I'm afraid Alex is off on his hobby horse. Valentina and I are only here to earn a shilling and stay out of trouble.' He held out his hand and Valentina took it. 'Come on, old girl, we'll leave them to it. Let's go and find you a drink or two – I've still got some vodka in my billet.' With a last poisonous look at Rosie, Valentina left with Monty.

Once they were alone, Alex reached inside his jacket and pulled out a map, which he unfolded and spread on the floor before Rosie. It showed Scotland, marked with red crosses. 'Since the end of the war, I've been working with your uncle and the Americans to set up a listening network around Scotland – SIGINT or signals intelligence to give its full name – to intercept foreign communications and monitor the movement of Soviet submarines. The race is on between the Russians and the USA to build nuclear-powered subs that can fire nuclear missiles at each other's shores without having to resurface to refuel. Scotland, sitting bang in the middle of Iceland, Greenland and

Britain, is all that stands between a Soviet stealth attack through the Northwest Passage.'

Rosie studied the map. Most of the red crosses were in the far north, with one in Shetland. 'Why are telling me all this? It must be classified information.' She pushed the map away from her and Alex put it back in his pocket.

'We monitor the comings and goings to and from Crail for security reasons. I spotted your name, made the connection with Bletchley Park. You were thoroughly vetted and signed the Official Secrets Act. I contacted Sir Raeside and got the go-ahead to approach you. He told me you help him with his work and that I can trust you.'

Ned's elegant town house in Charlotte Square had been the perfect place for Rosie to recover from her failed love affair with Frank. Ned had not let her wallow and put her to work transcribing the awful scrawl of his handwriting and turning the turgid legalese he favoured into plain English and documents fit for the eyes of civil service mandarins. Most of it was unintelligible, filled with coded language, but there were sensitive communiqués about defence policy and sometimes she would sit back and read on, absorbed.

Alex sat back in his chair and waited while Rosie mulled over his request. It was the chance for another adventure, but she wasn't sure she still had the appetite for it. At Bletchley the adrenaline of racing against the clock to decipher enemy messages had kept her going through the long hours, punishing shifts and broken sleep, but it had been exciting to know that she was playing a vital part in saving lives. Alex was watching her carefully, and she assumed there would be more to her role here than teaching art classes.

'If I agreed, when would you need me to start?' she said.

'As soon as you can.'

Rosie thought of St Leo's, of the days stretching ahead, one after the other, term after term, year following year, the routine only broken by weekends and school holidays. But this opportunity for change had come about so suddenly, and she had learned at the Park to control her eagerness to act on impulse. She would have to put in a call to Ned.

'How long would you need me?'

'For the summer, but you could start tomorrow as far as I'm concerned.'

'I have to be back for summer term. I can't just up and leave the school in the lurch. And after that, well, I'll have to think about it.'

'You can let me know.' He looked at his watch. 'I've a meeting with the CO. I'll get Monty to take you back to Crail.' Outside, Alex strode away without saying goodbye as Monty helped Rosie into the jeep.

Monty shook his head. 'I apologise for my friend. He has the manners of a baboon. To make up for it, can we tempt you with a night on the tiles in the fleshpots of Crail?'

She laughed. 'What fleshpots?'

'Well, there aren't many, I admit.' He ticked them off on his fingers. 'There are three deathly hotel bars, their only saving grace a seven-day licence to sell bad whisky and warm beer, one of which Alex has already inflicted on you. Then there's the Haven, if your fancy turns to a cream tea, and last but certainly not least, the Music Box, the *ne plus ultra* of decadent entertainment worthy of Weimar Berlin.'

Rosie laughed. 'I think I've walked past it. It's a café, a perfectly ordinary one.'

'By day, yes, but on a Friday night it comes alive to the sound of our very own jazz band, the Siberian Salt Sifters. We're all going – Alex, Valentina and yours truly, and you'll meet some of the students too. It's always great fun. What do you say?'

Rosie contemplated an evening spent alone in her room reading. The alternative was spending time with these intriguing new people. There was no contest.

Monty beamed at her. 'Splendid! Alex will pick you up at seven.'

Chapter 3

Rosie was clipping on her favourite diamond and emerald earrings when the throaty growl of an engine made her look out the window. Alex, astride a motorbike, waved at her to come down. After a last hurried look in the mirror to check her lipstick and smooth her favourite green satin dress with its fashionably nipped in waist and wide skirt, Rosie slipped on her heels, thankful she'd made a last-minute decision to pack one presentable outfit, and ran down the stairs.

When she opened the door, Alex stared at her. 'What happened to the crazy lady artist in her mannish attire?'

'Don't worry, she's still here, although I had a job persuading her out of brogues and into heels.'

'Well, you're a lot easier on the eyes this way. You'll be the belle of the Music Box. You'd better watch out for the young fishermen; they'll be eyeing you up like a prize turbot. Climb aboard my trusty steed and I'll deliver you safely to your prospective admirers.'

Rosie sat behind Alex, careful not to touch him. But when the motorbike lurched forward, she grabbed onto his waist. He was wearing a leather jacket that was so worn it was soft against her cheek. The wind had dropped, and the evening was mild. As they passed the harbour, Rosie looked out over the calm sea. The dying sun cast copper reflections onto the water and turned the clouds into peach confections. When Alex stopped the bike and switched off the engine, she was sorry the short ride was over. Once inside the café they were greeted with a blast of Brubeck, the musicians nearly hidden by the smoke from the cigarettes hanging from their lips. There was a gleaming Italian coffee machine on the counter, hissing and gurgling away like a miniature steam engine over the chatter. At the jukebox, two local girls in poodle skirts and twinsets were being chatted up by a couple of linguists. The tables were crammed with men from the camp, freed from their uniforms, their spirits high as they talked among themselves or to young Crail women squeezed in between them. Rosie heart sank as she realised that she was overdressed. No wonder Alex's compliments had held an edge of mockery. She hesitated at the doorway, wishing she hadn't come, until Monty rose from a table in the corner and called them over with a grin. He pulled out a chair for her and whistled in admiration.

'I say, what a smasher! I hope Alex behaved himself on the way over. I know I would have been tempted to ride off into that glorious Scottish sunset with you.'

'Shut up, Kusima, and spare Rosie your idiotic compliments,' Valentina said. 'You'd think you were French, not noble-born Russian.' She looked Rosie up and down with narrowed eyes. 'You're embarrassing her. It's worse to be overdressed than underdressed. Imagine wearing cocktail dress in this dump.' She picked up the satin hem of Rosie's skirt. 'This shade of green was the height of fashion in Paris . . .' Rosie brightened before Valentina dropped the material '. . . two seasons ago.' The Russian woman's painted mouth twisted into a smile. 'But I don't expect you to know much about fashion in Scotland, such provincial backwater, don't you agree, Sasha?' He ignored her until she poked his arm. Her manicured nails were painted the same blood red as her lips. 'Sasha! Get me drink before I die of thirst.'

Rosie tried to ignore Valentina's barbs and turned to watch the band. She'd seen girls at St Leo's be catty to each other but had never been at the receiving end, not since she was a young girl, anyway, and she was damned if she was going to play the victim now. She realised that far from being cowed back at the base, Valentina had only withdrawn temporarily before re-opening hostilities. She heard Monty clear his throat.

'Don't mind her, Rosie, she's in one of her vile moods. I beg your pardon, may I call you Rosie, or is that awfully impertinent of me?' Monty pulled a winsome face and she laughed. On the other side of the table, Alex and Valentina were talking in Russian. Ignoring their bad manners, Rosie turned her attention back to Monty who was now flirting with the waitress. He waited until she had put down their coffees and left before bringing out a hip flask and tipping its contents into their cups.

'Bottoms up!' he said with a wink.

Valentina took a greedy gulp and winced. 'Cognac – more French nonsense. We should be drinking vodka.'

'Bit hard to come by in Fife, unless you're at Kate's Bar in St Andrews,' Alex said. 'She always has a stash of Polish vodka for thirsty Russians and Poles who manage to escape Crail, even managed to get hold of slivovitz for the Yugoslavs and Czechs. I don't know why you have it in for the French, Valentina, you were brought up in Paris after all. And weren't your adopted parents French?'

'They treated me like dog.' She turned to Rosie. 'I was in state orphanage. My real parents, I don't know what happened to them. The bitch nurses told me my mother didn't want me, that she didn't know who my father was. They called her a *kurva*. How do you say this in English?'

'A working girl is the polite version,' Monty said.

Valentina ignored Monty. 'So, these bitches in the orphanage, they think to make money from me. When I'm six they sell me to rich French couple, who say they long for a child they cannot have.' She spat. 'Lies! They wanted a servant they did not have to pay. A little serf who would clean up after them and their spoiled brats.'

'They already had children?' Rosie said.

'Yes, it was all filthy lies they told the orphanage, not that they cared. I lived off scraps, like you would give a pig. They beat me, and when I got older, their ugly son got me alone in the kitchen one night, said as I was daughter of a *pute* I should service him the same way. I took the kitchen knife and cut him here in his . . .' She pointed to the back of her ankle. 'What is this called?'

'The Achilles tendon,' Rosie said faintly.

'Then I ran away, but he couldn't run after me.' She smiled triumphantly and tossed her hair. 'That is why I hate the French.' She spat on the floor again, narrowly missing Monty's shoe. He rolled his eyes at Rosie, who was staring at Valentina, open mouthed.

'Put a sock in it, old girl. We're here to cut a rug, not listen to your sob stories.'

Valentina shot him a furious look. 'Take care, Kusima, you know what happens when I lose my temper.' She turned her chair to face the band, so her back was to the other three, a vulture with its black feathers ruffled.

Chilled, Rosie leaned towards Monty and whispered, 'What happens when she loses her temper?'

'Fire comes out of her nostrils and she flies off in a mortar and pestle like Baba Yaga, another terrifying Russian witch,' Monty drawled.

Rosie couldn't believe he could make jokes about Valentina's horrible past. She glanced at Alex and thought she saw his mouth twitch, but he straightened his face. 'You shouldn't tease Valentina, Monty. Stop showing off in front of Rosie.'

Monty picked up his cup and drained it. He wiped his moustache with a neatly folded handkerchief. 'You're no fun, Alex, always so serious. Rosie will think us a dull trio.' He turned a mischievous smile on her. 'Do you? Are we?'

Valentina was now in conversation with the waiter and guffawed at something he said. Rosie relaxed, the Russian woman was obviously not upset any more. She smiled at Monty. 'I don't think you're dull at all. In fact, you're the most interesting people I've met . . .'

'How wonderful!' Monty preened.

'. . . in Crail.'

He pretended to look crestfallen. 'Oh, well, I suppose I asked for that.' He stared gloomily into his cup. 'I think I'll have another drop of that brandy. Rosie has scored a direct hit and I'm in need of some first aid.'

The evening passed quickly. Every now and then one of the linguists would come up to their table and say hello but would then beat a hasty retreat, frightened away by Valentina's poisonous glares.

'It's bad enough we have to teach *kursanty* without being forced to fraternise with them after work,' she snapped in a billow of smoke that did indeed make her look like a sulphurous witch.

'That's what the students are known as, *kursanty*. It's Russian for language cadets,' Monty explained to Rosie. He turned back to Valentina who was applying another waxy layer of crimson lipstick. 'You might be a bit friendlier to them, old girl. They're decent chaps, and I don't think they like being stuck out here any more than we do.'

Valentina snorted delicately through her perfect nose. 'Oafs and peasants, every one of them. They bastardise our beautiful language with their idiotic pronunciation. Most of them don't even speak French, just their yak yak yak English. Imagine speaking only one language. Philistines!'

'You might remember that we're the outsiders here, not them,' said Monty, giving Valentina more brandy. 'The Brits took our families into their country after we hightailed it from Russia, and they have given our countrymen and women these teaching jobs.'

'For which we slave for pittance, less than you would pay a servant.'

Monty shook his head. 'Drink up, old girl, and cheer up for Pete's sake. Most people liven up with a drink inside them, but not you.'

Valentina shook her head mournfully. 'I can't, I'm sad now Alex made me think about the orphanage and how I was taken away from Russia. I can never go back now to find my real mother because of the bloody Bolsheviks.' She bent her head for a moment and Rosie thought she might be crying. But when Valentina straightened up, her eyes were dry. Just then the band started playing a lively Russian folk song. Valentina swept back her dark hair and gripped Alex's arm. 'Dance with me, Sasha.' When he shook her off, she flashed her eyes at Monty. With her face no longer twisted with disdain, she looked like a beautiful, mournful raven. 'What about you, Kusima?'

Monty stood up and took her hand. 'Good idea, let's knock all this dreary talk about the past on the head and have a dance.' He signalled to some of the men and tables were pushed back. In the cleared space, Valentina was transformed into a whirling dervish, scarves flying, while Monty kicked and crouched like a Cossack. Soon everyone in the café was clapping along and shouting their encouragement. Even the local teenagers joined in. When the band took a break, a red-faced Monty led Valentina back to the table and someone put Elvis Presley's 'Heartbreak Hotel' on the jukebox.

'I love this song,' Rosie said.

Alex stood up and held out his hand, ignoring Valentina, whose face was like thunder. 'Would you care to dance, Rosie?'

'Are ye askin'?'

He looked confused. 'Of course, I'm asking. Didn't you just hear me?'

She laughed. 'It's what they say in Glasgow dance halls

– the man says, *are ye dancin'* and the woman replies, *are ye askin'*. As if they don't really care one way or the other.'

'I'll never understand the Scots.'

Rosie took his hand and stepped into his arms. 'We're a queer lot, it's true. We're backwards at coming forwards but we're always ready for a fight or a laugh, depending on the mood we're in, and how much drink's been taken.' Rosie was rewarded with another twitch that Alex tried to suppress, but the smile reached his eyes and she felt as if she'd scored a small victory.

'Not so different from the Russians, then,' he said. Elvis's voice picked up speed and urgency and Alex spun her around and brought her neatly into his arms again. He was a good dancer, moving fluidly and confidently, in control of their movements without pushing her around or standing on her feet. He drew her close. 'Heartbreak Hotel is what the *kursanty* call the camp. Not because they hate the place – it's seen as a cushy posting – but because of the émigrés who teach them. They will never see their homeland again, and like Valentina, mourn what is lost. You mustn't think too badly of her, she's had a hard life, like many of us exiles.'

Rosie searched his face and saw sadness for a moment. The jukebox played on, one hit after the other, and they danced to Frankie Laine, more Elvis, Louis Armstrong, more Elvis – someone was a big fan – and when The Platters sang 'Only You', Alex's arm tightened around her, and she allowed herself to lay her head on his shoulder. All too soon the song was over, and the band came back on, playing freeform jazz. Alex looked at her inquiringly, but Rosie only laughed and shook her head. As soon as they sat down at the table, Valentina stood up and kicked her chair out of the way and imperiously gestured Monty to come to the dance floor, displaying the behaviour of a queen bee used to being the centre of attention in a group of men. Rosie glanced at Alex and caught him looking back at her. He picked up his chair and moved it closer and put his arm around the back of her chair. Out of the corner of her eye, she saw Valentina dancing, her slender body jerking and twisting in time to the complicated rhythms. Monty danced as if he were a beatnik, a cool cat on the prowl in an avant-garde Paris nightclub, playing it for laughs.

Much later, breathless and laughing, they piled out onto the deserted street at closing time. Monty helped a rather unsteady Valentina into the jeep, and the pair drove off with one of his cheery waves. Rosie found herself alone with Alex. They walked down to the harbour's edge. The stars were bright in a clear sky now, the clouds of that morning had gone, and a full moon drew a silver path across the dark sea.

'It's peaceful now, but in a second the weather could change,' Alex said. 'Like peace. After two world wars, we've learned it is all too fragile. The Soviets want to destroy our way of life, everything we've salvaged from the last war.'

Rosie shivered in the chill air, and he took off his leather jacket and put it around her shoulders. She could feel the heat from his body and pulled it closer. The boats in the small harbour moved with the swell, their halyards clanking in the gentle swell. Alex gazed beyond them out to the open sea, where it stretched out darkly to the east. 'There could be a Soviet sub out there now, patrolling the deeps. They don't have nuclear missiles yet and can't reach America, but we're in the frontline here. We have to be vigilant, make sure things don't escalate the way they did in '14 and '39. This time, both sides have the A-bomb.'

Rosie shivered again, but this time not from the cold. It seemed that everyone, everywhere, lived in fear of the atomic bomb and what it would bring – the end of the world. She couldn't forget the photographs of the obliterated cities of Hiroshima and Nagasaki, and the survivors with their horrific scars. She had picked her way through bombed out London during the war, but nothing could compare with the devastation wrought by nuclear war. In a recurring nightmare, she watched, helpless, as a mushroom cloud bloomed in the sky before everything turned blinding white. Rosie knew the girls at school shared her dread as she was often asked about the A-bomb, and what would happen if they were attacked. She had tried to reassure them, but her words had sounded hollow to her own ears. The last war had been a long and arduous struggle for civilians, but there had been hope even in what Churchill described as 'our darkest hour'. This threat of the world's annihilation was different – intangible but all the more terrifying in its completeness. Rosie looked out to sea and tried to imagine an enemy submarine nosing its way through the black waters, armed to the teeth with deadly nuclear warheads.

Alex turned her to face him, his voice urgent now. 'We need to stop this insane escalation before it's too late. Will you help me?'

The wind picked up and Rosie took a step closer to him and searched his face. Her throat was dry. 'What can I do other than keep the troops' minds off their Russian studies with a few life classes? I'm afraid you're overestimating the power of art.'

He put a gentle hand under her chin. 'If you agree to join us, you'll see. I can't tell you any more than that just now.' He dropped his hand and Rosie caught her breath. She was right: there was more to this than teaching a bunch of conscripts the rudiments of art.

Chapter 4

For the rest of her Easter holiday in Crail, Rosie spent the days painting and sketching, inspired by the stormy skies and restless sea, the waves clashing and fighting each other to fling themselves at the rocks. Filled with a white-hot energy she hadn't known since her early days at art school, her pencil flew across the pages as she captured fishermen landing their catch down at the harbour among seagulls fighting for scraps on the slick cobbles. The birds' cries mingled with the raucous laughter of the fishwives on the harbourside, gutting the silver herring, haddock, ling and cod; their hands covered in pearlescent scales worked like lightning, wielding lethally sharp knives as they sang and shouted obscene taunts at the men. Rosie's sketch books and canvases filled with vignettes that caught the movement and vitality of the little fishing village clinging to the edge of the North Sea.

In the evenings, after a high tea of Dundee cake, ham, eggs and bread spread thickly with butter from local farms,

Rosie dashed out of the cottage at the sound of Alex's motorbike. A phone call to Ned had reassured her that Alex was 'a solid chap, one of the cleverest I've met to boot, would trust him with my life,' so any lingering doubts had evaporated like the haar under the midday sun. Rosie rode with Alex on his motorbike, arms wrapped tightly around his waist, the wind in her hair, as they sped through country lanes past hedgerows filled with yellow gorse, their coconut smell mixing with the petrol fumes from the Norton. Sometimes they'd meet Monty and Valentina in St Andrews and the four of them would go to the pictures. Valentina, so spiky at first, began to put her arm through Rosie's, charming her with confidences and compliments. Despite herself, Rosie began to warm to the Russian woman, whose penchant for drama and amusing barbs enlivened their little band. Valentina sobbed loudly during *A Town Called Alice* when she thought Virginia McKenna had lost her unrequited love, Peter Finch, and howled, 'How can noble Sergeant Joe Harman die? Why did idiot woman not tell him she is free to love him? Stupid bloody fool!' The scandalised shushing from the audience failed to quieten her, and Rosie, used to reserved Scots, envied the way Valentina never seemed to care what anyone else thought.

'Really, Val, why you didn't take up a posting in the diplomatic service is quite beyond me,' Monty said one night after they were ejected from the New Picture House for her outburst against John Wayne in *The Searchers*. An usherette had shone a torch in Valentina's face and told her to be quiet only to be met with a volley of colourful insults, some of the choicer Russian ones helpfully translated later by Monty.

'That imbecile cowboy! He must have heart made from stone,' Valentina said outside the cinema, furiously dabbing at her eyes. 'I need drink. But, please, vodka only, no American whiskey.'

'I think you're safe here,' Alex said. 'Kate's Bar doesn't stretch to bourbon, only good Scotch whisky.'

Rosie realised Valentina's sentimentality was just that – a melodramatic show of feeling that masked a heart so hard and cold it could have been forged in a Russian steel works. Once, when they were coming back from swimming in the sea, they had passed a veteran sitting on a makeshift trolley on the promenade. He was missing both legs. Monty had stopped to ask where he'd served and shared some war reminiscence. He shook the man by the hand, slipped him some money. They were barely out of earshot when Valentina laughed.

'You shouldn't waste your money, Kusima. He'll just use it to get drunk. Someone should put him down, like a dog. Or sell him to circus.'

Rosie hoped the wind had stolen her words to spare the poor man's feelings. Alex spoke sharply to Valentina in Russian, but Monty only shrugged and lifted his eyebrows at Rosie as if to say, 'What can you do?'

Rosie was able to put the unpleasant incident behind her back at the camp in the teachers' mess, where the émigrés, a curious mixture from the Eastern bloc, were gathered drinking tea and smoking. She loved these evenings, and listened, fascinated, as the older ones told stories about the past, before the revolution had turned these academics, writers and musicians from privileged families into desperate refugees, scraping and begging for food as they fled west to seek shelter and lowly jobs, until their language skills had rescued them from penury and been put to use by the Ministry of Defence.

Rosie went back to Edinburgh with her head full of Rimsky-Korsakov and Shostakovich, *Anna Karenina* open on her lap in the train as she watched the Fife coastline. Saying goodbye had been a wrench. At the railway station, Valentina had surprised her by clutching Rosie in a fierce embrace and calling her *moya sestra*, while Monty had solemnly kissed her hand in the French manner, Rosie suspected to annoy Valentina more than out of old-fashioned chivalry. Leaving Alex had been the hardest. She had cherished the times they were alone, walking in companionable silence, or reminiscing about Bletchley days, about their clever, odd colleagues, about boating on the pond and the winter it froze over enough to skate. Rosie didn't tell Alex that she and Margot had only strapped on skates when they saw him on the ice, skating effortlessly, oblivious to the cold and wearing a thin tweed jacket, as he had on the day she met him on the beach in Crail.

When she had jumped on the train, Rosie had been careful not to betray how much she had grown to care for Alex, but at the last minute her resolve wavered, and she leaned out of the train window to see him still standing on the platform, watching intently as if he were waiting for her to reappear. Rosie called out and he ran up to her. When she put her hand out, he clasped it with both of his as if he never wanted to let her go.

'You'll come back?' he said. 'Soon?'

On an impulse she leaned down and kissed him on the lips. Alex took her face into his hands and kissed her back, his mouth soft and warm. As the train whistle cut the air, they broke apart.

'I'll be back in the summer to teach your brainy conscripts,' she called.

'You will? That's marvellous! But wait, that's months away. It's too long!'

'Come and visit me in Edinburgh, then. Ned would love to see you.'

'And you, would you love to see me?'

'Yes, yes, of course! Goodbye, goodbye, goodbye!'

As the train carried her away from Crail, Rosie did not read a word of *Anna Karenina*. Instead, she looked dreamily out of the window and thought about Alex all the way back to Edinburgh.

Chapter 5

The house in Charlotte Square was in uproar when Rosie let herself in. Upstairs, there was the sound of running feet and a door slammed so hard the crystal chandelier in the hall shook and tinkled. She took off her gloves, hat and coat and set them with her case on the black and white flagstones before making her way up the curved staircase. On the landing she could hear raised voices from the guest bedroom, one muffled by sobs and the other shrill with fury and exasperation.

'Stella, ya cheeky besom! I swear, I'll swing for you one of these days.'

'Go away, Mama! I hate you and never want to see you again. You've ruined my life!'

Rosie shook her head. Stella and her mother, Jeanie Taylor, must be visiting and the fireworks had already gone off. Stella was ten years older than Rosie – although she would rather die than admit her age – but acted more like a petulant child than a mature woman. As the star of her mother's dance company, the Taylor Girls, Stella was a full-blown diva with an attitude to match. Jeanie was now too old to dance but was still as wiry, fit and driven in her sixties as she'd been when she'd started the company in her heyday as a celebrated principal dancer. The mother and daughter had a volatile relationship, not helped by Stella being spoiled and indulged from a young age by her showbusiness impresario father, Viktor Ivanov.

'I won't tell you again, missy, stop that carry-on this minute!' Jeanie shouted. 'You're giving me a right showing up – what will Lily's neighbours think?' Jeanie stepped out of the room, closing the door behind her, and caught sight of Rosie. Her face lit up and she opened her arms for a hug. Petite and lithe as a sprite, she only came up to Rosie's shoulder. Despite her age, she had held on to the striking looks that had once marked her out as 'a stunner' and enslaved the incorrigible womaniser Viktor.

'Rosie, darlin'! What a treat to see you again. Why didn't I get a lovely daughter like you instead of that monster?' Jeanie glared at the closed door. 'Her father, God rest his soul, ruined her.'

An outraged voice came through the door. 'I heard that, Mama! You're a fiend! You've never loved me!' A torrent of loud, rather forced sobs followed.

Rosie suppressed a smile and whispered, 'Off you go and have a cup of tea with Mother and I'll deal with this.'

'A cup of tea? That'll be right! Strong drink is what I need after dealing with that wee besom.' Jeanie's tone softened and she stroked Rosie's cheek. 'You look so like your ma, and you've her gentle nature and patience.' Jeanie smoothed back her own hair, still convincingly dark thanks to a skilled hairdresser. 'But you're not wrong, I need to calm down before I murder my only child.' She blew Rosie a kiss and clipped down the corridor in her high heels to Lily Crawford's drawing room. Rosie tapped on the door and the sobs escalated.

'Stella, it's me.'

The noise stopped abruptly, and the door swung open to reveal her friend, her powdered skin porcelain-white against her dark hair, eyes and delicately upturned nose, all unmarked by any signs of crying. Stella, despite being in her mid-forties, had inherited her mother's youthfulness, not to mention her skill with a make-up brush and hair dye. Bar a few crow's feet, she was still recognisable as the sulky fifteen-year-old Rosie had first met as a shy five-year-old recently landed in Scotland from Shanghai, missing her amah and bewildered by her father's death. Stella had taken the lost girl under her wing and Rosie had quickly become devoted to her, much to the delight of their mothers, themselves childhood friends.

Stella enveloped Rosie in a cloud of Worth's Je Reviens. 'Darling! You look wonderful, glowing, beautiful, gorgeous, divine!' She pulled back and held Rosie at arms' length to study her. 'Don't tell me! You're in love! I demand to know every detail at once! Who is he? Is he worthy of my darling Rosie? And if not, I'll kill him with my bare hands, as I should have done with that awful Frank.' She put her hand over her mouth, her eyes wide. 'It's not him, is it? Don't say you've been daft enough to take him back!'

Rosie laughed. 'Slow down! No, I haven't even thought about Frank for ages. And yes, there is someone new, but it's early days.' Stella ushered Rosie into the guest bedroom, where every surface was covered in piles of discarded clothes, spilled face powder and a jumble of various beauty creams, make-up and scent bottles.

'Go on, tell me everything! Don't leave anything out, not a thing, do you hear?'

Rosie lifted a tangle of stockings and silk underwear from a chair and sat down. 'First you have to tell me what this row with your mother is about.'

Stella waved her hand dismissively. 'Oh that! You know, the usual. She won't let go of the reins of the Taylor Girls, even though I should have taken over years ago. It's my time to be in charge.' Stella would never own up to the ageing process that overtook every dancer, but she looked in the mirror and pulled the skin at her jaw to tighten it, sighed and turned back to Rosie. 'Mama's ideas are outdated; she should just retire and get out of my way. I want to modernise the costumes, bring the dance moves up to date.' She swivelled round on her chair to face Rosie.

'What I really want is to get into films and take the troupe to Hollywood. Have you seen *Rock Around the Clock* with Bill Haley and His Comets, and The Platters?' Rosie shook her head, but Stella barrelled on. 'Well, it's the ginchiest with cool sounds. There's a follow-up coming out next month, *Cha-Cha-Cha Boom*.'

'Sounds riveting.' Rosie's tone was dry. Stella waved her hand as if to dismiss her friend's reaction as that of someone who clearly knew nothing about showbusiness, or rock 'n' roll for that matter.

'Don't be a snob – that's where the money is, not your dreary art house films with mournful Scandinavians. Honestly, that one you took me to last year was the living end.'

'*Ordet* won the Golden Lion at the Venice Film Festival.'

'Blah, blah, blah . . . it was all in Danish and about some lunatic who thought he was Jesus Christ. Give me *The King and I* any day, which won a Golden Globe, I'll have you know.'

'Never mind all that, go on with your plans to bring the Taylor Girls into the modern world.'

Stella leaned forward. 'Last year I had a call from someone in Columbia Pictures asking for dancers when they were about to start filming *Cha-Cha-Cha Boom*, but Mama wouldn't hear of it. She's stuck in the dark ages, thinks it's still all about the theatre and dancing girls in feathers and sequins high kicking to "She wears red feathers and a hula

hula skirt". I've told her until I'm blue in the face that we must move with the times or die, and film is the way to go.'

Rosie noticed that as usual when she was talking about work, Stella had dropped the pretentious way of talking peppered with French that she'd picked up over decades in the theatre. 'Then there's television, more families have them since the Coronation, and all the variety acts are desperate to get on the new shows. But Mama won't consider it, thinks it's all flash-in-the-pan, and that my "heid is full of mince". I'm afraid I lost my temper and called her a name I shouldn't.' Stella looked at her perfectly manicured pink fingernails and tried to look contrite.

Rosie hid a smile, sure that her friend had flung more than one salty epithet at her equally fiery mother. 'Oh dear, that's not good, but the two of you always spark off each other. You should talk to my mother; Jeanie always listens to her.'

Stella thought for a moment. 'You're right!' She stood up and checked her make-up in the mirror. 'You're a genius! I'll go and do that now.'

'And it wouldn't hurt to be nice to Jeanie every now and then. Why not use some of the famous Stella Taylor charm on her?'

Stella tipped an imaginary Stetson. 'That'll be the day!' Rosie recognised John Wayne's line from *The Searchers* and laughed. 'Wish me luck. And when I come back, I want to hear all about your mystery man.'

While Stella was negotiating with the two mothers, Rosie went to find Ned in his study. He was behind his desk, reading a document and taking notes but looked up when she knocked and put her head around the door.

'Am I interrupting?' Rosie said.

He came round the desk and took her hands in his. 'Not at all! My dearest darling Rosie, what a delightful surprise. I'd forgotten you were coming home today.' Despite the silver, he had what Jeanie called 'a fine head of hair' and, with his carefully trimmed beard and moustache and dapper dress sense, Ned was still a handsome and elegant man. As a sociable, worldly bachelor with finely honed conversational skills, a prestigious career in the law and now the government, and, most important of all, a sharp appetite for gossip, Sir Edward Raeside was much in demand by New Town grand dames at their soirées and at charity balls held in the Assembly Rooms. Ned wasn't really Rosie's uncle, but for as long as she'd known him, he had been her mother's close friend. They settled down in two wing armchairs in front of the fire that Ned kept well-banked all year round, and he poured them both a sherry.

'So, how was the Kingdom of Fife? Did the bitter winds of the North Sea sweep you off your feet?'

'No, but someone else did.'

'Oh. Hmm, let me take a stab at this. Who could you possibly meet in Crail? A visiting professor escaped from St Andrews University in ancient tweeds and leather elbow patches, or a burly fisherman, handsome but reeking of herring? Should I be looking out a sou'wester for the wedding at sea? Will we all have to start drinking rum?' He shuddered in mock horror. 'And are we to see you down at Leith fish market with a creel on your back?'

Rosie kicked off her shoes and wriggled her toes. 'Sounds delightful, but I think I'll stick with painting. Remember, I called you from Crail to see if you really did know Alex Kuznetsov?'

'Ah, I thought he might be the likely candidate. The dashing White Russian who set all the ladies' hearts aflutter at Bletchley.'

'Did he? I wouldn't know. He's asked me to give art classes at the Russian language school in Crail, but he's hinted there's more to it. He said you'd been working on listening stations in Scotland.'

Ned raised an eyebrow. 'My, you are well-informed. Just as well he remembered you'd signed the Official Secrets Act if he was spilling about SIGINT, or was this pillow talk?'

Despite her thirty-six years and experience with men, Rosie couldn't help blushing. 'No, it wasn't pillow talk, as you put it. As a matter of fact, we're at a rather delicate stage. It may turn out to be nothing.'

'With Kuznetsov, it's never nothing. If you've set a fire under him, you'd better hold onto your hat and get ready for a great love affair. Underneath that cool exterior beats a passionate Russian heart.' He sighed. 'So exhausting, these Slavs, with their sweeping emotions. Although, I do envy you the drama a teensy bit.' He took a delicate sip of his sherry and looked at the glass appreciatively. 'One of the few pleasures in life left for an old man.'

'Hardly old.'

'Too kind, my dear, but exactly so. Now, tell me more. How did you meet the dashing Kuznetsov?'

'His dog jumped on me on the beach, then he took me to the pub.'

'He picked you up? Hardly Anna Karenina and Count Vronsky, is it? And he took you to the local boozer? Not really his style, but I suppose caviar and vodka are in short supply in Crail.'

'We had both at the language school, where I was plied with vodka and Rachmaninoff, in equal measures.'

He made a face. 'You're a braver man than I, Gunga Din. Vodka will strip the enamel off your teeth. I am, however, partial to Rachmaninoff when I want a good cry in private. I take it Alex wants to use your considerable deciphering skills for SIGINT.'

'Perhaps, I must say I'm tempted. I've been a bit bored lately, you know, with teaching.'

'Ah yes, St Leo's. A fine educational establishment, but I can see why working alongside Alex would be more stimulating. I must say, I'm rather in favour of this turn of events. Most interesting! When are you seeing your Count Vronsky again? I trust you bid a suitably tragic farewell at the railway station?'

Nettled by the accuracy of his barb, Rosie said: 'I've invited him to come and stay.'

'Splendid!' Ned smiled wolfishly at her. 'I couldn't be more pleased. I can play the ogrish guardian and glower at him over the port. I'll be most disappointed if he doesn't sneak along the corridor into your room in the middle of the night. You'd better warn him about the creaking floorboard on the landing.'

'You will behave and be a charming host, as usual.' Rosie tried to look stern but failed.

Ned subsided into the wing-back chair. 'Yes, I suppose I will. How tediously predictable I've become in my twilight years.'

When Rosie went back upstairs, the earlier storm had quelled, and as she had predicted, Lily had brokered a temporary truce between Jeanie and Stella, who was now breaking and bending the soles of a new pair of pointes and stuffing the blocks with muslin to spare her poor feet. The two older women were talking, heads together, one copper streaked with silver, the other still the nut brown of her youth. Rosie stood in the doorway, unwilling to disturb the peaceful scene.

'I find lately that I've been thinking of the past more, about Jack,' Lily said. 'I wonder if he's happy in France, and if he ever thinks about me.'

Jeanie put an arm around her old friend. 'Och, Lily, there's no point looking back. You've got Rosie, and Ned, and me and Stella – we all love you.'

From the door, Rosie watched her mother carefully. Ever since she could remember, Lily had worn her sadness like a cloak. She'd try to be bright and loving to her daughter, but she kept something of herself apart and Rosie had never been able to bridge the distance. Over the years she'd heard about Jack, the man Lily had been with before she married Rosie's father. He'd been an artist too but had gone off to France to fight in the Great War and never come back. Instead, he'd abandoned her mother and had children with a French woman. Rosie knew only too well how much the end of an affair could hurt. It had taken all her strength of will to move on from Frank and she had been slow to trust Alex. Rosie would like to think that she'd learned from her mistakes and had become a better judge of character, but perhaps she was deluding herself and Alex would hurt her too. No, Alex was different from Frank. She couldn't imagine that serious man, a fellow veteran of the Park and a friend of Uncle Ned's, making a fool of her. Rosie shook off her misgivings and cleared her throat. Lily sprang up and put her arms around her daughter and Rosie tried not to squirm away as she had when she was younger, guiltily resentful of the sometimes overbearing love Lily fitfully lavished on her only child, only to ignore her other times. It was why Rosie liked Ned's company, he was always the same with her, affectionate but giving her room to breathe. Although Rosie had lived with Ned for nearly as long as she could remember, he'd never tried to be a father to her or anything more than a kindly uncle. Once, in a fit of adolescent pique, she'd shouted: 'You're not my father!' at him and he'd only replied: 'My dear, I'm far too good-looking to have sired a little hoyden like you.' There had been a pause while the young Rosie decided how to react. In the end, she'd fired back an insult about him looking like a worn-out old horse on the way to the knacker's yard, and the image had been so absurd and obviously untrue they had both burst out laughing.

Lily tucked her arm through Rosie's and led her to where Jeanie sat at a table with porcelain cups still fragrant with Chinese tea. 'The pot's nearly empty. Shall I make more?'

'I don't want tea. I had a sherry with Ned.'

Her mother tried not to show she was hurt that Rosie had gone to see her uncle first. 'That Ned! He's always ahead of the game when it comes to gossip, but now you must tell Jeanie and me all about your trip to Crail.' She hesitated. 'Did you meet anyone nice?' Lily winced, waiting for Rosie's usual impatience whenever the delicate subject of her romantic life was broached.

'Actually, I did.'

Lily's eyes widened and Jeanie leaned towards her. 'Who's the lucky man? He'd better be good enough for you and treat you right, or he'll have me to answer for. That sleekit Frank's lucky I didn't set some of my Glasgow pals on him. Some of the stagehands could give him a right doing, just say the word.'

Rosie and Lily exchanged looks. 'No, he's not a charming bounder like Frank. In fact, he's rather lacking in the charm department, so much so that I found him a bit abrasive at first.'

'That's no bad thing, I like a plain speaker. There's nothing sets my teeth on edge like a smooth-talking chancer,' Jeanie said. 'What's this rough diamond's name, then?'

'Alex Kuznetsov.'

Stella looked up from her ballet shoes. 'A Russian! Like my sainted papa.' She clutched her hands to her breast and gazed heavenward.

Jeanie snorted. 'Viktor was a good father, but he was always far too busy enjoying himself to be a saint. Just ask the chorus girls. He had quite an eye for the ladies, especially ones with slack knickers.'

'What does that say about you, dear Mother?' Stella spat.

'Why you cheeky wee . . .' Jeanie rose, about to lunge at her daughter, but Lily put a restraining hand on her arm and whispered something in her ear and she subsided into the chair, glaring at Stella, who smirked and went back to softening her pointe shoes.

Rosie sat down next to her friend and picked up one of the shoes. 'Are these new?'

'Of course. I get through a hundred pairs in a season. That idiot of a dresser can never get them right, so I need to stuff them with wadding until I break them in. I was bleeding through the silk last time I came off stage. More lame duck than dying swan.' Stella stretched out her feet in the high mules that she needed to wear for her shortened calf ligaments. Her feet were swollen with bunions and deformed from years of dancing en pointe. 'Look at these monstrosities. It's just as well the rest of me is perfect.'

Jeanie snorted. 'And modest, too.'

Lily looked from Stella to Jeanie. 'It's no wonder you and your mother rub each other up the wrong way. You're like two peas in a pod.' Stella and Jeanie exploded with protestations at the same time, until Rosie shushed them.

'Do you want to hear about my Russian or not?' Three heads swivelled towards her, and three pairs of eyes brightened with anticipation.

Chapter 6

The next Sunday, Rosie strolled to the West End of Edinburgh to see her old friend Margot Robertson. In William Street, she stopped to buy tulips and three paper bags of sweets, and when she reached Margot's townhouse in Grosvenor Crescent two little boys who had been sitting on the outside steps drawing in chalk jumped up and came down to meet Rosie on the flagstone pavement.

'Did you bring sweeties?' asked the younger.

'Daniel! Mother said we're not to ask,' said the older boy, but he turned to Rosie, hope written across his freckled face.

'Hello, my angels. I certainly did bring sweeties – dolly mixtures for Daniel and sherbet lemons for George.' The older boy's face fell, and she made a show of looking into her bag. 'Silly me! The sherbet lemons are for your mother. The liquorice allsorts are for you, George,' she said, and was rewarded with a huge grin.

'What do you say, boys?' Margot must have seen Rosie through the bay window of her drawing room and had opened the door, a plump toddler on her hip. When her brothers had chorused a thank you, they dashed across the cobbled road to the gated gardens and slipped through the open gate. Margot came down the steps and kissed Rosie on the cheek. 'It's such a lovely morning, I thought we could sit in the gardens while the boys run around and burn off some of their high spirits.'

'Wonderful. And how Susan has grown in the few weeks since I last saw her,' said Rosie as the little girl buried her face in her mother's neck.

'She's going through the shy phase. I only wish her brothers would, but they are wilder than ever.'

In the gardens, Margot spread out a blanket for them on the grass. Rosie picked daisies and made them into a chain for Susan, who babbled in delight and grabbed it in her chubby hands. Over the trees the three spires of St Mary's cathedral stood out against a blue sky and the bells rang out. Rosie waited while Margot handed a sandwich to Susan, who sat in her mother's lap and chewed with great concentration. After Margot had spotted the boys playing inside their favourite den, a massive rhododendron bush, she gave Rosie her full attention.

'How was Crail? Did it do the trick? Are you painting again?'

'Yes, thank you for suggesting it. I've a full sketch book and two seascapes on the go.'

Margot sighed. 'I only wish I had the time, but this lot keep me too busy.' She dropped a kiss on Susan's hair.

Rosie could wait no longer. 'You'll never guess who I met there – Alex Kuznetsov. Remember him?'

'No! Colonel Kuznetsov! How could I forget? We had such a crush on him. Is he still as good-looking as ever, or has he gone to seed? So many men do when they settle down. Look at my John with his pot belly and receding hairline.'

'John who adores you, and vice-versa.' Rosie was fond of Margot's husband, a rather serious shy man who worked in one of Edinburgh's august financial institutions. Rosie didn't know what he did but she knew he was sweet-natured, thoughtful, reliable and solvent, and that he was the polar opposite of the men they had met at art school.

Margot sighed. 'You're right. I wouldn't change John for the world, and of course I love my children, but I do miss my carefree youth.' She smoothed a curl from Susan's forehead. 'Tell me more about Colonel Kuznetsov, is he as handsome as ever?'

Rushing through her story – she knew from experience they could be interrupted at any moment by Margot's children – Rosie told her about their meeting on the beach, and how they'd grown closer over the fortnight, until she reached the kiss on the railway platform.

'My goodness, he certainly pulled out all the stops. Our eighteen-year-old selves would have died of jealousy. Are you seeing him again or was it just a holiday flirtation?'

'He's asked me to come and work this summer at this Russian language school he's helped set up in Crail. It sounds like fun.'

'For the whole summer?'

Rosie shrugged. 'It's a change. It could be fun.'

Margot looked at her for a long moment. 'It all seems a bit sudden. You hardly know this man.'

'We knew him at Bletchley.'

'Hardly. He was more a figment of our fevered young imaginations.'

'And Ned vouched for him – they're working together on some defence matters.'

'That's all right then. Ned is a fine judge of character.'

Rosie laughed. 'Yes, he's a great fan of yours – and of John.' The little girl had lost interest in her sandwich, now mashed to a pulp, and began fretting. A wail rang out from the bushes and George came running across the grass. 'Mummy, come quick! Daniel has tripped and grazed his knee.' Margot got to her feet and picked up Susan. 'Never a quiet moment. You are lucky, Rosie, to be at the beginning of an adventure.'

Chapter 7

Rosie ran down the stairs to look at the post on the hall table, but yet again there was nothing from Alex. Ever since she'd gone back to school, the days had dragged, and her usual patience had been replaced by tetchy bad temper, even towards her most talented pupil. That day in art class when Rosie showed her where she'd got the perspective wrong, the girl looked mutinous and begun to mutter about dropping art as soon as she could.

'If you're that easily put off, Anne Rankin, then art college is no place for you. The tutors there have no time for spoiled little princesses who need praised every ten minutes,' Rosie snapped, reducing her charge to tears. Seeing how miserable she had made her, Rosie repented and was kind to her for the rest of the term, giving her extra one-to-one lessons at lunch break and after school.

After several weeks of no word from him, she tried to forget about Alex, and about Valentina and Monty. To keep busy in her spare time she worked on a portrait of Stella, who was staying at Charlotte Square after refusing to go home to Glasgow with Jeanie while the dance company was between tours.

'I can't bear being in the same room as the old baggage, let alone sharing a house,' Stella said during one of their sittings. 'I'm never going home! I shall start my own company with modern choreography, unusual costumes and abstract sets. The critics will be astounded – that will show her!'

'I thought it was going to be all rock 'n' roll in Hollywood with American heart throbs in leather jackets and girls in bobby socks,' Rosie said.

'Don't be tedious, you know what I mean.'

Rosie smiled, knowing that mother and daughter would reconcile as they had countless times before. Meanwhile, she was glad of Stella's vivacious company and the chance to confide in her about Alex, or the *Russkiy*, as Stella insisted on calling him.

'Don't worry so much, you'll see him soon when you finish school for the summer and go back to Crail – when is that, the end of June? I never know these things, not having children, thank God. I don't know how you can bear teaching those callow young girls all day.'

'It's been weeks since I heard from him. What if he's forgotten about coming? I had planned on spending summer in Italy with a friend from art school but put it off because of this damn teaching job at Crail.' Rosie put down her paintbrush and pushed her hair out of her face. 'I'm such a fool, worse than the girls at school sighing over pictures of Dion and Ricky Nelson.'

'Who?'

'American rock 'n' roll singers – all the teeny boppers are mad for them. You should know that if you're going into the movies.'

Stella flicked her hands dismissively. 'Rock 'n' Roll – an infernal racket, it will never last. I've completely gone off the idea. Modern ballet with jazz is the way forward, like that scene in *Singin' in the Rain* with Gene Kelly and Cyd Charisse. Sheer genius! Anyway, back to your Russkiy. From what you tell me, he did all the running, and you played it cool. Very clever of you.'

'I didn't play it cool; I was wary because I didn't know anything about him, and because of you know who.'

'Frank.'

'Yes, Frank.'

'What's he doing these days?'

'From what I hear, he's still a journalist, writing about showbusiness, digging up the dirt on the stars.' Rosie's mouth twisted. 'He was always banging on about breaking important stories that made a difference. *News is what somebody doesn't want you to print, all the rest is advertising.* That was his favourite quote. He always made out he was the champion of the ordinary man in the street.'

'Well, he certainly wasn't your champion, the swine.' Stella, restless from sitting still for more than half an hour, jumped to her feet. 'Let's cheer you up. Why don't you get out of your dreary painting clothes and put on something a bit more glamorous? I'll do your make-up and we'll go out. There's a new play at the Lyceum. We could have gone to someone's house for cocktails, except all my dancer friends are back in Glasgow resting, *tant pis.*' She started rummaging in Rosie's wardrobe. 'Is this all you have? These awful flannel trousers and fisherman's jumpers are too depressing for words, and this tweed skirt is bagging around the bottom. Your emerald silk dress is the one lovely thing you have. Did Ned buy it for you?'

'How do you know I didn't pick it out myself?'

'I love you, darling, but your taste in clothes is *affreux*. And you would never spend a month's salary on a dress.'

Rosie, stretched out on the satin coverlet on her bed, threw a balled-up sock at her friend. 'How rude you are, and I do wish you wouldn't speak French at me. But you're right, Ned did buy it, he said it brought out the colour of my eyes, although I don't see how that's possible.'

'Such an exquisite sense of fashion, for a man. But then it's the male dancers I go clothes shopping with at the beginning of the new season. Shall we nip up to Jenners? There's a new sales girl who's from Paris.'

'There's nothing I would loathe more,' Rosie began, but stopped abruptly when she heard the doorbell. Her bedroom door was open, and she could hear voices in the hall – that of the daily who came in to clean and of a man. She whispered to Stella: 'It's him, Alex.'

'About bloody time. Let's find something half decent for you to wear . . .' But Rosie was up and halfway out the door. Stella sprang across the room and caught her by the shoulders. 'Oh no you don't. He's kept you waiting long enough, now it's his turn.' She steered Rosie to the dressing table. 'Now, let's do something about this hair.' Stella deftly twisted her friend's shortish hair and pinned it into the semblance of a chignon. 'Put on some lipstick and powder the shine off your nose while I dig out a sweet little summer dress that I picked up in La Samaritaine. You want to look chic but not as if you're trying too hard. Something I learned in Paris.'

'Paris, Paris . . . you're obsessed! We're in Edinburgh where a sensible tweed and twinset are the height of fashion.'

Stella rolled her eyes. 'Tell me about it! What I wouldn't give for a stroll down the Champs-Élysées or to be able to pop into Dior at Avenue Montaigne.' She went to her room and came back with a dress on a hanger. With a triumphant *voilà!* Stella deposited it on her friend's lap. A few minutes later, Rosie was admiring her reflection in the wardrobe mirror. Stella grinned like a chimp over her shoulder. 'Perfect! Now, go down slowly and remember, cool as a cucumber. What you're aiming at is hauteur if you can't manage froideur.'

'Do belt up, you goose.' Rosie gave her a peck on the cheek and, ignoring Stella's advice, ran down the stairs and arrived breathless and red-faced, skidding the last yard so she nearly slammed into Alex. Smoothing her hair, which was already trying to escape, Rosie attempted a careless tone.

'It's yourself, is it? What brings you here?'

He looked at her, amused. 'You invited me.'

Abandoning any semblance of hauteur or froideur, Rosie crossed her arms and glared at him. 'You said you'd write. You didn't. At all. And it's been ages.'

'I only write in emergencies – telegrams usually – but this is not an emergency. Or is it?' Alex grinned and put his hands on her shoulders. 'Did you miss me that much?'

Rosie shrugged him off. 'Not a bit. Why, did you miss me?'

'Of course not, I was far too busy.'

The daily shook her head at this nonsense and put out her hand. 'Your hat and coat, sir. I can't stand here all day, I've a whole house to clean,' she grumbled.

Alex smiled at the woman, and she looked mollified. 'Thank you, but I'll hold onto these, I'm sure you have more than enough to do.'

'Sorry, Mrs Jackson, I should have heard the doorbell,' Rosie said. Help was scarce these days, and it wouldn't do to annoy the daily, who was in high demand around Charlotte Square and the surrounding New Town streets and crescents.

When she had gone, Alex lowered his voice. 'Darling, don't be angry, it makes you so ugly.' He held out his hand and, undone by being called darling for the first time, Rosie found herself taking it. 'Come on, I'm parked outside.'

'Don't you want to have some tea first, say hello to everyone?'

Alex glanced upwards and Rosie turned to see Stella hanging over the banister clearly listening avidly. 'Later,' he said. 'There's someone I want you to meet first.'

Outside, the late May sun was warm, showing Charlotte Square with its garden at its best, the cherry trees heavy with pink and cream blossom. It was Rosie's favourite month, when Edinburgh shrugged off her drab winter coat and seemed young and gay again. Boris was sitting in the back of a smart open top car and barked happily when he saw Rosie. She tousled his curly head, and he wagged his rear end so hard she thought his tail might fall off.

'Good boy!' She laughed. 'You don't mind admitting that you missed me, do you?' She planted a kiss on his head and the dog rewarded her by trying to lick her face.

'You shouldn't encourage him. He's an awful old flirt.' Alex held the door open for her and Rosie got in, careful not to catch Stella's no doubt eye-wateringly expensive dress.

'Where are we going?'

'To the Old Town, where an American friend of mine likes to hang out – his ghastly phrase not mine – with theatre people.'

'Did you say theatre people? Then I'm in!' Rosie turned to find Stella wearing her most beguiling smile, a lock of glossy dark hair artfully falling over her eyes. Alex seemed to be immune to her friend's charms, which wasn't lost on Stella; the very embodiment of hauteur, she tossed her hair back and stuck her nose in the air. But when she spotted the car, she dropped the act. 'A Sunbeam, what fun!'

'How on earth do you know that?' Rosie said.

Stella shrugged. 'An old boyfriend had one. Smashed it up going too fast around a corner on the Côte d'Azur.' She climbed into the back seat and pushed a growling Boris along the tiny seat. 'Shove over, ya glaikit big lump.'

Rosie sighed. 'Alex, this is Stella Taylor. As her mother – who as you can see has passed on some useful Scots to her – would say, there's no show without Punch.' Alex scowled at Stella and got behind the wheel, ignoring Stella's prattling.

'Just as well I'm coming along. There isn't anything about showbusiness I don't know.' She thrust her head between the front seats and grinned at Alex, her charm on full beam. 'I'm a principal dancer, you know, star of the show, queen of the boards. Everyone who is anyone in the theatre and dance world knows me. Now put your foot down, *Russkiy*, and let's see what this baby can do.'

Alex started the engine and the car roared forward, propelling Stella backwards. He looked at her in the rear-view mirror and raised his voice over the noise of the gutsy engine. 'You know, you remind me of someone. A Russian friend of mine. She's also a pain in the neck.'

'No doubt, *moy drug*, because I'm half Russian.' Stella tied her hair back in a scarf and put on a pair of cat's eye sunglasses. '*Allons-y!* Put your foot down, buddy, and let's get out of Dodge,' Stella said, switching from her preposterous French to a cod American accent that could only have been learned from watching too many Westerns. Rosie smiled as they swerved around the gardens and down to Princes Street, holding her hair out of her eyes as she stole glances at Alex.

Chapter 8

The little car crossed Princes Street and sped up the Mound, bouncing over cobbles before turning into the Lawnmarket. Rosie looked up at the tall seventeenth-century tenements that made up the spine of the Old Town and at the wynds and closes leading off it like so many ribs, their gaping mouths disappearing into sinister darkness. The Old Town always made her think of the lurid Edinburgh of body snatchers and murderers Burke and Hare, and of councillor by day burglar by night Deacon Brodie. With its raffish air and winding medieval layout, this part of the city was only a mile away but a world apart from the geometrically laid out Georgian New Town. Rosie often climbed the Playfair Steps past the National Gallery and Princes Street Gardens to sketch the lively street scenes. On dark winter days, it was easy to imagine a time when the Tolbooth saw public hangings, and poor women accused of being witches were rolled in barrels down the Royal Mile, before being hauled back to the Castle gates where they were strangled to death and burned at the stake. All that seemed impossible now on this fine spring day, the sky high and cloudless and the view down to Holyrood ending in a hazy blue strip of sea. Alex stopped the car outside a crumbling tenement and called to a man standing in front of it, his hat pushed to the back of his head as he looked up at the building.

'Jim, I say, Jim!' The man turned and, when he saw who it was, grinned and waved.

'Well, hello there!' Alex got out and Rosie was surprised to see the two men embrace and slap each other on the back. She had never seen Alex so effusive. The American laughed and extricated himself. 'And this must be the talented Miss Anderson you were telling me about.' He opened the door for Rosie and offered her his hand. 'Jim Harrison.'

'Rosie, call me Rosie.'

'All right, I will. And who is this lovely creature?'

Stella smirked and tossed her hair. 'That's Boris,' Alex said, earning a muttered curse in salty Scots. Rosie bit her lip to stop herself laughing, feeling disloyal but at the same time gratified that Alex, unlike most men she knew, had not fallen at the first hurdle and succumbed to Stella's winning ways. Jim Harrison, on the other hand, was clearly entranced.

'Don't be a jerk, Alex,' he said and helped Stella out of the car, admiring her legs when her skirt rode up. Boris, not to be outdone, bounded out of the back seat and pushed

Stella aside to leap up and try to lick Jim's face. 'When are you going to train this mutt?' Jim pushed the dog down, but his tone was mild, and when Boris looked up at him beseechingly, head on one side, he crouched down to tousle his ears.

'Boris is impossible,' Alex said. 'But he was like that when I found him, abandoned. Monty tried to take him in hand, said he'd grown up with gun dogs, but Boris, who is of an indeterminable breed, defeated him.' Alex called to the dog, who ignored him and raced snapping after a pigeon that had unwisely landed near him. 'See, he's completely unbiddable, like a Russian, so we called him Boris.'

'Nonsense, he's a good dog, aren't you Boris?' Jim said. The dog skidded to a halt and turned to run back to him and sit obediently at his feet, eyebrows working like pistons as he gazed adoringly at the American. Stella cleared her throat, clearly annoyed that Boris and Rosie between them had stolen the limelight.

She offered Jim her hand, palm down like royalty. 'Stella Taylor. You may have heard of me?'

Jim shook her fingertips awkwardly and glanced at Alex for guidance. He shrugged. 'She's a friend of Rosie's, some kind of actress.'

Stella glowered at him before turning her most dazzling smile on Jim. 'Actually, I'm the principal dancer of the Taylor Girls.'

Jim's friendly face broke into a wide smile. 'Say! I've seen you dance at the Edinburgh Playhouse, and before that in Paris, up in Montmartre in the Moulin Rouge. Lots of feathers and va-va-voom, am I right?' He looked at her appraisingly. 'I'm looking to get into showbusiness myself, and I'd value your professional opinion.' He pointed a thumb at the building. 'She doesn't look much just now, but I'm hoping to turn this old lady into a theatre venue.' Stella immediately dropped her fancy-dan act and looked appraisingly at the derelict building. She narrowed her eyes at broken windows that gave it the look of a gap-toothed crone.

'Are you sure? Wouldn't you be better with a guild hall or an old church?'

Jim brought out a huge iron key and opened the sagging front door. 'Now where would be the fun in that? This used to be a brothel not so long ago. Perfect for the kind of plays I want to put on.' On seeing the women glance at each other, eyebrows raised, he laughed. 'No, not that kind of production, nothing sleazy. New plays written by new writers. It'll be a doozy, you'll see, just needs a lick of paint and some elbow grease.' The door swung open, disturbing dust that carpeted the flagstone entrance and revealing water-stained walls. Shafts of light streamed in from holes in the ceiling and the place smelled damp. 'After you, ladies.' Rosie and Stella gingerly stepped into the gloom, disturbing more pigeons roosting in the rafters that sent Boris into a frenzy of barking.

'Well, what do you think?' Jim said to them all once Boris had been bribed with a dog biscuit to quieten down. Rosie looked around uncertainly, but Stella was entranced.

'What a space! There's even a stage, and plenty of room for seating. It's perfect!'

Alex shook his head. 'You're as barmy as he is. Let's get out of here before this death trap collapses. I know a half decent restaurant where Jim can tell us all about his plans.' He glanced at the buckets that had been placed to catch leaks. 'No wonder they call it the theatre of the absurd. I'll see you outside.' Alex strode towards the door.

'Good idea, I'm starving,' Stella said, catching up with him. Rosie trailed behind with Jim.

'How do you know Alex?' she said.

'We're in the same line of work, really although he's military and I'm with the US Airforce based at RAF Kirknewton, just outside Edinburgh. When I was posted to Scotland, I told them it had to be near a university town so I could get another degree, and somewhere up to its neck in culture. Edinburgh came out tops. And when I got here, with the Fringe gathering strength, I realised it was the perfect place to start a new theatre.' At the door out to the street, Jim stopped for a moment. 'I don't know many people here yet. I'd like to get to know you better, I already know we're going to be friends.'

Rosie smiled. 'I'd like that too.'

After a lively lunch at the Oyster Café, Rosie was dismayed when Alex told her he was heading back to Fife. Jim tactfully offered to walk Stella back to Charlotte Square to leave the couple alone. Rosie found it hard to look at Alex.

'I'm sorry but I have to work. You understand, don't you?'

'I thought we would have more time together.'

'We'll have plenty of time when you come to Crail. You are still coming?' When she didn't say anything, he turned her chin so she would look at him. 'Have you changed your mind?'

'I'm not sure. I hadn't heard from you. I didn't know if I'd see you again, if you still wanted me to come.'

'Rosie, you must learn to trust me. I can't always be in touch and sometimes I'm gone for weeks. Of course I want you at the camp, I wouldn't have asked you otherwise.' He bent his head and Rosie leaned into the kiss. When they broke apart, he looked at his watch. 'I have to leave now.' He opened the car door for her, but Rosie shook her head.

'I'll walk home. Let's say goodbye now.' She clung to him for a moment before turning away.

Alex caught her arm. 'You'll come to work with me at the camp?' She nodded and he kissed her again.

Chapter 9

When the summer holidays began, Rosie put any doubts behind her and made the journey to Crail, eager to see Alex. Rosie found saying goodbye to the upper-six girls a wrench, but they were so elated by the end of exams and the prospect of leaving school that she couldn't help getting caught up in their excitement. Now she was looking forward to a complete change of scene, teaching the bright young conscripts at the JSSL. Alex had told her that one of the students, Gabriel Paxton, was a promising artist just out of St Martin's School of Art who was already beginning to make a name for himself. She was keen to meet him but didn't have to wait long: on her first day she saw a striking young man riding into the camp on a white horse, a Paisley pattern shawl wrapped around his uniform. When he spotted Rosie, he pulled on the horse's reins and dismounted.

'You must be the lady artist everyone is talking about,' he said, waving an amber cigarette holder about. 'I can't tell you how thrilled I am to meet you. Thank God for another artist! We've far too many playwrights and they have absolutely no qualms about press-ganging me into painting the sets. The next production is *Hamlet* in Russian – can you imagine! – and I'd appreciate another willing slave.'

'Happy to help. I'm an old hand at painting flats.'

'Marvellous!' He patted the horse's neck. 'I'm just back from St A's and need to put sweet Rocinante back in her stable, but if you come along to the theatre this afternoon, I'll introduce you to Michael, Alan and Dennis, all wonderful writers but, you know, writers.' He pulled a face and Rosie laughed.

When she made her way to the theatre later that day, she found a large room with the sort of raised stage found in a school assembly hall. Three men were sitting around a table covered in papers, some of which had fallen onto the stage floor, and she took them to be the playwrights Gabriel had mentioned. He was up a ladder, paintbrush in one hand and a pot of paint in the other, dressed in a boiler suit, a silk cravat tucked around his neck. When he saw Rosie, he climbed down and introduced her to the writers.

'Gentlemen, I'd like you to meet Rosie Anderson, a fine artist and the daughter of Lily Crawford, no less.' Rosie glanced at Gabriel. She hadn't told him about her mother, so he must have looked her up or asked about her.

'Never 'eard of either of 'em,' said one of the writers in a mournful Yorkshire accent. 'But charmed, I'm sure.' The trio shambled to their feet, knocking more papers to the floor, murmuring greetings with shy smiles. Just then an NCO strode into the building and barked at the men.

'Potter! Bennett! Frayn! Your presence *his* required for a spot of square bashing, *hif* you don't mind, ladies.' The writers gave half-hearted salutes and trailed after the NCO who could be heard shouting as they crossed the yard outside. 'Move hit, you bunch of useless eggheads. Strewth! I've inspected your kit and hit's not fit for a monkey to use. Plenty of brains but no common sense. What did I do to deserve being posted here? Get more discipline at Billy Smart's Circus. Garn, pick up yer feet!'

Once the others had left the theatre, Gabriel handed Rosie a paint-spattered boiler suit and she stepped into it.

'Don't you have a square to bash?' she said.

'They've given up on me, thank goodness. I'm so hopeless that I muddle up the other men, so I'm left to my own devices between Russian classes. I'm lucky to be posted here for my national service, although I preferred it when the language school was in London, I do so miss the art galleries and my friends.' Gabriel looked wistful and for a moment dropped his show of urbanity. He brightened. 'But you're here now and I'm sure we'll get on like a house on fire. Let me show you what I'm working on. It's the opening scene on the ramparts of Elsinore so lots of sinister indigo, poisonous viridian green mixed with the deepest, bloodiest magenta.' As they began working Rosie asked

Gabriel a question that had been bothering her since she'd heard about him.

'I was recruited to give the men art classes, but you're here already. I hope I'm not stepping on your toes.'

'Not at all. I shudder at the thought of teaching art to my dear brothers in arms, much as I'm fond of some of them. I wasn't asked, thank goodness. But it's rather an odd assignment if you don't mind me saying. Although, delighted to have your company, not to mention another pair of hands and eyes.'

Rosie thought it was odd too but kept her thoughts to herself. Alex had hinted that there might be more to her mission than art classes and she was determined to pin him down about it, if, that is, she could find him. She had written to say when she'd be arriving and expected him to be on the railway station platform to meet her earlier that day, but there was only a private in a jeep waiting to take her and her suitcase to the base. He'd dropped her off at the classroom building and shrugged when she asked where she was to be billeted. The teachers' mess had been empty, and everyone was either teaching, being taught, or doing military exercises, so she'd been glad to bump into Gabriel. After a couple of hours working on the sets, just as her back and arms were beginning to weary, he suggested they finish for the day. As they cleaned their brushes, he said, 'I'll walk you over to the NAAFI for a bite to eat and then to your billet. You must be tired if you came up on the early train. Where have they put you?'

'I have no idea, nobody's told me, and the person I was expecting to show me round is nowhere to be seen.'

'Typical shambles. You'd think the military would be a model of efficiency, but this place didn't get the memo. Who was supposed to meet you?'

'Alex Kuznetsov.'

'Oh yes, not exactly a ray of sunshine, is he? Do you know anyone else?'

'Cosmo Montgomery, and Valentina Something. I'm afraid I can't remember her second name, something Russian.'

Gabriel laughed. 'It's Nazarova, but we students call her the Black Death. She would appeal to my sense of drama if she wasn't so terrifying.'

'Valentina's all right when you get to know her. She can be quite charming when she chooses.'

'Never lingered in her company long enough to see that side of her, but I'll take your word for it.' Gabriel looked at his watch. 'Classes should be finished by now and the tutors will be gathered round the samovar, reminiscing about Mother Russia and cursing the stupidity of us *kursanty*. I'll walk you over, and hopefully see you in the theatre whenever you can spare a moment from your duties.'

There were several people in the tutors' mess all talking in Russian. Through the fug of cigarette and pipe smoke, she spotted Alex in the corner and waited for him to look up from his newspaper. When he saw her, he sprang up from his chair and led her out of the room to his jeep.

'I'm pleased to see you.' He helped her into the jeep, and Rosie tried to ignore how his hand in hers made her feel.

'Really?'

'Of course, I said I was, didn't I?' Alex turned the key in the ignition and drove them down the road to Crail, the noise of the engine and the wind whipping past them making conversation impossible. He stopped outside a two-up-two-down slate-roofed cottage and pulled down Rosie's suitcase. 'In here,' he said and opened the door that led straight into a small sitting room. He closed it behind them and took Rosie in his arms and kissed her so thoroughly that any doubts she'd had about his feelings for her were forced into retreat.

When she could catch her breath she said, 'You didn't meet me at the station.'

'Couldn't get away. But I'm glad you're here.' He brushed her hair back from her forehead and laughed when it sprang back. 'The wind has turned you into a wild creature.'

Rosie tried to smooth her coarse springy hair. 'Stella is always telling me it's too short, too boyish, that I should have it set into luscious curls like Gina Lollobrigida.'

'I like it the way it is. There's no artifice about you, you're as transparent as a glass of water.'

'Is that one of your strange compliments? I'll take it in lieu of anything better.'

'I don't waste time on sweet nothings. Let's go upstairs.' Rosie hesitated until he turned back to her on the stairs and smiled. It was like the sun coming out. Unlike Frank who was all charm and style and no substance, she knew this was a man she could trust to mean what he said. She put her foot on the first step and followed him. Under the eaves, Alex carefully undressed her, kissing her and touching her with a sure and expert hand but with such tenderness that Rosie, nervous at first, let herself be taken over by an urgent desire she had not felt for a long time.

Much later, as she lay in the big brass bed, drowsy and replete in his arms with the sound of the sea coming in through the open window, Rosie roused herself enough to ask Alex if there really was more to her mission than giving conscripts art classes.

He sat up in bed and sighed. 'You want to talk business now? I thought the Scots were a wild, romantic race.'

'We are, sometimes, but we're also hard-headed and practical. You'd know that if you'd ever read Robert Louis Stevenson – we can be both Alan Breck Stewart and David Balfour.'

'If you say so. It's true, though, that I owe you an explanation about why I wanted you here – apart from being madly attracted to you.' He tilted her chin towards him and kissed her gently. 'Once you've heard what I've got to say you can still walk away if you wish. I won't hide the fact that there's an element of danger in what I'm about to ask you to do.'

Rosie sat up on her elbows, suddenly alert. 'I did my bit at Bletchley. I never baulked at the round-the-clock shifts when a particularly tricky coded message came in.'

'I know, I remember. I read your slips. Even Turing was impressed.'

'So?'

'So, there is something we need you to do over and above the art classes. In fact, the art classes are more of a cover. There's a chap I'd like you to keep an eye on, one of the students, Simon Fairweather. He's close to Alistair Baird. Have you heard of Baird?'

'Of course. He's an art historian and a critic who seems to take delight in savaging an artist. He's just been knighted, I think. Ned knows him.'

'I know, it's one of the reasons I thought you'd be perfect for this job. Baird was in MI5 during the war, and we suspected he was passing ultra intelligence from Bletchley to the Soviets, but we could never pin anything on him or find his mole. We suspect he's recruited Fairweather to the KGB and he's feeding information back to the Soviets from here – they're suspicious of the JSSL and what we're up to. If we can get solid proof that he's spying for them it will lead us back to Baird, and we'll have enough leverage to finally nail him.'

'What do you expect me to do? You can't possibly want me to follow him around, I wouldn't know where to start.'

'No, of course not, just befriend him and watch him. Young Fairweather's wet behind the ears, hasn't been in the game long. He's no artist but he loves art, having been schooled by Baird, in more ways than one, I might add. You're not shocked by that sort of thing, are you?'

'Please! You have met Ned, haven't you? And I run with artists, actors and dancers. I'm not naïve.'

'You'll do this, then, keep an eye on Fairweather and report back if he lets anything slip or does anything out of the ordinary?'

'If it helps, yes.'

'There's one more thing I need you to do, which is a lot trickier. But let's see how you get on with Fairweather first. While you're here I'll teach you some basic surveillance techniques, show you the whole bag of tricks, leaving coded messages and drop boxes, that sort of thing.' Rosie wanted to hug herself with glee. She felt as if she were fully awake for the first time since she'd left Bletchley Park. Alex smiled. 'If you could see your face, like a child on Christmas morning.'

'Hey, you don't get to patronise me just because we've slept together.'

'I don't think we've done any sleeping, not yet anyway. I could do with some shuteye, budge over a bit.'

'I thought you Russians were meant to be a wild, romantic race?'

'We are when we've had a proper kip.'

Alex kissed her again and Rosie closed her eyes. She sighed and lay her head on his chest, and soon his breathing steadied. When the doorbell jangled, he didn't stir, so she slipped into a man's dressing gown hanging on the back of the bedroom door and left him sleeping. Valentina and Monty were at the door. They hugged her and barrelled in with bottles of wine and fish suppers that made Rosie's stomach rumble. She realised she hadn't eaten all day. Valentina arranged herself on the sofa while Monty fetched plates, glasses and a corkscrew from the tiny scullery.

He shouted up the stairs, 'Alex, get down here, old boy. We've brought fish suppers from that place in Anstruther, and they'll get cold if you don't get cracking.' With the bottle in one hand and four tumblers in the other he sat down next to Valentina, who sulkily pulled her legs out of the way. They looked quite at home and Rosie realised that they had been in the cottage many times, that it was Alex's cottage, and she was to live with him. Rosie shook off a stab of apprehension – after all, nobody knew her in the village, and Valentina and Monty certainly didn't care about her morals. The arrangement made sense, she told herself, and this way she would see Alex every day, eat with him, sleep with him, wake up with him. It was perfect.

Chapter 10

As the summer rolled on, Rosie soon settled into teaching the men who proved Gabriel Paxton wrong by being eager to try their hands at different media, whether it was clay, water colours or charcoal. She even had them out picking up driftwood and pebbles from the beach to make their own sculptures. They were more than ten years younger than her and were like puppies when they got near the water, stripping off down to their underwear before running into the waves, oblivious of the cold, shouting 'Come on, Miss, the water's lovely!' at Rosie, who shook her head and sat in the dunes, sketching them. She only swam with Alex, in a sheltered cove they'd discovered further up the coast, gasping as they dived into the breakers, salt on their skin and in their mouths.

Befriending Simon Fairweather had been much easier than she'd imagined. He had the clear blue eyes and golden skin of a young, country-bred Yorkshire lad, and far from being a sophisticated art lover, he didn't show the slightest interest in or any aptitude for drawing. Simon was the most high-spirited and playful of the young men she taught, turning the art class's beachcombing trips into impromptu games of cricket on the sand. During one of these games, he threw himself down on the sand next to Rosie, and she thought it might be time to ask a few probing questions.

'How are you finding the language classes?'

'Horrible, worse than Latin at school, which I hated but I was good at, for some reason. Suppose that's why they picked me.'

'Would you like to go to Russia one day? I would.'

'Not me, England is where I'm from and England is where I'll stay, can't abide abroad, or foreigners, no offence.'

Rosie laughed. 'I'm Scottish, not a foreigner at all.'

'Well, you're not English. Although, I'm more of a Yorkshireman than an Englishman, truth be told. Why'd you want to go to Russia, anyway? It's full of Reds. Here, you're not one of those commies, are you?'

Rosie smiled. 'Don't be daft.' A shout came from the beach. 'I think it must be your turn to bat. Away you go, Simon.'

He grinned at her and saluted before racing back to the water line. Rosie lay back against the sand, sheltered by the dunes and the marram grass. The sky was high and clear of clouds, a perfect Scottish summer's day. She closed her eyes against the sun and pulled the brim of her straw hat down over her eyes. Simon Fairweather seemed straightforward, as far as Rosie could tell, and she couldn't imagine what secrets he would have to divulge other than the long lists of technical and military Russian vocabulary the linguists had to learn by rote.

Despite not being able to report anything back to Alex, over that long summer he insisted on teaching Rosie what he called tradecraft. He showed her the dead letter box, a hole in a drystone wall under a sycamore tree and they practised sending and receiving notes in tiny writing on tightly rolled up scraps of paper that could be easily disposed of to avoid detection. If one of them wanted to signal that a letter had been dropped, they had to leave a chalk mark on the wall of one of the disused huts. Alex showed her how to use a microdot camera, so small it could be hidden in the lining of her pocket. In the privacy of their cottage, she practised taking photographs with the fiddly little camera, as well as making key impressions and lock picking. Alex would drop her off at the edge of coastal towns along the East Neuk of Fife, St Monans, Elie or Anstruther, and she would walk through the streets, trying to spot him as he tailed her, and doing her best to lose him, which was tricky in a small town but not impossible as she found. He taught her how to slip into a hotel, turn her coat inside out and don a cap, and come out again a few minutes later. Sometimes she took an item of clothing off a washing line as she passed or hid under an upturned rowing boat until her hamstrings ached from crouching in a corner.

Rosie crowed with delight the first time she managed to lose him but wished she hadn't when he told her she was ready for the next stage.

'I'm going to blindfold you and take you into the countryside, a good hour's drive away, and in the middle of the night. I'll leave you there with nothing but the clothes on your back and I want you to make your way back to Crail as best you can. Do you think you can manage? You can always duck out if you're not up to it.' Alex looked at her steadily, as if he didn't care either way. Rosie opened her mouth to protest and then shut it. She'd signed up for this and she wasn't going to give in now.

The summer days are long in Scotland, and it was after midnight when Alex woke Rosie and she climbed groggily into her clothes. She was about to pull on a jacket, but he stopped her.

'Just as you are. I know it's chilly but you're going to have to survive the night on nothing more than your wits.'

'I'll need a torch.'

'There's a full moon tonight, that should be enough. If you were on a clandestine mission, a torch would give you away.' He handed her a small disc. 'A compass. Do you know how to use one of these?'

'Yes. I've taken the girls at school on camping trips and hill walking.'

'You know how to follow an Ordnance Survey map, then?'

'Of course.'

'Well, you won't have one of those. You'll have to rely on . . .'

'I know, my wits.'

'Look out for landmarks and follow rivers downstream. But don't go into villages, skirt around them and, whatever you do, stay out of sight.'

By the time the jeep stopped, after what seemed much longer than an hour, Rosie was already so cold she couldn't feel her nose and her ears were painful, and she wished she was wearing the woolly hat she'd sneaked into her pocket before they'd left Crail.

'Here we are,' he said and undid her blindfold. 'Jump down. I'll see you back at the cottage. Good luck.'

'Cheers,' she muttered as the jeep drew away, leaving her in a country lane surrounded by fields. A sharp cry startled her, and she couldn't make out what it was. Not a fox's unsettling scream or an owl's soulful hooting but a sharp warning cry, perhaps from some kind of bird of prey. Rosie stood still and tried to get her bearings. She set off in the direction the jeep had gone and tramped for a while along the lane. A snuffling noise from behind the hedgerow made her stop in her tracks. It grew nearer and the hairs on her neck stood up. The sound receded and she walked on. A rumbling engine sounded in the distance behind her, growing louder as it drew near and, mindful that she was to stay hidden, she ducked into the field and lay low while a van stencilled with Dundee's Land o' Cakes passed. If she was near that city, she'd have to travel in a south-easterly direction to get back to Fife. Rosie squinted at her compass and decided to strike out across country, travelling as the crow flies. After an hour of scrambling down the sides of burns and splashing through them she was wet, tired, covered in sweat and cuts, and hopelessly lost. The moon, which had been shining brightly, disappeared behind dark clouds and it began to rain. In the dark, Rosie could no longer read the compass to see which way to go.

'Perfect. Bloody Alex bloody Kuznetsov, you could have let me have a torch or a box of matches at the very least. Maybe it's a test and I should have thought about matches or a lighter. No, definitely a torch would be the sensible option. Who's going to see me out here in the middle of nowhere?' Talking out loud made her feel better. If there was an enemy spy lurking in the undergrowth, good luck to him or her, she thought. The oaths she'd learned during the war came back to her as she stomped through mud and clambered up the slippery side of a stream. 'Bugger this for a game of soldiers, I'm going to find somewhere to kip. And you'd best get your head down too,' she told the imaginary enemy tail. After another miserable trek following the burn downstream, she came across a shepherd's hut and climbed inside. Ignoring the smell of greasy fleeces, she bedded down on some rancid old blankets and rolled herself up in them to try to keep out the cold, wishing again she'd thought to bring something to light a fire. The wind picked up outside and the rain pattered against the tin roof and slowly her body heat warmed her inside the blanket.

When Rosie woke, the sun was breaking over the treeline at the far end of the field. Stiff from her night on the floor, she stretched and went down to the burn to wash her face and drink some water. Her stomach rumbled and she spied wild blaeberries and spent a while picking them and eating them. Rosie wiped her stained hands on her jumper and set off again, following the burn and heading due east towards the rising sun and, she hoped, the East Neuk of Fife. If she hadn't travelled far enough south, she'd still come to the coast and from there make her way round past St Andrews to the East Neuk. When she came at last to a country lane, she kept to it and, like a mirage, saw a bus shelter and a timetable that promised a bus that stopped at all the towns along the East Neuk, first stop Crail, along at eight in the morning. Without a watch, she couldn't guess the time, but she didn't mind waiting and sat down heavily in the shelter. The paintwork was covered in scratch marks proclaiming Shirley's undying love for Tommy and crude drawings illustrating comments that called Marilyn's virtue into question. Rosie was dozing when a bus came to a stop with a screech of brakes and a pneumatic hiss. She climbed aboard and handed over some coins.

'Alex need never know.'

'What was that? I'm Shuggie, nae Alex,' the bus driver said.

'Sorry, I was talking to myself.'

He took in the straw and burrs in her hair and jumper and the mud spattered from her thighs to the hiking boots she was glad Alex had made her borrow. 'Are you all right, hen?'

'I am now, thank you, Shuggie.'

Rosie sat down next to an open window and turned her face to the wind as the bus picked up speed. It wasn't until they were turning into Crail that she noticed the jeep following the bus. And when she got off, she waited until Alex pulled up.

'No need to ask how you did,' he said. 'I was tailing you all night, and you were so slow I was able to double back on foot to where I'd left the jeep. May I say, you're a sorry sight.'

'Oh, shut up. I'm never doing that again,' she said and climbed into the jeep.

'No,' he said. 'I don't think orienteering is your forté. You wouldn't have lasted a minute at Achnacarry Castle where I did my basic commando training during the war. Never mind, you don't really need those skills.'

Rosie punched his arm. 'Now you tell me! You mean to say I went through a night of hell for nothing?'

He winked and put the jeep into gear. 'Hold onto your hat. Although you seem to have lost yours. I think there's a shepherd wearing it now, and wondering who was sleeping in his bed.'

Chapter 11

Not all of Rosie's time was spent teaching or learning tradecraft, and the overnight yomp was thankfully the last part of her training. For the rest of the summer, when she wasn't on duty, Alex would take her off in his sports car with Monty and Valentina to Kingsbarns beach where they liked to set stones in a circle and burn a fire in the dunes and swim in the North Sea. Except for Valentina who preferred to sit fully clothed as near the fire as she could get. Rosie worried her many scarves would go up in flames one day.

On weekends, Rosie and Alex drove to Edinburgh and met up with Stella and Jim Harrison, who dragged them to every play and show in town. In August, the Festival transformed the austere city into a vibrant Camelot, where actors, musicians, artists and performers from all over the world vied for the crowds' attention. Jim's enthusiasm was infectious, even when a play was a baffling avant-garde Fringe event involving mime, white face paint and sometimes, shockingly according to *The Scotsman*, nudity. Rosie tried to appreciate the modern plays, but much preferred the claustrophobic kitchen-sink dramas, and was spellbound by a production of *Look Back in Anger*, the vicious insults doled out by Jimmy Porter to his middle-class wife all too painful a reminder of her relationship with Frank, who liked to think of himself as a down-trodden worker when in fact he was a well-paid journalist with a private school education.

Stella and Jim between them knew many of the performers and, after a show, they often met them at the Café Royale or the Supper Room at the Assembly Rooms where, among the fluted Corinthian pillars and beneath the sparkling chandeliers, Rosie loved being part of the noisy group spinning stories and jokes. Stella was the most vivacious and sometimes outrageous, always with one eye on Jim. Rosie knew from experience that it was only a matter of time before he was completely under her friend's spell. Alex didn't join in with the general hilarity, preferring to talk intensely with Jim and any musician or director who had joined the party, and more often than not would forget about Rosie. Although she was usually happy to observe rather than take centre stage in a gaggle of people, she was grateful that Jim noticed and would draw her into the conversation without making it too obvious. He was a true southern gentleman with the manners to match his easy charm and she welcomed his kindness.

Rosie couldn't resist taking Alex to visit Margot at her home in the West End. If she thought her friend would be bashful meeting the object of their youthful infatuation, she was mistaken. Margot was red-faced and harassed when she came to the door, Susan crying on her hip and Daniel and George a tangle of arms and legs as they fought like puppies.

'I'm sorry, the children are playing up,' she said as she ushered them inside. When Rosie tried to introduce Alex, the toddler opened her mouth, took a huge breath and howled. Alex fished in his pocket and brought out a wooden carving of a bear. He held it out to her, and she abruptly stopped crying and took the bear, which was small enough to fit into her fist. The two boys, sensing their little sister had stolen a march on them, appeared at Alex's side and looked up at him expectantly. He crouched down to their level and shook them each by the hand.

'Do you like Dinky cars?' he asked them. They nodded, too shy to speak. 'Well, that's lucky as I brought a couple with me.' He made a show of patting his pockets. 'Now, where did I put them? They're good ones, too. Don't say I've dropped them on the way here.' George and Daniel came closer, watching his every move. The older boy pointed.

'There! In your jacket pocket!'

'This one?' Alex said.

'No, the other one!'

'Ah, here is one at least. A Ford Capri, if I'm not mistaken, a red one. Now where could the other one be?' Daniel lunged forward and patted the bulge in Alex's breast pocket.

'There it is!'

'So it is. Well observed,' Alex said, and brought out an identical model. He handed them out and the boys thanked him and ran off to race the cars on the stone hall floor.

'Thank you,' Margot said. 'And it was a stroke of genius bringing them exactly the same toy, otherwise they'd be fighting again. And the little bear is adorable.' She put Susan down and the little girl sat and began to babble to the bear. 'Let's go in while they're quiet,' Margot said, and led them into the drawing room where John was reading a newspaper. He leapt to his feet and the two men shook hands, and within seconds were discussing that day's financial news.

'Dear Lord, he's even more amazing than we could ever have dreamt, I've never seen John look so animated when he meets a new person,' Margot whispered to Rosie as the men talked about the Dow Jones and the currency market. 'I thought he'd be formidable and aloof.'

'I'm as surprised as you are. He's never usually this relaxed.' She put her arm through Margot's. 'It must be the warmth of your home.'

'The chaos, more like. It's impossible to be formal here, not with these marauding barbarians,' Margot said as the boys rushed in to show their father their new cars, followed by Susan who was now chewing on her bear.

As they walked back to Charlotte Square, Alex was still in a mellow mood.

'I like your friend Margot. Much more sensible than Stella.'

'Everyone is more sensible than Stella, but I love them both. Do you remember Margot?'

'I've never met her before, so how could I?'

'She was at Bletchley Park.'

'No, I can't say I do. I wish I'd known you though, properly I mean, not just through reports.'

'You were far too grand and important.'

'But not now?'

'Well, only sometimes. I liked seeing you at Margot and John McDonald's. You were wonderful with the children. I thought you were an only child.'

'I was, but I have a whole tribe of cousins, nephews, nieces and too many uncles and aunts, who had all settled in London. It was nice being with a noisy, messy family again.'

Rosie enjoyed these outings with friends, but she liked best the times when she was alone with Alex, walking around the city, peering into the windows of Georgian houses in the New Town, or strolling along the Water of Leith. Sometimes Alex would fall silent, his expression was unreadable and his thoughts elsewhere.

One afternoon, after they had climbed Arthur's Seat with the wind cutting through her like a knife despite the warmth of the day, Alex lapsed into one of his thoughtful silences as they looked out over the church spires, crescents and squares laid out in patterns below them. It was late summer and her time teaching at Crail was coming to an end. The Festival was packing up that week and Edinburgh would retreat into autumn, hanging up her dancing shoes and pulling on worn, comfortable slippers Rosie wanted to ask Alex what would happen next. Would she continue to see him, and Valentina and Monty? Jim had already told her he would be sure to be a regular visitor at Charlotte Square. Ned and Lily had taken a great shine to the American and had told him not to stand on ceremony – unheard of in the New Town where nobody popped in without prior warning.

Rosie was already dreading the time when she would have to say goodbye to Alex. He had mentioned he would be going north soon, to check on the SIGINT listening stations, but other than that she didn't know if she was part of his plans. After her experience with Frank, she was reluctant to show any dependence on a man. If Alex wanted to carry on seeing her, if this was more than just a summer fling, then he'd have to make that clear. The alternative made her feel even colder and she cocried into Alex. A new school term would be starting soon, and Rosie didn't relish the thought of going back to its routines. She nudged him and asked a question that made her cringe even as she said it.

'You're a million miles away – what are you thinking about?'

Alex turned to her, his expression grim. 'How all this could disappear one day. If there's another war.'

Rosie shivered and burrowed her chin into her scarf. 'Don't say that! Nobody would be barbaric enough to destroy this city. Even the German bombs hardly touched Edinburgh.'

'Only because it was out of range for the bombers' fighter escorts, and other than the Naval yard at Rosyth, which the Luftwaffe attacked at the beginning of the war, the city was more or less left alone after a few failed air raids. Goering thought Edinburgh would be undefended, so his light bombers were easily shot down over the Firth of Forth.'

'But if there's another world war, Edinburgh still won't have any strategic importance.'

'This would be different. Edinburgh wouldn't survive an atomic blast.' Rosie folded her arms to stop herself trembling at the words that struck terror into everyone's heart. She thought of the news reels and horrific photographs of Hiroshima and Nagasaki, of the dead in their hundreds of thousands and those who had sickened and died from radiation, the cities turned to rubble. Her stomach felt like lead. Another war! The country was still on its knees from the last one, cities like Coventry and London full of the ragged gaps left by German bombs. She remembered the nights she spent on watch on the roof of the art school in her first year, before she left for Bletchley Park, and how the sky lit up over London as people huddled together in shelters listening to the wail of air raid sirens and the heavy drone of enemy bombers. Everyone had tried to put the worst of the war behind them but they'd only buried it deep. The fear and dread of those days ran through the country, even as it shook off the austerity of rationing and began to rebuild. Now here was Alex telling her he was convinced war would come again, and this time nowhere would be safe, not Edinburgh, with its breath-taking beauty spread out before them, not pretty little Crail with its harbour and fishing boats, not peaceful Kirkcudbright in Galloway, with its pastel-coloured houses where she had spent her childhood, not the bleak magnificence of the Highlands and islands, and not Glasgow and her beloved art school, which had miraculously escaped the bombs last time round. Rosie imagined it as a smouldering, burnt-out wreck, Charles Rennie Mackintosh's masterpiece reduced to rubble.

She made Alex turn to face her. 'This arms race, it's madness, an invitation to catastrophe where we will all be killed and there will be nothing left other than a poisonous wasteland. Surely there's something we can do to prevent war, some sort of campaign. There are plenty of good people who are fiercely against nuclear arms.'

'There's a new movement starting with scientists, artists, writers, musicians, some members of the Labour Party and trade unionists, people who are anti-war and want to get rid of all nuclear weapons, but it won't work.'

She clutched at his sleeve. 'How do you know that?'

Alex shrugged. 'The campaigners are well-meaning, but ultimately their efforts will be futile. The Soviets and the Americans face each other across the Atlantic with Europe in between, both equally eager to extend their influence over the world. Neither of them will listen to a bunch of high-minded pacifists. Nobody listened to them in the first or second wars, why should the third be any different? There will always be war. It's the human condition.'

Rosie buried her face in her hands and tried to blank out his words. 'I wish there was something I could do. I couldn't bear how useless I felt towards the end of the war, how everything was out of our hands, and we just had to wait to see if we'd be invaded, if Hitler would win. It's why Bletchley meant so much to me, we were saving lives, helping. But what can we do now? Wait for Khrushchev to bomb Scotland into oblivion? I'd do anything, anything to stop another war.'

Alex took her by the shoulders. 'If you're serious, there is something you can do, a heroic, selfless and dangerous act that will put a stop to this madness and prevent another war.'

Rosie waited. She watched trams and cars crawl along Princes Street, as miniature as the Dinky toys Alex had given to the McDonald boys. 'I'll do anything.'

'If you agree to do this, you couldn't tell anyone, not even your mother or Ned.'

'Just tell me what I can do.'

'You know Angus Sinclair and his wife, don't you?'

Rosie frowned. 'Sir Angus and Lady Moira? He's high up in the MoD, and they have a marvellous house on Loch Ewe, in the Highlands. I went there a lot when I was growing up. Ned took me to stay, and I remember being fascinated by all the curiosities the Sinclairs had collected.'

'I knew their house too, during the war, when it was the headquarters for the Russian Arctic Convoys and controlled the North Atlantic convoys entering and leaving Loch Ewe.'

Another blast of wind whipped around the crag, making Rosie pull her jacket closer. 'I remember always being absolutely freezing at Summer Isle House in the winter. It's perishing in these big, draughty country houses because nobody can afford to heat them. Ned would shut himself away with Angus in the library for hours on end, talking shop no doubt, and I was expected to play with the son, Duncan, an annoying boy who was always wanting to play kiss-chase.'

'Precisely why I need you to go there. There might be some more of that sort of thing.'

She took a step back. 'Whatever do you mean?'

'I need you to get something from the Sinclairs' house, and their son could be the way in.'

'I don't understand.'

'We know there's a mole, high up in the MoD, so embedded in the establishment that nobody would suspect him of handing our secrets over to the Russians. We strongly suspect it's Angus Sinclair.'

'No! But he's one of Ned's closest friends.'

'Your uncle doesn't know about our suspicions. He's too close to Sir Angus, we didn't want him to behave differently with him, so we've kept it quiet. Only a handful of people are in on this.'

Rosie thought hard and pictured Sir Angus. Saw him making a cutting remark to his son, despised for not being any good at games, for clinging too much to his mother. Small and unobserved as a child, she had seen what had been hidden from Ned – the casual cruelty he doled out to his wife and son with disparaging comments and indifference. 'Angus always terrified me when I was a child. He stomped about the place making me think of the giant in Jack and the Beanstalk. He was awful to his son too, ridiculed him at every turn, thought he was a milksop of a boy. It almost made me feel sorry for Duncan.'

'Sir Angus heads up the nuclear submarine base project. His people have been all over Scotland, looking for a suitable location, one deep enough for nuclear subs. My contacts have spotted his scouting teams near Edinburgh, in Rosyth, and as far north as Orkney and the Shetland Islands, and in various places along the west coast. The intel points to Sinclair having reached a conclusion, and that he has a set of encoded plans for the new base, which we understand he intends to hand over to the Soviets. I need those plans, as proof. It's the only way we'll convince the prime minister that he's the mole.'

'How do you know all this?'

'I set up the anti-Soviet unit, early in the war, when everyone still thought Stalin was our friend.'

'I knew that – it was common knowledge in Bletchley.'

'It was no secret. We intercepted and decoded Russian signals, but we also planted agents in Moscow under deep cover to keep an eye on Uncle Joe. They've been in there since they joined the NKVD, now the KGB. When the war ended, we knew we had to be ready for the next one, and that it would be the Soviet Union we'd be fighting this time, so I was seconded to the Secret Intelligence Service.' He paused. 'That's who I take my orders from.'

Rosie's voice was faint. 'MI6, not just an intelligence officer?'

'That's right.'

'This is the mission you were training me for, why I was learning tradecraft.' Rosie instinctively looked around, but there was nobody else on the crag where they were standing. 'Should you be telling me this? You could go to prison if they found out you'd broken the Official Secrets Act.'

'I've been sanctioned to recruit you. And you signed it too, at Bletchley.'

She gaped at him. 'You want me to be a proper spy, not just keep an eye on some lad at the camp? But I'm a teacher, an artist. What could I possibly do? I don't have any of your commando skills, jumping out of planes and so forth, and you know how awful I was that night when you left me in the middle of nowhere.'

'Don't worry, I don't need you to be that kind of agent. You're close to the Sinclair family, you said yourself that the son is an admirer. We need to see those plans, and nobody would suspect you.'

'You want me to get hold of them? How?'

'The Sinclairs are throwing a New Year's Eve party.'

'Their Hogmanay bash is a tradition, but I haven't been to one for years.'

'A member of their staff, who also works for us, has drawn up the guest list and you and Ned are on it. Have you kept that microdot camera I gave you in Crail?'

'It's in with my paints, next to a putty rubber in its box.'

'Good, you're going to need it. The blueprints are kept

in a safe in the Sinclairs' library. I want you to copy them and bring me the film.'

Rosie looked at Alex, wondering if this was an elaborate joke. But he was deadly serious. 'How on earth am I supposed to get to them? I don't recall safe cracking being part of my training.'

'The plans are kept in the same safe as the Sinclair tiara, the one Lady Moira wore when she was presented to Queen Alexandra. It's worth a fortune and Duncan Sinclair likes to show it off to impress people, particularly pretty women. If you flirt with him a little and ask to see the tiara, he'll open the safe. It's up to you to come up with a story to get him out of the library long enough for you to photograph the plans.' Rosie examined her lover's face, looking for any signs he might falter at the thought of her more or less seducing another man to get what he wanted.

'Alex, that's so grubby. I'm surprised that you'd asked me to do something so vile.'

He touched her cheek. 'I know, my darling, but you have to overcome your squeamishness. It's a matter of life or death, and I know you can take care of yourself, that you won't let it get too far. If the Sinclairs' son looks as if he is getting out of hand, there will be people around you, and I won't be far away. We'll work out a signal and a meeting place, like we did at Crail.'

Rosie grimaced. 'I still think it's an underhand way to

behave – I've known the Sinclairs since I was a child and I'm very fond of Moira, who always treated me like the daughter she never had. And Duncan was a bit wet, but harmless.'

'They'll never know it was you. Nobody will know where we got hold of the proof that Angus Sinclair is betraying his country, and you'll single-handedly stop a significant leak to the Soviets about your country's defence, potentially saving millions of lives.' He took her hands and kissed them. 'And I'm afraid that being underhand and duplicitous comes with the territory when you're a secret agent.'

'Why did you say it was dangerous?'

He dropped her hands. 'We don't know what Sir Angus will do if you get caught, but we do know that the Soviets won't hesitate to eliminate anyone who gets in their way. But don't worry, I know what I'm doing, and I would never let anything happen to you. I'll be nearby to make sure you get away if there's a problem.'

Rosie hesitated, trying to take in what he had just told her. He trusted her, didn't see her as a spinster teacher but as someone who had toiled at Bletchley Park, someone brave and capable. If she did this for him, she would be protecting her countrymen and women, her family and friends. Rosie made up her mind.

'Well, I guess I'd better not get caught, then.'

'You'll do it? Are you sure?'

'Yes.'

Alex placed his hand gently behind her head and kissed her. He murmured into her hair. 'Did I mention that I love you?'

She smiled up at him. 'No, you didn't. I was beginning to think you never would.'

'I've never said that to anyone before.'

'You're not going all soppy on me, I hope, Alex Kuznetsov? Perhaps school and Cambridge didn't knock all the Russian out of you after all.' He seemed to be waiting for her to say something. Rosie laughed. 'All right then, I love you too.'

Chapter 12

Summer was nearly over, and Rosie knew it would be soon time to say goodbye to her students at the camp. She tried not to miss Alex, who had left for the Highlands, or think too much about the mission he'd given her and was glad to be kept busy painting the last of the flats for *Hamlet* and putting together an exhibition of her students' work. Simon Fairweather had volunteered to help her hang the paintings and sketches and place the driftwood sculptures for the exhibition. Rosie was watching him at the top of a ladder as he hung a portrait of the commanding officer in full fig when Gabriel Paxton strolled in. He took a long drag of smoke from his cigarette holder and let it out in a thoughtful stream as he looked at the painting.

'The CO looks constipated. He should have had a dose of Andrews Salts before he sat for his portrait. And would you look at the size of his chin. I take it,' he squinted at the signature on the painting, 'Lieutenant

Mellis was absent the day you covered the Golden Ratio?'

'Don't be unkind and give poor Simon a hand before he falls and breaks an ankle,' Rosie said.

'And such a well-turned one at that.' Gabriel looked up at Simon, whose khaki T-shirt had risen to expose a stretch of smoothly tanned skin. Rosie could swear Simon winked at Gabriel before climbing down from his perch. He ran a hand through his sweat-darkened blond hair, and grinned.

'Mellis is no great shakes at art, but he makes a first-class silly mid-on.'

Gabriel shook his head at Rosie. 'What is this delicious Adonis talking about?'

'Cricket. It's his one true love.'

'Next to artists,' Simon said. 'Can't get enough of them.'

'Is that so? You must come and sit for me.'

Rosie wiped her hands on a rag tucked into her boiler suit pocket. 'If you two have quite finished, I'd appreciate Gabriel casting his eyes over the rest of the exhibition.'

'I'm off to the NAAFI for some scran,' Simon said, his eyes still on Gabriel. 'Might take you up on your offer. I'm used to nude modelling for my artist friends so I'm not at all shy.' Before Gabriel could pick up his dropped jaw, Simon turned on his heel and left with a backwards wave.

'Not being a regular at the more physically demanding aspects of national service training, our paths have not crossed, alas. What a delectable specimen of manliness,' Gabriel said to Rosie.

'Never mind him, he's a lovely young man and a terrific sportsman, but absolutely no artistic talent.'

'Even better. Now, show me the rest of this so-called work, if you must,' he said with a shudder. In fact, Gabriel was generous in his appraisal of the men's amateur efforts, merely grimacing at some of the more tragic exhibits without comment and finding warm words for some of the harbour watercolours. 'Not bad. There's a couple that wouldn't look out of place in a provincial gallery. Although I do loathe a bobbing boat, on principle.'

The opening, or *vernissage* as Gabriel insisted on calling it as if it were at the Royal Academy, was a tremendous success. Word had got round that the catering corps had managed to get hold of sherry to hand out with the sausage rolls, and the exhibition was packed. Rosie's students beamed with pride and were happy to be the butt of the good-natured ribbing from the rest of the troops. Surrounded by the young men, some of whom had only just started shaving by the look of it, Rosie was beginning to feel old and was pleased to see Monty standing next to Valentina, who was scowling at a piece of driftwood draped with dried seaweed. Monty abandoned her and moved to Rosie's side.

'I say, where's Alex? You'd think the old misery guts would be here in your moment of triumph.'

'He had to leave and said he wouldn't be back until after I'd left.' Rosie remembered how distracted Alex had been as he packed his kit bag, barely taking the time to look at her as she sat in front of the fire, twisting a handkerchief to stop herself crying. At the door, he'd turned for a last word.

'I won't be able to see you for a while, not until after the Sinclairs' party.' He took her hands. 'Listen to me, Rosie, this is important.' She blinked away her tears and nodded wordlessly. 'There's a fisherman's hut down at the shore of Loch Ewe down from Summer Isle House. I'll meet you there as soon as you can get away. Don't forget the camera and everything we went through.' A final peremptory kiss and he was gone. Rosie realised that Monty was studying her. She gave him a tight smile and he relaxed into his usual affable self.

'Alex and his mysterious ways,' he said. 'It's a shame he won't be here when you leave, but never fear, I'll take you to the train station. Can't have you going without a proper send-off.'

The next few days were a flurry of packing and last-minute reports on the men's artistic efforts, which Rosie doubted would ever be read. She couldn't bear to say goodbye to everyone at the camp, so she asked Monty to collect her from the cottage in Crail for the earliest train. As she closed the door behind her, she felt a pang of sadness. She was shutting the door on a time of intense emotion and new-found closeness with Alex. By asking for her help, he'd had to open up and share the secrets that had made him seem aloof and sometimes, she admitted, cold and indifferent. Rosie shook herself. He had promised that after this mission was over, there would be other times, and that a whole lifetime lay ahead of them. Still, she couldn't help the tears that finally came as Monty drove her out of the little town. He pretended not to notice and kept up a steady stream of silly remarks on the way to the station.

Here we are again, happy as can be, all good pals and jolly good company,' he sang as the jeep stopped.

Waiting on the platform were all her students from the camp, who crowded around her, patting her on the back and taking turns to shake her hand.

'Thought you'd slip off without saying goodbye, eh?' Gabriel said as he pulled Rosie into a hug, elbowing one of the students out of the way. Simon stepped forward and shyly handed her an enormous bouquet.

'For our favourite teacher,' he said to cheers and a hearty chorus of *for she's a jolly good fellow*. Even the stationmaster, notoriously bad-tempered, smiled at the ruckus.

'Haven't seen such a good turnout since the end of the war,' he said. 'You take care, Miss. And you'd better hurry along now if you want to catch the Edinburgh train. I'm about to shut the doors.'

'Goodbye! Goodbye! I'll never forget you!' Rosie shouted and waved as the train pulled away and she blinked back yet more tears.

Chapter 13

The summer may have been over, but Edinburgh was showing off its autumn colours, the trees wearing their burnished cloaks of copper, gold and scarlet. The girls at school were full of chatter and buzzing with excitement after the summer holidays, and Rosie's most promising pupil, Anne Rankin, asked to use the art room during breaks and study periods. Crail had made Rosie a better teacher. With the conscripts, she'd been faced with the challenge of making art lessons interesting rather than daunting or a chore, and now she incorporated those methods into her teaching. She took the girls for walks along the Water of Leith in Dean Village to pick up fallen leaves and other found objects and turn them into art. They responded to her new-found zest with their own natural enthusiasm and curiosity.

Her life outside the school also picked up in a surprising way. Stella was back on tour, but that didn't stop Jim Harrison coming over to Charlotte Square most evenings and weekends. She found herself enjoying his company as a cultured man with a keen eye for art, leavened with a sense of fun. She didn't like to admit it, but sometimes she had found that Alex could be too serious, and often overtaken by strange, black moods. Jim, on the other hand, was always the same way – cheerful, kindly and interested in what she had to say. He insisted on going to every gallery opening and on seeing the premiere of every play. His tastes were catholic, and he was as enthusiastic about a foreign art-house film at the Cameo as he was about the latest Hollywood movie at the New Victoria, where he indulged his weakness for musical comedies. After one of these, they'd walk back to Rosie's home, their breath foggy in the cold, singing the latest musical hit to the bemusement of people hurrying past in their winter coats, collars up against the haar that hung like a ghostly veil over the city. Jim would come in for a nightcap and was never in a rush to go home. He was easy to talk to, a good listener, and a thoughtful, entertaining conversationalist. Rosie was fascinated by his knowledge of the rebel American artists and together they pored over art magazines showing the work of abstract expressionists, and found they had both been to the Tate to see 'Modern Art in the United States' earlier that year.

'If only the exhibition would come again, I'd love to spend more time with Rothko's colour-field abstracts, not to mention Jackson Pollock's work,' Rosie said wistfully.

'Well, we'll just have to go to New York to the Museum of Modern Art,' Jim said. 'I could show you the sights, we'd have a swell time.'

Rosie sighed. 'That would be lovely, but it's impossible.'

'Nothing is impossible.'

'You Americans are always so positive; it can be quite exhausting.'

'Hey, who are you calling positive? I've been in Scotland for long enough now to learn how to be a gloomy cynic.'

'Why, Jim, don't tell me you've gone native. You'll be talking about the weather next,' Rosie said with a laugh.

If Ned was home, the conversation would turn to politics and world affairs. Now that she knew more about Alex's work, she found herself listening closely one evening when Jim and Ned discussed USS *Nautilus*, the world's first nuclear-powered submarine armed with nuclear cruise missiles.

'The Soviets must be spitting blood,' Ned said. 'Your *Nautilus* revolutionised naval warfare when it was launched two years ago.'

Rosie pretended to mark her pupils' essays on Giotto and listened carefully.

Jim leaned forward in his armchair. 'Yeah, and now we've gone from atomic power to a hydrogen bomb, a thousand times more powerful than the ones dropped on Hiroshima and Nagasaki. The tests went well at Bikini Atoll, but the Russians are catching up with Joe-19.'

'We're not doing too badly ourselves,' Ned said. 'The boffins have been working like mad and they'll have something similar ready to test next year.'

Jim raised his glass. 'Welcome to the most exclusive club in the world – the thermonuclear club, membership of three.'

Ned and Jim were making light of it, as if nuclear annihilation was quite a normal state of affairs. They had moved onto the Suez crisis and the likelihood of war in the Middle East when Rosie could keep quiet no longer. She was in a bad mood as once again there was radio silence from Alex, with not a letter or a phone call from him.

'How can you talk so calmly about these awful bombs and the prospect of another war that could mean the end of the world?'

Jim shrugged. 'As long as our side has the best weapons and the latest technology, we can keep the Soviets at bay. Khrushchev won't risk defeat, not when we have the advantage.'

Rosie set aside the school work she was marking. 'I think all this brinkmanship is utter madness.'

'True,' Jim said, replacing a jotter that had tumbled from its pile. 'But old Ike knows what he's doing. He won the war for us in North Africa and Normandy, after all.'

Ned raised an eyebrow. 'I wouldn't go that far, although we're of course grateful to our American cousins for their contribution, even if you were a little late to the party.'

Jim laughed good-naturedly, showing once again how impossible it was for him to be offended. 'All the best guests are.'

The two men changed the subject to talk about Jim's progress on his theatre and Rosie went back to her marking, her resolution to help Alex protect her country stronger than ever.

One late, darkening afternoon, when the wind was hurling the rain at the windows, Rosie and her mother were leafing through Lily's old sketch books from their time in China, something they liked to do from time to time.

'Look at me, upside down and looking through my legs, such a scrap compared to the roly-poly boy I'm playing with,' Rosie said.

'Sweet little Beauregard, his amah used to stuff him with dumplings. His mother was my dear American friend, and we spent so much time together, the two of you were inseparable. Perhaps that explains your affinity for Jim Harrison.'

'I can't think what you mean, Mother. Jim is just a friend. I have Alex, and even if I didn't, he's keen on Stella.' Lily raised her eyebrows and Rosie ignored her, bending her head to look more closely at the drawing. 'You've captured the sense of movement, the children's energy and mischief bursts out of the page. Tricky but you've pulled it off.'

'Oh, I'd had plenty of practice sketching moving subjects with Jeanie and the first dance troupe she got into, and before that when we were girls. She'd do all sorts of acrobatics – somersaults and handstands, pliés and pirouettes. Jeanie Taylor was another child who could never sit still.'

Rosie reached the end of the book. 'Why are there no drawings of my father? I've only got that formal photograph of him and you. What was he like?'

'He was tall, and good looking, fair like you, and you have his strong jaw and blue eyes. I don't know why I didn't draw him. I suppose because he was always working. When he was at home, he was always so tired, or closeted in his study.'

Rosie closed her eyes and tried to picture her father, but she could only see a shadow figure in sepia tones. 'I wish I could remember him, but I only have a few vague memories of Shanghai.'

'You were only five when he died. I'm sorry you've had to grow up without a father.'

Lily sighed and took the sketch book from her daughter. The movement dislodged a sheet of paper that had been tucked inside an envelope at the back of the book. She bent to pick it up, but Rosie got there first. It was a sketch of a young man, his hat tilted to the back of his head. Amusement creased the skin around his eyes and his lips seemed to twitch with suppressed laughter.

'Who is this?'

Lily took it from her and smoothed a foxed edge. 'Jack Petrie.'

'Your first love.'

'Yes, my first and last.'

'Not my father, then?' Rosie couldn't understand how her mother had never got over Jack Petrie, even after all this time.

'Did you marry Father as a way of forgetting Jack?'

'I would never have used your father that way. He was a good friend to me when I needed one. I thought Jack had died in the war, that there was no hope. I was grieving and Hugh was kind to me, helped me live again.' She took Rosie's hand. 'And he gave me you.' Rosie gave the sketch back to her mother who once more smoothed its foxed edge.

Ned sauntered into the drawing room and squeezed between them on the sofa.

'A tender moment between mother and daughter, how lovely! But I'm so bored I'm going to ruthlessly break it up and make you pay attention to me. I'm the luckiest man in the world to have two beautiful girls in my household. Whatever did I do in my long and sinful life to deserve you both?'

Lily smiled at him. 'We are happy, aren't we, in this funny little family of ours? If only . . .' She picked up the sketch and her eyes filled.

'I know,' Ned said, looking at the drawing. 'I miss him too.'

Rosie tried to remember what she'd been told about Jack over the years. He was an artist who had gone missing in the war. The details were hazy, but she knew he'd turned up alive in France after the war and had started a family with another woman. She found it hard to understand why her mother still carried a torch for the love of her youth – perhaps that was sometimes the way with first love – and not only Lily, but Ned, who had been a close friend and who she suspected had also been in love with him. She had always envied her mother having someone who had been – and clearly still was – the love of her life, but now she had Alex, and because of him she understood how you would do anything to hold onto that kind of love.

Rosie, preoccupied by school and trying to put Alex's silence down to the fact he was travelling between listening stations, had put the talk of Jack Petrie out of her mind. A few weeks later, when the trees had nearly lost all their leaves, she was once again marking books in the evening while Lily and Ned played cards in the lamplight, and they all heard the doorbell followed by a murmur of voices in the hall. Mrs Jackson poked her head around the door, looking crosser than usual.

'There's a queer-looking chap asking for Sir Edward.'

'Who is it?' Ned said.

'A foreign-sounding name, but he doesn't sound foreign.'

'Well, be a dear and show him in. It's a dreich day and the poor chap must be cold standing in the hall.' Ned got up to stir the fire into life and Rosie and Lily looked at the door expectantly, curious to meet this stranger who had put Mrs Jackson out of sorts.

When the visitor came in, he stood at the door for a while, as if unsure of his welcome. Rosie realised why Mrs Jackson had called him 'queer-looking'. Half his face was covered in burn scars, he leaned heavily on a stick, and there was a hang-dog melancholy air about him. She waited for Ned to spring forward in his usual affable way and usher the man over to the fire and offer him a dram, but he and Lily seemed frozen. Really, Rosie thought, they have forgotten their manners. She got up and went over to the stranger, her hand outstretched.

'I'm Rosie Anderson. Do come in and get warm.' The man tore his eyes away from Lily, whom he had been staring at, and blinked at Rosie.

'I'm terribly sorry to barge in like this. I'm an old friend of Ned's.' He stumbled over his words. 'I, I didn't expect to see Lily here.' A faint noise came from the sofa and Rosie turned round to see if her mother was all right. She had gone white, and her hand shook as she put it to her throat.

'Jack?' Lily said.

'I go by Alain Bourret now,' he said and bowed his head as if in shame. Rosie looked from one to the other. How could this be Jack, the hero of her mother's youth? He was an old man, broken and bent, but her mother sprang from the sofa and embraced him. He put his arms around her, hesitantly at first, and then more fiercely, a drowning man clinging to a raft. Lily touched his ruined face and murmured his name, over and over, as if chanting a spell to bind him to her. Jack dropped his cane and cupped her face to kiss her. Rosie felt a hand on her shoulder.

'Let's leave them alone,' Ned whispered It was only when the door had closed that he buried his face in his hands and his shoulders heaved. Her uncle, usually so composed, sagged so that Rosie had to catch him and lead him to his study. She knew from the way Lily had clung to the stranger that she had never stopped loving him and that her father would not have stood a chance against such a ghost. And now, after more than forty years, the ghost had returned.

Chapter 14

The next morning, Rosie walked into the dining room to see Jack sitting at the table reading *The Scotsman*, in front of him a plate with a smear of marmalade and a scattering of toast crumbs.

Jack folded the newspaper. She noticed his hands trembled as he put it down. He smiled nervously at her. 'Good morning.' Rosie nodded and sat down, busying herself by scraping butter onto what was left of the toast in the rack. 'I'm afraid Ned and I made short work of breakfast before he had to dash off,' Jack said. 'Shall I make some more coffee?'

'It's fine,' Rosie said, taking a tepid sip.

'You're right, I'll wait until Lily comes down, or better yet, I'll take her a tray. She's having a long lie.' Lily was usually up before Rosie, pausing only to swallow a cup of Chinese tea before heading to her studio in the mews. The thought of her mother spending the night with Jack made her feel uncomfortable. It was ridiculous to feel this way;

Lily was entitled to her own life. Rosie excused herself, her appetite gone, and crossed the garden to the studio. She was slashing blues and greys on a stormy Crail seascape when Jim pushed open the door to the studio.

'My, don't you look a million dollars! Only you could make a boiler suit sexy.'

'It's handy for painting.' She smiled and beckoned him in. Jim was exactly the person she needed at the moment. Rosie put down her palette and looked in the small cracked mirror tacked on the wall. There was a blue streak of paint across her forehead, and she'd managed to give herself a charcoal moustache. She groaned and reached for a rag, but they had all been drenched in turps at some point and were stiff and dry. Jim handed her a navy and white silk spotted handkerchief from his top pocket, but she batted it away.

'I'll only ruin that thing of beauty.' She headed over to a paint-spattered sink where the brushes were cleaned, wiped her face and scrubbed her hands. 'Careful you don't get paint on your suit in here. Honestly, the only other man I know who is as elegantly dressed as you is Ned. I thought Americans were supposed to favour the casual look.'

'I'm from the South, where gentlemen are required to look immaculate all day, even in ninety degrees.' He wandered over to Rosie's easel and looked at the canvas with a practised eye. 'You capture the exact colour and movement of a restless winter sky.' He glanced out of the window and shivered. 'No wonder you're so good at painting bad weather, living in Scotland. It's the rain in the wind I can't stand. On days like this, the swampy Savannah heat doesn't seem so bad. Aren't you freezing? You should be wearing that awful greatcoat I've seen you in, no doubt bought from your favourite lady's outfitter, the Army and Navy Store.'

'I don't mind the cold, and it's cosy enough in here with the paraffin heater. Tea?'

She lifted a battered aluminium kettle onto the electric plate and pulled out a couple of rickety kitchen chairs. Once they were seated with the chipped enamel mugs of strong tea that reminded her of the NAAFI brews at Crail, Rosie sighed extravagantly. Jim winced at his tea and put it down at his feet.

'What's eating you?'

'An old flame of my mother's is staying. Someone she cared for a great deal when they were both at art school.'

'And you don't like him? Is he what Ned would call an awkward customer?'

'He seems perfectly nice, but I'm worried about Mother. He's turned up out of the blue after all this time, and she's welcomed him with open arms.'

'What does Ned say?'

'Jack Petrie was Ned's oldest friend. Mother met Ned through him.'

'So, this Jack Petrie is her first love. That's some powerful juju.'

'But they're both so old!'

Jim laughed. 'Listen to you, Rosie Anderson! Love doesn't have an age limit. When they look at each other, Lily and Jack won't see two people in their sixties. Finding each other again after all these years means they are still young in each other's eyes. The wrinkles and grey hairs won't matter.'

'I suppose you're right, as usual, oh wise one. How do you know so much about all this?'

'After my mother died ten years ago, my father married his high school sweetheart. It was a bit of a scandal because they carried on behind her husband's back until he found out and there was a divorce. My stepmother is still considered a Scarlet Woman by the good ladies of Savannah, but her and Pop don't care.'

'What about you? How did it make you feel?'

Jim shrugged. 'She makes the old man happy. He was miserable after Mom died.'

'Mother has always had bouts of being sad and distracted, ever since I can remember, but Jack made her light up last night. I should be happy for her, but I don't know much about this man.' Rosie drank her tea. Outside, the wind beat at the glass panes and moaned as it raced across the slate roof.

'It's understandable if you feel a little jealous,' Jim said.

It was a comment that would have made Rosie defensive

a few months ago, before she'd met Alex. But now she was able to answer calmly. 'No, I'm happy for them.'

'Well, I hate to admit it, but I was jealous when Pop and Melissa got together, at first anyhow. He and I had gotten used to rattling around together in that big house, and then Melissa came along, and Pop only had eyes for her. I felt like a gooseberry in my own home. But I soon realised it wasn't so much that I was jealous because my father had been taken away from me, I was envious of how much in love they were. I didn't have that. Not then.'

'But you do now?'

His eyes softened. 'Yes, I guess I do.'

Rosie smiled. 'Stella's performing at the Pavilion Theatre in Glasgow. Shall we go and see her? I'm sure you miss her as much as I do.' Jim lowered his eyes and picked up his mug of tea before putting it down again and returning her smile.

'Sure, why not?'

Chapter 15

Bundled up against the cold, Rosie waited outside the Pavilion Theatre, having sent Jim to congratulate Stella in her dressing room on his own. She yawned, suddenly tired. The three of them had a late table booked at Rogano and it would be hours before she was heading towards her own bed in Edinburgh, with Jim behind the wheel of the tiny Morris Minor he insisted, rather unconvincingly, was a refreshing change from the Cadillac he'd left behind in Savannah. Rosie was worried about Stella. At forty-six, despite the assiduous beauty regime that made her look a decade or so younger, she was old for a dancer and tonight she had been slower on the stage with some of the trickier moves no longer in her repertoire. Instead, the audience was artfully distracted by enormous frothy ostrich feathers and glamorous costume changes. It was time Stella retired but she couldn't envisage her friend giving up the spotlight after so many years as the Taylor Girls' star turn.

Rosie shivered despite the well-cut winter coat and fur stole Jim had insisted she borrow from her mother so she wouldn't, he said, be mistaken for a 'hobo'. She should have remembered that Stella always took ages to leave the theatre, surrounded by bouquets of flowers and admirers toasting her with champagne. Hope Street was bustling with crowds coming out of cinemas, variety theatres and dance halls and Rosie smiled at the groups of spirited young Glaswegians calling out to each other. The cold was beginning to seep up through the thin soles of the heels and nylon stockings she'd swapped for her usual brogues. At least her dress was woollen, but it didn't keep her as warm as her trousers. Rosie shifted from foot to foot to ease the chill and when someone knocked into her, she nearly lost her balance. A strong hand caught her by the arm.

'Sorry, Miss, didn't see you there.' Rosie turned to face a man, whose affable grin only grew wider when he saw who it was. 'My, my, don't you look a picture! Quite the elegant lady, my gorgeous Rosey-Posey.'

Frank! She shook him off. 'Not your anything, not anymore.'

'Now, now, no need to be like that. We're old mates, aren't we? I always said that no matter what, we'd still be part of each other's lives. And here we are! You can't argue with fate, me bumping into you like this.'

'Hardly unusual to find me here, given that Stella was on

stage tonight, and you usually cover the first night of her new show.'

Frank grimaced and glanced at the billboard. 'That harpy! She never did like me. She used some choice language last time I saw her at a gallery opening. I had to be quick on my feet or I'd have been drenched in lukewarm Blue Nun.' Rosie's mouth twitched. Frank noticed and pressed home his advantage. 'Come on, darling, can't you let bygones be bygones? After all, we were together a long time, and I've missed you.' His eyes twinkled. 'Admit it, we had a few laughs together. Nobody is as good company as you, Rosie. Most other people bore the backside off me. Let's have a drink or two for old times' sake, what do you say? I'll treat you to champagne cocktails at the Grand Central Hotel. Then I'll see you safely onto your train back to Auld Reekie, and I promise I won't try it on, no matter how much I'm tempted.'

Rosie found her bitterness over Frank's betrayal had gone, that she was finally free of him. What harm would it do to catch up? It was true that in the early days she'd had good times with Frank, who could be entertaining when he wanted with his gift for gossip and irreverent observations. It would be healthier to remember those days rather than dwell on the unpleasantness of their final days together. What's more, by being cool and breezy, she could show Frank how little he meant to her now, which would give her a modicum of satisfaction. Besides, she didn't fancy being what Jim called a gooseberry with him and Stella. A part of her, too, was angry that Alex still hadn't been in touch. A drink with another man, even if it was Frank, would soothe her pride.

'All right, we can go for a drink, but only for one and somewhere close by. I'll leave a note for my friends and catch up with them later.'

'Splendid!'

After Rosie had had a word with the doorman, Frank offered his elbow, and she reluctantly put her hand through his arm. By the time they had pushed through the doors and into the warm fug of a Victorian pub round the corner from the theatre, Frank was making her laugh so much she'd nearly forgotten what a heel he was underneath all the charm and chat. He found them a table in a quiet corner and brought over their drinks.

'Well, it's not the Grand Central Hotel,' he said, eyeing the pools of spilled beer, 'but I suppose it will do.'

'That's a huge brandy,' Rosie protested.

'All the better to warm you up, my dear.' He treated her to a lascivious grin, and she rolled her eyes. 'Besides, they're out of champagne cocktails, funnily enough.' Frank leaned towards her and pulled out all the stops, launching into scurrilous gossip from the newspaper world about the famous people who had stayed at Glasgow's most glamorous hotel that year, fed by a string of chambermaids and a chatty concierge, all paid retainers for his newspaper.

'Gene Kelly was a real gent; the staff were all charmed by his impeccable manners, you can just imagine, but as for –,' he mentioned one of Hollywood's most coveted female stars whose curves and dangerous beauty had entranced the entire male population on both sides of the Atlantic. 'She was a complete diva, a monster! The suite was an absolute zoo cage with fags squashed out in the butter, dirty knickers hanging from the chandelier, cocaine spilled everywhere, and a steady stream of hot and cold running call girls – girls mind you, not male escorts. I was on duty every night she was there and bunged the doorman a few quid extra to let me hang around, no questions asked. The snapper hid behind a potted fern and got some cracking pics of her being helped up the stairs to her room by a couple of tarts from the Drag.'

Rosie's eyes were wide. 'I don't remember reading about that.'

'The paper didn't dare print the story. Bloody cowards! I'd made a call to her agent for a comment, and he complained to the editor, threatened a lawsuit, no less. The boss tore a strip off me, scared we'd be blacklisted by the studio's publicity department. I've been in the doghouse ever since.' He suddenly looked serious. 'What I really want to do, rather than all this celebrity fluff, is proper investigative journalism, you know, the kind of thing that wins you prizes. That would show everyone what I'm capable of, but they won't even consider it. I've asked for a transfer off the features desk back to hard news, but old Wilson won't have me back. He's got his favourites, but I know I could write the chief reporter under the table given half a chance.'

Rosie found she could find it in her heart to feel sorry for Frank. She knew he'd worked hard to get a coveted spot on the Glasgow broadsheet where he worked and was desperate to be taken seriously. But his flair was for entertainment, was known disparagingly on the editorial floor as the lights and brights, no matter how much he yearned to emulate his hero, James Cameron. Frank had told her often about his admiration for the Scottish journalist acclaimed for his brilliantly written first-hand reports of the Bikini Atoll nuclear experiments and the atrocities committed during the Korean War. But Frank, never one to be despondent for long, brightened. 'Never mind, swings and roundabouts, I'll be back in the good books before you know it, and as for the chief reporter, everyone says he's lost his bottle, and you know, you're only as good as your last story in this game. Never say die!' He swallowed the rest of his brandy and jumped up. 'I'll get another round in. Same again?' Before Rosie could say no, he was at the bar. When Frank shouldered his way back through the press of Saturday drinkers and sat down, Rosie was careful to only take a few sips from her drink, but she was already feeling the effects of the brandy on an empty stomach.

'I'll have to go in a minute,' she said.

'Not yet surely? I haven't heard what you've been up to. I hear you're teaching in one of those terribly-terribly Edinburgh girls' schools and living with your mother. Bit boring for you after raffish Garnethill and the life of a bohemian artist, isn't it?' There it was: Frank's trademark cruelty, like a stiletto slipped between the ribs.

'I love teaching, and I'm good at it.'

Frank raised his eyebrows. 'If that's what you need to tell yourself, be my guest, but I can't imagine you're having a lot of laughs, not compared to some of the wild times we had.'

Rosie was stung. 'Actually, there's been rather a lot of excitement recently.'

'Oh? Do tell. Did the neighbours finally invite you in for a nice fruit scone, or had you had your tea, as they say in Edinburgh?'

'An old flame of my mother's, from before the Great War, has turned up on the doorstep, and they're madly in love again.'

Frank narrowed his eyes. 'How interesting! I'm sure you mentioned him before, Jack something.'

Rosie hesitated, remembering she was talking to a journalist, not just her own old flame. 'It doesn't matter, it's not really that interesting, I'm making too much of it.'

Frank turned the brandy balloon in his hands. 'Petrie, that was his name.' He looked up and smiled disarmingly. 'Sorry to change the subject – and I didn't mean to imply your life is dull without me, that's my vanity speaking – but did you see the profile I did on your uncle getting his knighthood?'

'I did, actually, it was very well written. You got him down to a tee.'

Frank tried to look modest. 'I told them I had a personal connection, let on that I'd met him. The news editor didn't need to know it was only through you, that I'd never actually met Sir Edward Raeside. The desk loved it, Glasgow man rising through the ranks of the Ministry of Defence, they love a local hero.' He picked up his nearly empty glass and drained it. 'Listen to me, bumming myself up, and even worse, boring you about my work. As we say in the journalists' boozer, no shop talk in the mess. Tell me what you've been up to. Anyone lucky enough to have claimed your heart, or are you still young, free and single?' He waggled his eyebrows like Groucho Marx and Rosie suppressed a smile. Frank was fun to be with, but she knew she couldn't trust him. He was right to be frustrated; he was good at his job and had a keen nose for a story. She had never told him about Bletchley Park – even her mother thought she'd worked in a propaganda film unit in London during the war – and she knew it would be dangerous to talk about Alex in case Frank started sniffing around and caught wind of his intelligence work.

'I've had a few offers, but I like the single life,' she said.

'Do you, aye?' He stubbed out his cigarette and patted

his waistcoat for the cigarette packet and lighter. 'I'm surprised nobody has snapped you up. These Edinburgh men must be blind.' He covered her hand with his. 'You're an exceptional woman, Rosie, and deserve to have an interesting life.' She withdrew her hand. Little did Frank know just how interesting her life had become this year. He pulled back her hand into his.

'I do miss you. I was a fool to let you go. I know, it was all my stupid fault, but do you think you could give me a second chance? It would be for keeps this time; I promise.' He smiled but tightened his grip on her hand. 'Remember, I always said no matter what happened between us, we'd end up together.' There was a time when her heart would have leapt at these words, but not now. Rosie wrenched her hand away and stood up.

'I've moved on, maybe you should too.'

He leaned back and took a drag of his fresh cigarette. 'Have it your way, but you can't blame me for trying,' he drawled, smoke curling from his nostrils. 'Go back to teaching spoiled little rich girls. A perfect career choice, I might add, for a spinster and failed artist. What is it they say about those who can't ending up teaching?'

Rosie bit back a reply and picked up her coat. By the time she reached the pub door, Frank was already chatting up two pretty women at the next table, shaking their hands. She heard him say, 'What are you charming ladies doing in a place like this? I'd love to take you away from all this and treat you to champagne cocktails at the Grand Central Hotel. I'm a journalist and would love to hear your stories.'

Rosie was still in a filthy mood when she stormed into Rogano, pink-cheeked from the walk down the hill, darting between trams and merrymakers. The rich aroma of lobster bisque greeted her as she made her way through the restaurant, but she was no longer hungry, her appetite soured by her encounter with Frank. She'd been a fool to lay herself open to his barbs, to believe that they could have a friendly drink without descending into rancour. When she reached their table, Jim and Stella had their heads together, looking so intimate that Rosie couldn't bear the thought of intruding. It would have been different if Alex were with her, and suddenly she missed him unbearably. When Stella looked up with bright eyes, the picture of joy, Rosie made up her mind.

Kissing her friend on the cheek, she said: 'Well done, your act was perfect, as always. I'd love to stay and celebrate, but I'm going to have to get the train home, I have a crushing headache. You don't mind, do you?'

Stella pouted. 'But I haven't seen you for ages, darling.' She frowned. 'You do look a bit peaky. You should wear more make-up, a brighter lip. Is everything all right?' Before Rosie could reply Stella put her hand up as if to stop her. 'Don't tell me! You hated the show. You're right, it was dreadful, so old-fashioned. I keep telling Mama we should change direction and do some of the new dances in the style of Margaret Morris, with all those artistic classical Greek postures, but will she listen? No, all she's interested in is giving the punters a cheap thrill.' She turned to Jim, who looked as relaxed in the Art Deco plushness of Rogano as he did with his sleeves rolled up on the stage of his draughty, half-finished theatre. 'Thank goodness for you, Jim, I don't know what I'd do without you.' Rosie stopped herself from rolling her eyes. As usual, Stella had turned the conversation back to herself.

'Don't be silly, Stella, you were marvellous tonight, as always. I'm just not feeling terribly well.'

Jim started to get up from the table. 'We'll forget dinner, in that case, and I'll drive you home.' Stella looked mutinous and Rosie hastily put a hand on his arm.

'Please don't, I wouldn't dream of spoiling your evening. I know you've both been looking forward to it. The railway station is only around the corner and if I'm quick I'll catch the next train to Edinburgh.' Before they could protest, Rosie blew them a kiss and went back out into the cold.

Chapter 16

She brooded all the way back on the train, first about Frank and how he still managed to make her feel small even after all this time, and then about Alex and how he could disappear for nearly two months without a single word, and finally her thoughts turned to Jack Petrie, hoping he wouldn't let her mother down again. In Lily's eyes he was clearly still the handsome young man she'd seen off to war, but to Rosie, he seemed damaged, broken even. So many men of that generation carried scars from the trenches, not only physical ones. Ned, too, had fought in that war, and sometimes, at night, she heard him crying out in his sleep.

There was a light on in the study when Rosie got back. She walked past the half-open door and saw Jack sitting with his back to her by the fire, talking to Ned, their voices a low, comfortable rumble. Ned spotted her and beckoned her in, but Rosie only shook her head, not wanting to interrupt. She hadn't seen her mother much lately and knocked and went into her bedroom. Lily was standing at the window, wrapped in a Chinese peignoir, its red silk embroidered with a gold dragon, her hair tumbling down her back. She turned round and Rosie was struck by how radiant she looked. Lily held out her arms and Rosie went to her.

'I'm sorry, darling, I've been neglecting you,' Lily said.

'Not at all. You've been catching up with Jack.'

Lily smiled uncertainly and they sat down together on a silk-covered chaise longue. She smoothed her daughter's hair. 'What's the matter? I didn't expect you home for hours. Did Jim bring you home?' She sighed. 'I do like that American. Such beautiful manners! And he's so thoughtful and cultured and well-read. Ned adores him.'

'So does Stella. Why don't you ever say anything nice about Alex? I don't think you like him.'

Lily hesitated. 'He's a little imposing with those haughty Russian looks.' She reached for Rosie's hand. 'But if you like him – and I know Ned thinks the world of him, which is always a good sign – then he must be wonderful. I just want you to be happy.'

'I feel the same way about you and Jack. But it's been forty years since you last saw him. I don't understand why he's come back now. You said he had a family in France.'

'His wife died a couple of years ago and his children are grown. Jack came back for a reason that I'm not at liberty to tell you about. He didn't expect to see me here, but being together is as natural for us both as breathing.'

'Surely you can trust me. You talk so little about my father; I don't want any more mysteries about the past.'

Lily took a deep, trembling breath. 'Jack disappeared because he was badly wounded at the front; we were told he was missing in action, assumed dead. Ned was in the same regiment and when he came back from the war, he told me how brave Jack had been.'

Lily told her how Jack had put his life on the line for his men, volunteered to go out into No Man's Land to see where the enemy were holed up. When a body was found with his jacket and Lily's letters and picture inside it, everyone assumed he had died in battle. The dog tags around the disfigured corpse were Jack's, confirming the identification. Years after the war, Jeanie, on tour in France, came across Jack and he had told her what had happened. A grenade had gone off next to him and he had been badly wounded. When he woke up in a French hospital, he'd lost his memory, and the nurses called him Alain. By the time he remembered who he was, and that he'd been in a foxhole with a wounded French soldier, the war was still far from over. When the grenade went off, killing the Frenchman, Jack had swapped his jacket and dog tags. He knew his actions would mark him out as a deserter and he would be shot.'

'So, he ran, rather than facing the music.'

Lily bridled. 'It's easy to blame deserters but ask yourself if you'd have been any braver, if you wouldn't have taken the chance to get away from all that slaughter and terror? None of us back home knew what they had to go through. You should have seen Ned when he came back from the war, he was like a ghost, as if he'd been hollowed out. It took years for him to recover, and he's never been quite the same since. Under all that joking, there's a terrible sorrow and anger.'

'I hear him at night sometimes.'

'Yes, his night terrors. I go in and sit with him sometimes until he wakes.'

Rosie had seen what war can do when some of the injured men were sent to Bletchley Park, but she could never fully understand what they had been through.

'There's one thing I don't understand. Why didn't Jack send word if he loved you so much?'

'He was ashamed of how he had left his men, of being a cripple, and of how his face looked. He didn't want to be a burden to me.'

Rosie met her mother's eyes. 'You found out he was alive before you met Father so there was nothing to stop you going to him.'

'I did, after Jeanie eventually told me about him, before I married your father. I didn't care what he looked like, about the burns, the wounds, his poor shattered mind. Jeanie and I went together, but by that time, he had met a French woman who was kind to him. And there was a child and another on the way. I saw them all together and he looked if not happy then at peace. I would have shattered that little family. I knew he would have gone with me if I'd asked him to, but I couldn't do that to another woman, to those children. I left without him seeing me.'

Rosie's felt a catch in her throat. 'That must have been hard.'

'I wasn't the only one. The war did so much harm to so many men and women.'

'But why is Jack back now, if it wasn't to be with you?'

'He wanted to see Ned, to see Scotland again. He didn't know I was living here, that I was widowed too. That I still love him, that I will always love him, no matter what.'

Rosie smoothed her mother's hair from her forehead. 'I'm sorry if I sounded judgemental. I think I understand now. But I feel so sorry for Father.'

'I should never have married him. He thought that in time I would come to love him as much as I loved Jack, and that he could live with it, but it ate away at him. There are no innocents in this story, I'm guilty for being a coward and letting Hugh marry me even though I didn't love him, not the way I loved Jack.' Lily began to sob, and Rosie took her mother in her arms.

'Jack's back now, you're together again. It's all ended well.'

Lily shook her head. 'You don't understand. If the army find out he didn't die on the battlefield, Jack will be sent to prison for desertion. It would kill him. I can't bear the thought of losing him again.'

Rosie froze. She remembered Frank's expression, studiously casual, as he remembered the name, Jack Petrie.

Chapter 17

A few weeks later, Rosie woke to the sound of raised voices. It was morning but still winter-dark and she nearly tripped over a chair as she pulled on her dressing gown and tried to find her slippers. Reaching the landing that overlooked the hall, she saw Ned at the front door gesticulating at someone.

'I have no idea who or what you are talking about. For the last time, there's no one of that name here,' he said. Rosie ran down the stairs only to stop at the sight of Frank leaning on the door jamb. He smirked when he saw her.

'Here's Rosie now. Perhaps she can help. Only the other day, she was telling me all about her mother's old boyfriend coming back after forty-odd years. I made a few inquiries around here and imagine my surprise when I found out Jack Petrie now goes by Alain Bourret.' He turned back to Ned. 'I'm sure the Home Office would be intrigued by his new French identity. I did some digging at Register House, where they keep the national records, and blow me if Jack

Petrie wasn't declared dead in 1915.' Frank pulled out a notebook from his coat pocket and consulted the scrawl of shorthand. 'According to my source in the army, his body, conveniently missing its facial features, was recovered from the Battle of Loos after his men risked their lives to retrieve it from No Man's Land. In fact, one of those brave boys was shot through the head by a sniper just as they got back to their trench. But I'm sure the lad's mother was comforted by his courage in rescuing the body of his commanding officer. Oh no, wait a minute!' Frank struck his forehead dramatically. 'I forgot, it wasn't Petrie's body, was it? It was some poor French sod who just happened to be wearing his tags and jacket. I believe Petrie stole Alain Bourret's identity and legged it. I wouldn't be surprised if he didn't finish him off to get out of doing his duty.'

It happened so quickly, Rosie didn't have time to blink: Ned punched Frank in the face and sent him sprawling down the steps onto the flagstones below.

'How dare you!' he shouted. 'Jack's the most courageous person I know. He was awarded the Victoria Cross and put his life on the line countless times for his men. What did you do in the last war that makes you think you can tarnish a man's name?'

Nursing his jaw, Frank grinned up at them with bloodied teeth. 'I know your game; you're trying to intimidate me. You may be some government high-heidyin, but I don't scare easily.' He took a few steps towards them. 'I notice you used the present tense when you were talking about Petrie, so you know fine well he is indeed alive and well. Not only that but I understand from Rosie he's living under your roof, *Sir* Edward.' Frank brushed off a sleeve. 'Give Monsieur Bourret my best regards and tell him I'll be in touch once he's ready to talk. Make no mistake, it's all going to come out now. There's no death sentence for desertion these days, but two years in the pokey can be made into a life sentence if the offender intended to avoid action, and I do believe that when he swapped his dog tags and took off, Jack Petrie had just that in mind. But you'll know the law better than me, Sir Edward, and no doubt you're well aware of the consequences of harbouring a deserter.' He tutted. 'A man in your position too. Think of the scandal! You'll have to stand down from the MoD, at the very least, and you might even end up sharing a cell with your pal. How cosy!' Frank walked up the steps and handed his card to Ned, who had gone white. 'Here are my details. I'm Frank Galbraith, of the *Daily Journal*. Things will go better for you and Petrie if you let me tell your side of the story. It'll get the public on your side and the judge might go easier on you if I dress it up in hearts and flowers. Rosie tells me there's a real love story there.'

Ned looked at the card with disgust. 'You know as well as I do that you can't print a word about an active court case.'

Frank tapped the side of his nose. 'Ah, but it hasn't gone to the cops yet. As there's been no charge, I can say what I like, and if it goes to trial and I get exclusive background interviews done and dusted beforehand, we can go to town after the verdict.'

'This is an outrage! I'll sue, you miserable heel.'

'Be my guest.' Frank tipped his hat. 'But the facts are on my side. Give me a bell once you've talked it over with Petrie.' He looked pious for a moment. 'I'm only after the truth, you know.'

Ned ripped the card in two and let the pieces drop. Frank was about to go when he turned back for a parting shot.

'And by the way, your friend isn't the only one who was decorated in the war. I did my bit, only I don't shout about it.'

Ned shut the door and, without looking at Rosie, stalked into his study. She stopped at the closed door and took a deep breath before turning the handle and going in. Ned was sitting at his desk, his head in his hands. Gingerly, she sat down opposite him.

'Ned, I'm sorry.'

He looked up at her. 'It's just as well Jack didn't hear any of that. He went out with Lily early this morning.' Ned leaned towards her. 'Do you have any idea what you've done? What were you thinking, talking to that odious hack?'

'I hardly said anything – just mentioned that Mother's old boyfriend had turned up, didn't even tell Frank his name, but he remembered. I must have told him about Jack at some point in the past. I certainly didn't know the full story, that Jack deserted, until Mother told me last night, so Frank must have found all that out under his own steam. He's been looking for a big story to prove himself, and I handed it to him. I've been such a fool.'

Ned sighed. 'You weren't to know, but it's landed us in the most God-awful mess.'

Rosie looked up. 'Maybe it's not as bad as Frank's making out. After all, Jack was badly injured by a blast, and later he was shell-shocked and couldn't remember who he was. Perhaps he'll leave it at that.'

Ned grimaced. 'I'm afraid Galbraith is on the right track. Jack told me himself that he came across the wounded Frenchman and gave him his jacket to try to keep him warm; it had a photograph of Lily in it with a message to Jack. When Bourret died, Jack swapped dog tags with him before shooting him in the face so everyone would think it was him. He knew what he was doing.' Rosie hid her eyes as if to block out the pictures that were spooling in her mind. 'Jack had every intention of running, but a grenade went off near him and he ended up in a French hospital. By the time he recovered his memory, he was Alain Bourret and deemed too badly wounded to go back to the front to fight with the French.'

Rosie swallowed. 'I don't blame him, but Jack will be branded a coward if this gets in the press.'

Ned stood up and passed a weary hand over his eyes. 'Don't use that word, I beg you. You have no idea what it was like fighting that wretched war, how terrified we all were, the hopelessness, pain and death. The filth and the cold and damp that got into your bones. It was like people imagine Hell to be, only worse. It marked us all and those of us who survived, well, we were never the same. Jack didn't want to take that back to Lily. He thought he'd ruin everything, he'd disgraced himself, and didn't want to ruin her life too, so he let everyone think he was dead, because in a way the old Jack Petrie had died.' Ned sat down with a shuddering sigh and Rosie realised he was crying.

She went round to his side of the desk and put her arms around him. 'I'm sorry, I'm an unfeeling idiot. I spent the last war safely tucked away in Bletchley Park and the men who saw action never talked about it. You never talk about the trenches.'

'We want to forget, those of us who can. That's why Jack is the bravest man I know. He came back to Scotland to confess. That's why he wanted to see me, to turn himself in to the Home Office. He's been ashamed all these years and once his wife died, he wanted to make a clean breast of it and take the consequences. He didn't realise Lily would be here, that she was free to be with him, and that they would be as much in love now as they were all those years ago. Lily's been trying to persuade him to go back to France together, back to his village, where Jack can continue living as Alain Bourret.'

Rosie was hurt. 'Mother wants to leave? She didn't say anything about it last night when we were talking about her and Jack.'

'She hadn't convinced Jack, and then that louse turned up on our doorstep.'

'So, Jack is running away again, and taking my mother with him.' Rosie couldn't stop the bitterness creeping into her tone.

'It was her idea; she wanted to save Jack and spend what is left of their lives together. But I know Jack, and he won't do it.'

Rosie sat down heavily. 'I'm sorry, I wasn't thinking. If Mother has the chance to finally be with the person she loves, she should take it.' She thought of Alex, of how she was risking so much to help him. 'I'll help her pack.'

'I'm afraid it's too late for that. Galbraith already knows too much. It won't be long before he contacts the authorities.'

'Could we buy him off? He was always skint and borrowing money off me.'

'That's not an option. I've never paid off anyone in my life and I'm not about to start now. Besides, as much as I loathe journalists like him, I know none of them would ever take a bribe. Even the most unscrupulous are single-minded when they get their teeth into a good story. They value seeing their name in the paper and being the envy of their peers far more than any sum of money. With my name in the mix of this story it becomes a government scandal, a story that would make Galbraith's name.'

Footsteps crossed the hall and Rosie heard her mother and Jack talking; they were back from their outing.

'What can we do?' she whispered. The study door opened, and Jack came in. He was still laughing at something Lily had said but his smile faded when Ned and Rosie turned to look at him.

'What's happened?' he said.

'My dear fellow,' Ned said, and quickly told them about Frank's visit.

Jack was pale, but he stood straighter than before. 'I knew it was only a matter of time. I told Lily I didn't want to run this time, that I was wrong to have run all those years ago.'

Rosie heard a whimper. Her mother was in the doorway, her hand covering her mouth, her eyes huge. Jack turned to her and took her in his arms. Watching them, Rosie felt a stab of anguish. What had she done?

Chapter 18

Rosie closed her bedroom door and let herself cry. Once the storm had passed, she curled up on the armchair next to the window and looked out over Charlotte Square gardens. The elms were bare against the winter sky and the sandstone buildings that surrounded the square were grimy with soot and drab in the grey light. Rosie had never felt so alone or lonely. She was too ashamed to face Lily, Ned and Jack, Jim Harrison was no doubt with Stella, and she had no idea where Alex was just when she needed him most. Feeling desperately sorry for herself, Rosie caught sight of her reflection in the wardrobe mirror. Crying had made her blotchy with reddened eyes, a concertina of frowns on her forehead, and her hair was standing on end. What a fright she looked. A frumpy spinster, just like Frank had said. Well, he could get lost; she wasn't the same person who had let him walk all over her. What on earth was she doing, waiting for a man to get in touch with her? It was time she took control of her life.

Rosie blew her nose, splashed cold water on her face in the bedroom sink, and pulled on a pair of flannels, an old cricket shirt of Ned's and her old jumper that had gone ragged at the wrists. She ran her hairbrush under the tap and tugged it through her hair. *There*, she told her reflection. *That's better*.

Downstairs, Rosie ducked into the cubby hole under the stairs where the house telephone was kept and started dialling. After a few rings it was answered by a woman in a clipped Home Counties accent.

'Name please?'

'Rosie Anderson, I'm one of the JSSL teachers. I'd like to speak to Cosmo Montgomery.'

'What's this about?'

'I'd rather not say. It's urgent though.'

A sigh. 'Very well, stay on the line.'

It seemed like an age before Monty came to the phone. 'Rosie! What's the matter? Are you all right?'

'There's been some trouble. I need to see Alex, but I haven't heard from him in weeks.' Her voice wavered but she cleared her throat and carried on. 'Please, Monty, can you get hold of him for me?'

There was a moment's silence. 'I can get a message to him.'

She closed her eyes and let out a breath. 'Thank you.'

Breezy again, he said: 'Righto, look after yourself, and don't do anything I wouldn't do.'

Rosie spent the rest of the day hidden away in the studio, trying to work but mostly staring miserably out of the window. It was early evening when she trudged back through the back garden to the house. Alex was waiting for her. She ran to him, and he opened his arms.

'*Moya dusha,*' he whispered. My soul. He had only called her that when they were at their most intimate. Rosie's doubts evaporated. He loved her and he'd come to her when she needed him most. Alex pulled away and looked closely into her face, as if examining her for signs of damage. 'What is it? Monty said you were in trouble.' His brow creased. 'Are you pregnant?'

She nearly laughed. 'Not that kind of trouble, and it's not me that's in hot water.' Resting her forehead on his chest she said, 'I've ruined Ned and my mother's life and put someone they love in danger.'

'Tell me about it and I'll see if I can help.' They went into the morning room where she knew they wouldn't be disturbed. When Rosie had finished telling him the whole story, she sat with her head bowed, ashamed all over again.

'I'm such a fool, mentioning Jack to Frank. What was I thinking? Now Jack could end up in prison and my mother, well, I can't bear to think what I've done to her.' Rosie bit her lip. She wouldn't cry; she didn't deserve to feel sorry for herself.

Alex tilted her chin, so she had to look at him. 'Don't worry, I'll help.'

'How?'

'I need to speak to Ned, and to Petrie.'

The three men had gone into Ned's study and closed the door behind them. Rosie stood for a moment in the cold hall before squaring her shoulders and going upstairs. She would have to face her mother. Lily was sitting up in bed, Jack's coat around her shoulders, going through a box of papers. Her face was still far too white, but she managed to smile when she saw Rosie.

'Come and see.' Some of the letters were illustrated with thumbnail sketches of soldiers in kilts and Glengarries, some leaning on their bayonets and asleep on their feet like horses, others hunched over billycans or playing cards. 'From Jack when he went to war.' Lily picked up a small album. 'And these were taken at art school.' Rosie leafed through sepia photographs of young men and women in fancy dress posing as gods and goddesses from classical or Celtic mythology; a flyer for an exhibition and an invitation to a masquerade ball, both illustrated in the Glasgow Style, and a menu for the Willow Tea Rooms. The last photograph was a year group of students in embroidered dresses and collars, the women with their hair piled up and pinned with elaborate pieces of jewellery, or in loose waves on their shoulders in the style of the pre-Raphaelites, the men in tweed jackets and soft neckties or suits and stiff collars. It was a glimpse into another time, before war had torn Europe apart. Rosie peered at the rows of students until she identified her mother, laughing at something the handsome young man next to her was saying.

'Is this you and Jack?'

Lily took the photograph from her. 'Yes, that's my Jack. For years this box of memories was all I had to remember him by, when I thought he was dead, and then later, after I'd found him but couldn't be with him. Perhaps I should have been braver, more selfish, for both of us, insisted he come home with me. But it wouldn't have been fair on Justine or the children.' She glanced at Rosie's stricken face and put an arm around her.

'I'm so sorry,' Rosie said. 'I should have been more careful. I let my guard down and let slip that Jack had turned up and Frank figured the rest out.'

'You weren't to know what would happen. I should have been more open with you. I'd spent so long missing Jack, I'd become used to it, and it was almost a comfort to keep all that sadness to myself.'

'What will you do now? What will happen to Jack?'

'I wanted us to run away together, hide in France or further away, somewhere nobody could find us. There's all the more reason now, but Jack insists on turning himself in. He says he's sick of hiding and he doesn't want that for me, looking over your shoulder all the time and living a lie. He's been eaten up with guilt and shame for half his life and now he's come home and wants to live honestly and with dignity.'

'Even if it means going to prison?'

'Yes, even that. He says it doesn't matter now that we're back together. He's Jack Petrie again.' They were quiet for a moment. Lily gathered the letters and album and put them back in their box. 'I see your Russian is back,' she said.

'I sent Alex a message that there was trouble, and he came straight away. I thought there might be something he could do as he's with the MoD. He's in with Jack and Ned now.'

'I wasn't sure about him at first, but he clearly loves you if he came when you needed him.' Lily picked up Rosie's hand and they intertwined their fingers as they had when she was a girl. 'You're bold and single-minded, like your father, and like him you can be fiery and impetuous. You have the best of both of us.'

'I have to say, I was dismayed when Ned said you wanted to get away to France. I'd miss you terribly. It's just been you and me for so long.'

'And Ned, of course.'

Rosie laughed. 'Where would we be without Ned?'

'Let's go down and see if they've come up with a plan.'

When they walked into the study, the three men turned to face them. Ned was holding a legal tome he'd pulled down from the shelves that lined the room.

'I've been looking up what the law says about, ah . . .' he said and glanced at Jack who sat staring into the fire, lost in thought. '... um ... desertion. Section 37 of the 1955 Army Act states that anyone who deserts shall, on conviction by court martial, be liable to be imprisoned or any lesser punishment.' He pushed the reading glasses he was usually too vain to be seen in further up the bridge of his nose. 'Here's the important bit: the longest sentence is two years, but it's up to the court's discretion. It could be less, or no custodial sentence at all.'

Lily sat down heavily. 'Two years! Would it be in Scotland?'

'Depends on where our old regiment will be when he faces a court martial, could be England if they're abroad or if they're back in Scotland it would be in the Maryhill barracks in Glasgow,' Ned said. 'I'm afraid they'd hold Jack in prison until the trial. That's if you turn yourself in, Jack.'

'I told you, I'm not running away again. I should have handed myself in during the war as soon as I regained my memory.'

'If you had, you would have been shot by a firing squad,' Ned said. Lily gasped and he turned to her and his expression softened. 'Don't worry, Lils, they outlawed the military death penalty in 1930.' He turned back to Jack. 'If you're sure you want to stay and stick it out, I'll phone the MoD and represent you in court.'

Jack frowned. 'I can't let you do that, Ned. Didn't you also say,' he pulled the legal book towards him, 'that any person subject to military law who fails to report a deserter without delay could also be imprisoned for two years?'

Ned took the book back and closed it. 'I'll take my chances. We're too long in the tooth to wait around for a snake like Frank Galbraith to go slithering to the authorities.'

Jack struggled to rise from his chair, groping for his stick. 'I don't want you to get in trouble on my account.'

'I can look after myself. And may I remind you that I've been looking out for you since we were boys. I'm not going to leave you to face this alone.'

The two old friends glared at each other. Alex raised his hands to calm the situation. 'I'll make the call to the MoD. I have a few favours I can call in, and it will sound better coming from me, Ned, as you're in the middle of all this.'

Rosie reached for her mother's hand and squeezed. 'I told you Alex was a good man,' she whispered. 'He'll do what he can, you'll see.'

'What if Jack goes to prison? And Ned too? I don't think I could bear it,' Lily said. She hurried from the room and Jack went after her. Rosie could hear the rise and fall of their voices in the hall. She turned to Alex. 'Do you really think you can help them?'

'I will do everything I can.'

Ned sighed and rubbed his eyes. 'It all hangs on who we get as the Judge Advocate General and whether he takes into account mitigating circumstances.'

'We'd better go through those in detail before I make the

call,' Alex said.

Ned managed a smile. 'A debrief, eh? Just like the old days at Bletchley Park.'

Alex put a hand on his shoulder. 'Exactly so. We'll get through this together. You distinguished yourself in both wars, and that should count for a lot.'

'Thank you, dear boy.'

The men seemed to have forgotten Rosie, who slipped out of the room to make coffee. It was going to be a long night.

Chapter 19

Alex was buttoning his shirt when Rosie woke early the next morning. He hadn't come to bed until late, the heat of his body rousing her from sleep. Afterwards, she'd fallen asleep in his arms as she had so often in Crail. She clicked on her bedside lamp and sat up to watch him dress.

'Can you tell me where you're going this time?'

He reached for his jacket. 'London. It's better if I speak to the top brass in person. I'm afraid I'll have to go straight back to work from there. I'll call Ned and let him know the upshot.' He glanced at the door. 'Meanwhile, don't forget what we talked about. I still need your help.' His mind clearly already on the day ahead, Alex kissed her briefly and left. Rosie sank back against the pillows. It was too early for the fire to have been lit and the room was cold. She shivered and hugged her bare arms. There was nothing she could do but wait it out.

After Alex left, the Charlotte Square house sank into a tense silence with Ned in his study reading up on military law and preparing Jack's defence, and Jack and Lily spending as much time together as possible while they could. In the weeks since Alex's departure, Rosie was busy at school as the longest term marched towards the end of the year. The school's ancient iron radiators were lukewarm and barely gave out any heat even when the girls sat on them, tucking their fingers into the ends of their cardigans. At home, Rosie escaped to the studio for hours but couldn't settle to painting, staring at the canvas, unable to concentrate as her mind whirled with what lay ahead for Ned and Jack, and how it would affect her mother. The invitation from the Sinclairs came as a welcome distraction. Rosie took the thick, gilt-edged card with embossed lettering to Ned, who was having breakfast with Lily in the morning room. He looked up from his newspaper and smiled, but his eyes were tired.

'What have you there?'

'An invitation.'

'I hope it's not another bunfight at the Signet Library. I don't think I could face m'learned friends in their cups.' He took the card and his expression cleared. 'Just the ticket! A delightful few days of fishing and deer stalking at the Sinclairs', rounded off with their famous Hogmanay ball.' He raised his eyebrows. 'And you are invited too, my dear Rosie. I know you find the Sinclairs a bit stodgy, but can you bear coming with me? I'd love your company; we've seen so little of each other lately, what with one thing and another.'

Rosie lowered her eyes so she wouldn't betray her excitement. 'I'd like to come. It would be good to get away, and I know you're fond of Sir Angus and Lady Moira. Although it's a pity it must involve the slaughter of defenceless animals.'

'Really, Rosie, you are becoming dreadfully judgemental,' Ned said. 'Rather a bourgeois attitude for a bohemian artist to affect, wouldn't you say? It must be Alex's influence. The younger Russians can be awfully serious about the decadent pastimes of the aristocracy, even the ones that hate the communist regime are a bit sniffy about blood sports.' Ned waved away her indignant response. 'I'm only teasing, you know I'm as fond of Alex as I am of your charming American friend. So refreshing to have young people about the house again! Your mother and I were creeping towards our dotage before you lot woke us up.'

'Speak for yourself,' Lily said, mustering a smile.

'And as for those poor defenceless animals,' Ned said, 'they will be quite safe. I only agree to country pursuits so I can wear my pretty Norfolk jacket. I must say, Stewart Christie have outdone themselves this season,' he said, referring to the traditional gentlemen's outfitters in Queen Street who were too discreet to object to Ned's demands for tweed jackets with coloured piping and Liberty print silk linings. 'Anyway, my darling Rosie, it will be wonderful to have you at Summer Isle House.

You can keep me in check and away from the handsome beaters. There was an absolute stunner there last year. Now, before I write back, are you sure you don't want me to send your regrets?'

Rosie tried not to sound too eager. 'No, no, count me in.'

'I am glad, but are you feeling quite well? Lily, do take your daughter's temperature at once; she must be feverish. I thought you hated these house parties. What about the Sinclairs' son and heir, Dreary Duncan?'

'Duncan isn't so bad. He can be quite sweet, really.'

Ned shook his head sadly. 'Lily, I urge you to call a psychiatrist. Do we know any psychiatrists? Hmm. I must look one up, they must be awfully good company at dinner, if one could get them going on their more colourful cases. The university is bound to be teeming with them.' He got up, heading for his study, and Rosie knew her eccentric uncle would soon be looking up eminent Edinburgh psychiatrists for his own amusement. At the door he turned and spoke to Lily. 'No invitation for you, my sweet Lily of the Valley. Are you feeling terribly snubbed?'

'Not in the slightest, and I'm more than happy to stay here with Jack. Besides, I don't think the Sinclairs have recovered from my last visit.'

Ned chuckled. 'That fool of a groom should have locked the door. The sight of his naked body gave Moira's housekeeper the vapours.'

'Silly woman. She fled before I could explain he was only posing for me. You know how I like defined musculature.'

'Don't we all, my dear,' Ned said as he left.

On a crisp morning in late December, Ned and Rosie motored north towards Poolewe to the Sinclairs' home in the Highlands.

'I do love Summer Isle House,' Ned said, one eye on the road that hugged the coast towards the north-west Highlands. 'There's always something to look at and new to discover among all the curiosities.'

'When I was little, Moira used to let me play with the antique dolls houses she collected.'

'She must have been pining for a daughter to let you do that. One of those dolls houses belonged to Queen Victoria's daughter, Princess Louise, the Duchess of Argyll.'

'I hope they put me in the Chinese bedroom with the boxed-in carved bed. It made a great den when we were little.'

'We? Did you let Duncan into your den? Was that quite safe knowing his undying love for you?'

'I suppose he did have a crush on me even when we were little. I shouldn't have agreed to play kiss-chase with him and his cousins.'

'You weren't to know you'd start his little heart a-hammering. I remember he'd follow you around like one of the Sinclairs' slobbery blood hounds.'

'Unfortunately for Duncan, he still bears a remarkable resemblance to that breed.'

'Poor chap. He never did get married. It must have been all that unrequited love for you.' Ned glanced at her, taking his eye off the winding single-lane track and narrowly avoiding a sheep standing defiantly in the road. It was just as well that, other than cyclists and a postman's van, they hadn't passed another car for miles. 'Perhaps you'll take pity on Duncan now? You could throw Alex over and be the next lady of the house. Moira would be delighted,' he teased, nudging Rosie and making the car swerve.

'In the unlikely event we ever make it to Poolewe in one piece, Duncan still has no chance, even if Alex weren't on the scene.'

'There's no denying your Russian is the more exotic dish, but perhaps some plainer fare and a great helping of financial security might be the wiser choice?'

'Ned! You old materialist! What about love?'

'Ah, love. Now there's a big word. The highs are exhilarating but the lows . . .' They were quiet for a while as Rosie thought of Lily and what she had been through with Jack, losing him during the war and what she was facing now. But when it came to her and Alex, she knew that she'd finally found the right person and that she need never be alone again.

In the distance, a hazy line of blue water appeared on the horizon, the only colour amid the brown hills. In late summer, Rosie knew, the heather would burst into a blanket of mauve, pink, red and white, and from January to June, the gorse would put out its garish blooms, as yellow as the sherbet lemons she used to eat from paper pokes as a girl. But now the countryside wore its balding winter furs like a dowager on her uppers. The clouds were low and heavy with snow and the first flakes began to fall as the car crested a hump on the road. Rosie could see the deceptively ordinary-looking house with its simple white gables and slate roof on the shore of Loch Ewe, an upside-down mirror image reflected in the water. A long time ago it had been an inn, and then a hunting lodge, before it was titivated up for a summer house for the Sinclairs that became their permanent home when they had to sell their other properties in the hard years between the wars. They had made up for the loss by filling it with treasures and curios from all over the world, including a collection of antique toys that had fascinated Rosie as a child, from porcelain dolls dressed in lace and satin to ingenious puppet theatres and mechanical animals playing instruments.

Ned pulled the car up to the house. 'There she is – a sight to gladden the heart. I remember coming here as a boy in the school holidays with Angus during those gay years between the wars, when the Sinclair parties were quite wild, nothing like the grand, respectable affairs Moira holds today. Funny how people get so serious as they get older, except for me, thank goodness.'

The snow was falling steadily and beginning to carpet the gravel and lie on the fierce-looking stone mastiffs that guarded the entrance to the house, giving them comical schoolboy caps. A man in tails came to take their bags, and another in working clothes took the key to drive the car to the old stables Rosie had played in as a child. She remembered the horses snorting and whinnying while she chalked the beds for peever – or hopscotch as Duncan's cousins called it as they went to boarding school in England – and how slippery the cobbles were as she hopped up the chalk bed. The Sinclairs still kept horses, but not as many since the Second World War, when the Royal Navy had requisitioned the house as command headquarters and for officer training. Since then, the stables for the hunters and race horses, their coats gleaming from daily brushing, had been converted into garages to house Sir Angus's collection of vintage cars, an enthusiasm he shared with Ned.

Rosie and Ned followed the butler up the steps to the main door. The Sinclairs were one of the few old families in Scotland to still have staff, even if they were much reduced in numbers from the house's heyday. She paused and turned to look at the loch sweeping into the blue-grey horizon and wished she was staying longer to paint. They were ushered into the drawing room where Sir Angus and Lady Moira were drinking tea in front of the fire, logs crackling under the carved chimney piece and spreading warmth through the charming room. Three elderly labradors at the couple's feet looked up with clouded eyes, their tails thumping, before putting their greying muzzles back on their front paws and going back to sleep. A blood hound lay on its back on a sofa snoring, its long ears fanned out on the faded embroidered silk as it twitched and chased rabbits. Pictures covered the walls – Rosie spotted a Gainsborough and a Reynolds – and every corner, table and glass-fronted display case was crammed with curios and ephemera collected by Sir Angus's well-travelled forbears. Despite the grandeur, it was a cosy, domestic scene. Angus wore a moth-eaten cardigan over a checked shirt and moleskin trousers that had seen better days, and Moira was comfortably upholstered in the baggy tweed skirt, twinset and pearls, and sensible calfskin walking shoes deemed essential wear for every country gentle-woman from Wester Ross to the West Country. Her kindly face creased into a smile as she rose creakily to her feet, but Angus remained impassive. He shook Ned's hand and only nodded briefly at Rosie. As if to compensate for his coldness, Moira clasped Rosie to her shelf-like bosom, enveloping her in a cloud of lavender cologne, mothballs and damp dog.

'My dear chap!' Ned beamed at Angus. 'How the devil are you? How's Whitehall treating you these days?'

'I'm afraid they're rather chasing their tails in London. What do you make of how Eden's handling Suez? Bit of a pig's ear, wouldn't you say?'

Moira said, 'Really, Gus, if you're going to discuss politics I'll take Rosie for a turn around the grounds.' Her husband ignored her. Moira took Rosie's arm and led her through the French doors.

'You are a tonic,' Moira said, stopping just outside. 'Lovely to have another woman about the place, I'm afraid Gus isn't much company for me, too tied up with his work, as usual. But listen to me grumbling on, you're looking wonderful, Rosie. Has some young blade snapped you up yet?'

'I'm very happy as a spinster.'

'Hardly a spinster, my dear! Plenty of time – only don't leave it too late. Listen to me, an old bat handing out advice. Oh, look, the snow has stopped, we can walk along the shoreline.' She poked her head back into the drawing room and called to the dogs. 'Benji! Ralph! Maisie! Jupiter! Walkies!' The three labradors lumbered to their feet and looked expectantly at their mistress, except Jupiter the blood hound, who paddled his paws, still deep in slumber on the sofa. 'Gus, I've told you about spoiling that beast. Look at him sprawled there like a pasha.' Sir Angus, deep in conversation with Ned by the fireplace, only waved his hand at her.

The two women crunched over the gravel down to the pebble beach, the labradors waddling and panting after them. 'I know I'm a meddlesome old woman, but if you could bear it, I would like a little chat.' Rosie waited, knowing what was coming next: a refrain that she'd heard often at Summer Isle House over the years. 'Rosie dear, you should be settled with a husband and in pup by now. You don't want to leave it too late. I did and then nothing happened for years until Duncan arrived, and after that I couldn't have any more.'

Rosie looked away, embarrassed. She had never talked to anyone about wanting a child, not even to Lily, who had come late to motherhood and was far too sensitive to press her about marriage and babies as her friends' mothers had. Rosie had put it out of her mind entirely while she was with Frank, who would have been horrified at the thought of a pram in the hall, let alone nappies and a teething baby. But now, with Alex, she had started to long for his child. The thought had begun as a small light she guarded in private until it had grown brighter and stronger. They stopped at the water's edge and Rosie pointed out a sailing boat. Moira shaded her eyes to peer into the distance.

'Oh, that's only old Calum and his two sons pulling up their lobster pots. I've ordered some for dinner in your and Ned's honour.' Undeterred by Rosie's attempt to change the subject, Moira turned to face her and took her by the arms. 'My dear, I'm going to come straight to the point, and never mind the niceties. What about my Duncan? He's about the same age as you, he's always adored you, from when you were both little babbies, and he'll inherit all this once we fall off our perches. You've a good head on your shoulders, not like some of these silly gels he brings up from London. And you'd bring some much-needed vigour into the Sinclair line. We're getting to look far too much like our dogs.' She eyed Rosie's hips. 'You're neither of you in the first flush of youth, but plenty of time yet to have children. A good match all round, I'd say.' Rosie smiled at the thought of toughening up the Sinclair bloodline, as if she were a brood mare. They carried on walking along the shoreline. 'Do think about it, dear girl. You could paint and not have to worry about money as Angus has been careful with investments. He lost almost everything in '29 but didn't panic like some others, kept his nerve and our stocks have recovered since the war. I know it's supposed to be vulgar for women to talk about money, but that's poppycock, men talk about it all the time.' She went on without drawing breath. 'You'd be good for Duncan. He'll need a strong woman by his side when he becomes clan chief and has to manage the estate and the mine and chemical works. You may be a bit dreamy, as is only to be expected of an artist, but you've a steel core. I remember when I first met you as a child, only a little thing and still hankering after your poor dead papa, but full of spirit, and I knew then you'd never have any trouble standing up for yourself.'

Rosie was trying to think how to answer Moira without hurting her feelings when they heard a 'halloo!' and turned to see Duncan. As he drew near, panting as hard as the labradors, she noticed he'd put on weight and his jowls had begun to sag, making him look more than ever like the Sinclairs' blood hound. His hair had receded, and his face was deep red with exertion. The lavish dinners at Summer Isle House with their generous decanters of claret and port wouldn't have helped, nor his lunches at the New Club or the East India Club when he went down to Edinburgh and London. He was dressed like a pauper, in true aristocratic fashion, in an ancient kilt and cashmere sweater that moths had gone to town on, leaving holes large enough for his elbows to poke through. On his feet were battered tackety boots that he'd inherited from some distant Sinclair that were so down at heel even Charlie Chaplin's little tramp would have turned his nose up at them. Rosie painted on a smile and tried not to mind when Duncan pressed a moist cheek against her face.

'Rosie! Terrific to see you again! How long has it been? Three years?'

'Five, I think.'

He grinned at her, with adoring puppy eyes. 'Well, you don't look a day older – fresh as a daisy! Or should I say a rose?' Duncan said and laughed, a high-pitched silly giggle. Rosie tried not to wince. He had a nervous disposition, his confidence eroded by his father. Duncan clearly still had a thing for her, and it would be all too easy to bend him to her will. Rosie felt herself blushing and bent to stroke the dogs to hide her face. It had been easy to agree to Alex's plan in Crail, but now that she was here, with well-meaning Moira and Duncan, who was annoying but had never meant her any harm, she was ashamed. She thought back to what Alex had said and made herself remember why she was here, that Angus was the worst kind of traitor and was endangering the safety of everyone, even his own family. No, the mission was too important to be squeamish now.

Rosie stood and smiled brightly at Duncan. 'You're looking well, yourself. All that stalking has kept you in fine shape.' He looked delighted and Moira nodded her approval.

'Why don't you two young things walk to the folly and catch up while I change out of my gardening clothes.' She patted her son on the cheek and smiled fondly, only to be rewarded with a scowl. 'And then, darling boy, we must let Rosie bathe and dress for dinner. Our other guests are arriving in time for cocktails.'

Rosie noticed Duncan looked terrified. No doubt bullied at school and at home by his father, he didn't have the confidence and easy manners displayed by the likes of Alex and Monty. She would have to tread carefully not to frighten him off.

Rosie thought quickly. 'Do you mind if we catch up a little later, Duncan?' She turned to Moira. 'I'd love a bath now, if you don't mind. The drive from Edinburgh was a bit of a strain. You know how fast Ned likes to go and he's even worse in his new car.'

'Has he the new Bentley?' Duncan said, relieved to be on more familiar ground. Rosie remembered that he was fascinated by cars and as a boy had spent hours painstakingly making models of them, much to his sporty father's disgust. 'I'll just pop over to the garage to have a peek before dinner,' he said.

As they watched him hurry up to the house, Moira sighed. 'My poor boy. I blame that school, all that hiking and cold showers at dawn. It wasn't right for a sensitive boy like Duncan, but his father insisted, said generations of Sinclairs had thrived at Glencaple. What he needs is the love of a good, steady woman, you'll see.' Moira took her arm. 'Your room is the same one you've always had – the Chinese room. And it won't be so cold now that we have central heating. Can you imagine? No more stone pigs to warm the bed or dashing through the cold to get to the bathroom. It's positively tropical!'

Rosie smiled at Moira. She was so much nicer than her awful husband. It must be a trial being married to such a tyrant. She squeezed the older woman's hand. 'Lead on, Macduff.'

'Yes, once more unto the breach! Or is that *Henry V*, not *Macbeth*?' Moira said. 'I was hopeless at Shakespeare, much rather be out hunting than have my nose stuck in a book in the schoolroom. Did I ever tell you about the awful governess I had as a child, who taught me and my brothers to swear in Gaelic? I can still shock the housekeeper. Now there's a woman you wouldn't take a broken pay packet home to.'

Rosie laughed. 'Where on earth did you pick up that expression?'

'My new lady's maid, Baxter, is from the Gorbals. Rough as a badger's arse but a genius with a needle and thread. She's patched up all my evening dresses. Would you like to borrow one?'

Rosie, still recovering from the badger's arse, shook her head. She had seen Lady Sinclair's wardrobe of grand dresses from before the Great War, which had been let out and had panels added to them over the decades. 'That's kind of you, but Ned took me shopping before we came.'

'Oh good, you're all fixed up. As you say, Ned has such impeccable taste – so unusual for a man. If I asked Gus to take me clothes shopping, he'd head straight for Campbell's of Beauly, who do, I must admit, a beautiful tweed, and some lovely cardigans.'

Rosie gave the older woman's arm a squeeze. She felt another pang about being in her home under false pretences but remembered what Alex had said. She looked back at the loch, stretching out to meet the skies, a sight that made her catch her breath. It was inconceivable to imagine a deadly nuclear armour stored in these waters. They reached the flagstone terrace. With the light fading, Rosie could see through the French windows into the wood-panelled library where Ned and Angus were drinking whisky and deep in conversation in front of the fire. She'd have to think of a way to lure Duncan into the library later. She didn't relish the prospect, but it had to be done, for her country, if there was to be a Scotland for the child she longed to have with Alex.

Chapter 20

Dinner that night brought a surprise. As Rosie came downstairs, she heard a familiar laugh coming from the drawing room and quickened her step. A handsome head turned when she walked in. Simon Fairweather bounded towards her and crushed her into his arms.

'Why, it's Rosie! Hello, gorgeous! Look at you all dolled up like a Scotch Princess Margaret, if she were a blondie, that is.' Simon's blue Yorkshire eyes were bright against his tan and his golden hair. He looked dashing in white tie, and she had to stop herself melting under his charm onslaught. She knew he wasn't interested in women, but it didn't stop him being a terrible flirt.

'I thought it was you,' Rosie said. 'How lovely to see you again! And you don't look so bad yourself out of army fatigues.'

'Oh, I just threw this on.' He lowered his voice. 'So glad you're here, the average age is about seventy.'

'Who are you here with? I didn't know you knew the Sinclairs.'

'Come and meet my friend,' he said, leading Rosie to an older man who was staring at them superciliously. 'AKA my current meal ticket,' he whispered to Rosie who had to stifle a laugh as she approached Simon's austere friend. He stared down his sharp nose at her, his eyebrows raised, and thin lips pressed together, like the Tusculum bust of Caesar she'd had to copy at art school.

'This is Sir Alistair Baird, but you can call him Ally, I always do,' Simon said.

The downturned mouth pinched even more. 'I prefer Sir Alistair. And you are?' He jabbed the question at Rosie as if he were poking a broom handle at vermin. Rosie bridled but forced herself to be polite. Alex had said this man had been suspected of trading in state secrets; she would have to be on her guard.

She held out her hand. 'Rosie Anderson. I understand you're an art collector and connoisseur. I'm an artist.'

Baird ignored her hand. 'An artist? Are you sure? I've never heard of you.'

She swallowed a sharp retort. Really, he was the most dreadful man. 'You may know of my mother, Lily Crawford. She's on the board of the Royal Society of Artists.'

Baird sniffed. 'I have, as it happens, heard of her. I'm not terribly convinced by that rather over-enthusiastic gaggle of women artists from before the Great War – all those damsels in distress and painted crockery – but Crawford stood out as a talented portraitist. Her later Chinese scenes, on the other hand, are too sentimental for me, like something out of an amateur production of the *Mikado*.' He waved his hand. 'And now of course, she's completely out of fashion. Bit of a has-been, I'm afraid.' Rosie felt her face heat up, but Baird didn't seem to notice. He peered at her. 'What sort of thing do you dabble in?'

Rosie gritted her teeth. 'Landscapes, seascapes mostly.' Baird didn't bother hiding his boredom. He looked over her shoulder to see if there was someone more important to talk to and moved away without another word. She felt dismissed and shot a look at Simon, who grimaced apologetically.

'He's like a bear with a sore head before he's had something to eat,' he said. 'I'd better go and find out when it's going to be served. The staff are a friendly bunch, especially that gorgeous butler.' He winked at Rosie.

'You're as bad as Ned, who I can see has been trapped by Duncan, who will no doubt be quizzing him endlessly about his car. I'd better rescue him.'

'You do that,' Simon said distractedly, already signalling to the butler who had come in with a tray of drinks. He sighed. 'What a smasher! Wasted up here in the wilds, though. The London nightclubs I could take him to! Look at that neat figure and the way he glides about the room. I bet he does a mean tango.'

Rosie was making her way over to Ned when Moira stopped her and introduced her to the rest of the dinner guests: the local minister and his wife, a fiercely shy composer who had come to the Loch Ewe to work on a new symphony that seemed to involve traditional fiddle music, and a hearty couple from a nearby estate, the woman with a complexion as ruddy and hair as heathery as Moira's, and her husband squeezed into a pre-war dinner suit. After what seemed like an interminable exchange of pleasantries, Rosie excused herself and reached Ned, only to be immediately whisked into dinner by Duncan. At first, she was dismayed to find she was seated next to him, but soon realised this would be to her advantage. She waited until he'd ripped apart his bread roll.

'Are you looking forward to the shoot tomorrow?'

Duncan leaned back to let a server put his game soup in front of him. 'Rather! Always love a day out on the hills. Can I persuade you to come?'

'You know I don't know anything about guns.'

He looked earnest. 'I found it tricky at first, when father tried to teach me, I'm afraid I was all fingers and thumbs. But then one of the ghillies took me aside and spent an afternoon showing me how to steady my breath and aim, and I got the hang of it. I could show you, if you like that is.'

'That's kind, thank you, but really, I'd rather spend the day in the library reading. There are so many amazing books.' She tipped her head shyly and looked up at him through her lashes. 'Although I'd love to have some company.'

Duncan went bright red and looked at his soup plate. 'Um, yes, reading, rather fond of that sort of thing myself, although I don't think Father quite approves of having my nose stuck in a book when there's plenty to do in the fresh air.' Rosie could hear Angus's strident tones echoed by Duncan. She thought she had persuaded him to stay behind with her in the library, where the safe was, but her hopes were dashed. Duncan looked rueful. 'I'd stay with you in a heartbeat any other time, but I'm afraid I can't miss this shoot. There's a wily old stag Father has been after for weeks and the ghillie says he's finally tracked him down, but he won't stay in one place for long.'

That evening, after the minister and his wife and the composer had left, she realised Simon and Alistair Baird were also house guests and were staying for the Hogmanay Ball. The staff retired for the night or left for their homes in the village, and the men sat around the dinner table with their port and cigars. A drooping Moira, never good at late nights, went to bed and Rosie pretended to do the same. She waited half an hour before slipping out of her room and creeping downstairs to listen outside the dining room in the shadowy hall. She heard the men discussing the Suez crisis for a while and was about to leave when her ears pricked up.

'Of course, once we have the Americans' submarines here, armed to the teeth with nukes, we'll have a much stronger hand and our reputation as a world power will be restored,' Sir Angus said.

'Interesting theory.' Ned's voice.

And then Baird's. 'But where would you put them? I suppose the Royal Navy bases at Portsmouth or Devonport are the obvious choices?'

'Not at all! Too far away from the Soviet patrols. We need to guard the North Atlantic, so it must be a new base, here, in Scotland,' Sir Angus said. 'Plenty of deep water around our coasts, that's why the MoD chose this house during the last war. You could fit a whole fleet in the sea loch.'

'So, the base would be built here on Loch Ewe?'

'Oh no, it was bad enough having the place requisitioned during the war.'

'But you have found somewhere?'

'Indeed, we have . . .'

Ned interrupted. 'Best not to say too much, Gus.'

Sir Angus harrumphed. 'Quite right, quite right, old boy. Need to know only.'

Baird's voice was smooth. 'I quite understand. But I assume you have found somewhere? I suppose it's only at the back-of-a-fag-packet stage, though.'

'Hardly, we have the plans down to the last tooth mug in the barracks. Ned and I were making a couple of last-minute adjustments to the plans earlier today.'

'They're safe from prying eyes, I trust?'

'Safe as houses! Can't be too careful, Reds under the bed and all that, although I can't imagine the minister's KGB,' Sir Angus said.

The talk then turned to the shoot and Rosie crept back to her room. She lay in bed staring at the carved wooden canopy over her bed. The plans must be in the safe, the very plans that Sir Angus wanted to hand over to the Russians. And now Baird seemed inordinately interested in them.

The next morning, Rosie went on a recce to the library and found the painting that Alex had described. Behind it, she supposed, lay the safe with the blueprints for the nuclear submarine base. Rosie put her hands on either side of the heavy gilt frame and was about to lift it off the wall to make sure she had the right one when she felt the air change in the room. She thought everyone was at the shoot but someone else was in here with her. Rosie lowered her hands and pretended to examine the painting.

'Dreadful daub, isn't it? The Sinclairs are convinced it's a Reynolds, but it's a fake, and not a terribly good one at that.' Rosie turned to see Baird rising from a wing-back chair that faced away from her and towards the view. He strolled over to a telescope by the window and peered out over the sea loch. 'Not much to see in this weather.'

'There's a haar today, but when it's clear you can see for miles.'

Baird turned to Rosie. 'What did you say? A hare? What on earth are you talking about?'

'That's what we call a cold sea fog in Scotland, a haar. I believe it's Old Norse, leftover from the Vikings.'

'How interesting,' he said, sounding anything but.

'You didn't fancy the shoot?'

Baird shuddered. 'God, no! Trudging through the damp and dreary hills and glens with a bunch of philistines is not my idea of fun. I'm strictly an indoor creature.' He approached her with delicate, cautious movements and Rosie was reminded of a cat. And like a cat, he could be charming if he wanted, when he was talking to someone of rank like Sir Angus; he didn't bother sheathing his claws for her. Rosie thought she had managed to stay under his radar, but she was wrong. Under his hooded eyelids, Baird didn't miss a trick.

'You seem awfully interested in that painting when there are so many other real gems in this house.' He gestured towards the door. 'There's a Gainsborough in the hall and a Boucher tucked away in the corner of the drawing room, and I spotted eighteenth-century Meissen porcelain figurines and Sèvres tableware in the dining room.'

'Sounds like you were making quite the inventory.'

'Comes with the job – a little side line at Sotheby's. I have quite an eye and I notice everything, absolutely everything, don't you know. For instance, last night, I saw you wandering about in your dressing gown like Rochester's wife escaped from the attic. You should be careful in case you catch cold; these old houses can be terribly draughty.'

Rosie ducked her head to avoid his gimlet eye. 'Right, well, I'm off for a walk, see you later.' She hurried out of the room to avoid any more questions and went down to the kitchen and servants' quarters where she knew he wouldn't follow. She pulled up short when she saw Simon going into the room where the silverware was kept. Hurrying past, she saw him with his arms around the butler, their mouths locked together. As she escaped into the kitchen garden, she wondered if Alex had been right about Simon and Baird being enemy spies, and her heart sank. Simon with his breezy, friendly ways had been one of her favourite students at the JSSL and had become a friend. If Alex was right and Sir Angus was handing secrets to the Russians, the others must be working for some other shadowy organisation, that or they didn't know about each other's involvement with the KGB.

Rosie's suspicions about Simon and Baird were confirmed later that day, after the hunting party had returned and everyone was resting before dressing for dinner. Rosie saw Simon go into Baird's room. He left the door ajar and she could hear them if she stood flat against the wall in the corridor. She held her washbag in case someone else came along and she could pretend she was on her way to the bathroom.

'It was just as I thought, the safe is behind a painting in the library,' Baird was saying. 'All we need now is the combination. Did you get it out of that idiot of a butler?'

'Give me a chance, I'm still warming him up.'

'And no doubt enjoying every minute.'

'Are you jealous?' Rosie heard a soft thud and then another as one of them dropped his shoes to the floor. 'Look, Ally, I don't know if my charms alone will work on Hamish.'

'A bribe, then?'

'No chance, jobs like his are scarce around here and he knows on what side his bread's buttered. Tell you what though, one of my pals was a safe cracker and taught me a thing or two. I think I can get it open and take what we need.'

'Too risky, although when we do get it open, we can make it look like a jewellery theft to cover our tracks.'

'There is something else. Hamish has a wife.'

'Now, that is interesting.'

'And a baby on the way.'

'Even better. I'm sure the little woman wouldn't be too pleased if she were to find out that her husband bats for the other side. I do like a spot of blackmail, so effective. Just as long as he doesn't top himself first – remember that politician destined for the cabinet we thought would be a good source?'

'Spent months grooming him. Waste of bloody time. Mind you, we had a good laugh at the grieving widow at the funeral. I was one of the coffin bearers and you read the eulogy, what larks!' Rosie heard Simon's pleasant baritone of a laugh and Baird's high-pitched donkey bray, and shivered. 'I don't think Hamish is the type to end it all, doesn't have the imagination for that.' There was a lull in the conversation before Simon started speaking again. He had moved further away, and it was harder for Rosie to make out what he was saying. She edged closer. 'His father . . . stalwart . . . church . . . elder like a church warden . . . find out his only son . . . light on his highly polished loafers.' Rosie heard a drawer opening and a curse.

'What are you looking for, dear boy?'

Simon was clearer now, nearer the door. Rosie inched back. 'The camera that can be worn as a buttonhole. I was just thinking, what if there were some compromising photographs of Hamish on his knees? And I don't mean in prayer.'

Baird's laugh grated on her ears. 'Talking of which, get over here. Lock the door first, would you? Bloody hell, you left it open! How many times do I have to . . .' Rosie heard footsteps cross the room and hurried to her own. She would have to work quickly to find a way to stop Simon and Baird from getting their hands on the plans. And she would need to start soon.

Chapter 21

Rosie got her chance sooner than she'd thought possible. When the guests came down for breakfast next morning, she pulled Duncan aside and piled on the charm. She thought she had gone too far when she breathlessly egged him on to tell her every stultifying detail about how he'd stalked the stag over what sounded like every hill and glen on the estate, only for the beast to get away when his shot went wide.

'I'm afraid I made a bit of a hash of it. Father was so furious he told me to stay behind today.'

'So, you're not going out today?' Rosie asked, hating herself for manipulating him so shamelessly.

'We were going to take the *Angelina* out on the loch, but the forecast is for a snow storm.' Rosie glanced at the large bay windows to a sky covered with blue-grey clouds heavy with unfallen ice crystals. 'Mummy is setting up the drawing room for bridge.' He sighed. 'I find card games boring – I'm afraid I'm not terribly competitive – but if I drop out, the numbers will be odd.'

'What if I duck out too to even things up? Then we can spend some time together, like we used to when we were little. Remember tea and scones in the library as a special treat when the weather was bad, and we couldn't get out to play? We could have a cosy time in the library. Do you still have the Blue Fairy book? I loved that when we were small.'

Duncan's face lit up. 'The Blue, the Red, the Olive, the Brown, the Green – we have most of them, and first editions at that.'

'Let's do that, then, if your mother can spare us?' Rosie said, knowing full well that Lady Moira would be only too delighted for the two of them to spend time together alone. Duncan readily agreed and went off to tell his mother that she would be two short for cards.

Back in her room after breakfast, Rosie dabbed on some powder to take the shine off her nose but decided against lipstick as too obvious, and likely to scare Duncan off. He'd met Stella in her stage make-up at the Charlotte Square house once and had turned quite pale and stammered that she was *terribly glamorous*. It wasn't a compliment and Stella had despised him ever since. Rosie gathered her resolve and went downstairs. In the library, the Sinclairs' ancient tabby cat was curled up on the sofa by the fire and half-opened an eye when she sat down and scratched behind its ears, until it rumbled contentedly and went back to sleep. Back issues of *Scottish Field* were stacked on a low table next to the sofa and she was leafing through one when

Duncan appeared at the door. Rosie patted the cushion for him to sit next to her and smiled warmly.

'There you are, at last!'

'Am I late? Sorry to keep you waiting. I bumped into that Fairweather chap, and he wanted to know if he could browse in the library. I made up an excuse, said I had some work to do. He seems quite jolly but, well . . .' Duncan ground to a halt, too embarrassed to admit he wanted to be alone with her.

'You're quite right, we called dibs on the library first,' Rosie said, using a much-loved phrase from their childhood games at Summer Isle House. She patted the sofa next to her again and he sat down gingerly with a hesitant smile. Rosie suppressed her irritation; she understood why Sir Angus lost patience with his nervous son. 'You're so lucky to live in this magnificent house with all its treasures.'

'I suppose I am, although I don't really notice them after all these years. I feel a bit hemmed in by so much clutter. You know what I'd really like? A modern house with clean lines and everything tidied away in cupboards. It would be so peaceful.' He looked around the library, at the marble busts, porcelain lamps, Persian rugs, countless ornaments on every surface, and the paintings crowding the walls. 'One day I'll inherit this house and everything in it.'

'A big responsibility,' Rosie said, feeling sorry for the next Sinclair Clan Chief. But she must not let herself be dissuaded from her mission. 'Do you know what I've always wanted to see? The famous Sinclair tiara. Didn't the diamond come from a Maharaja?'

'Yes, the Maharaja of Jaipur. He gave it to the Empress Queen Alexandra, and she gave it to Mummy. They're related you know, Mummy and the Empress Queen.' He looked downcast. 'It's why I'm such a disappointment – Mummy says I'm quite the catch and she was sure I'd be married by now. She tried to matchmake me with countless debs, but, well, none of them were quite right.' He looked at Rosie longingly, his thoughts as clear as if he'd said them aloud. If she let him, he'd kiss her, but she couldn't bear going that far, it would be too cruel. She played with the catch on her watch to defuse the tension in the air.

'I do so wish I could see the tiara, such a romantic story behind it! But I imagine it's locked away in the bank with your mother's other jewels.'

'Oh no, the tiara is right here, in this very room.'

'You don't say!'

Duncan beamed, eager to please her. 'Would you like to see it now?'

'I'd love that.'

He heaved himself off the sofa and lifted the not-Reynolds off the wall. Behind it lay the safe, which he opened with a few turns of the combination dial and then pulled out a black velvet bag. Duncan looked shyly at Rosie. 'The girl I marry will wear this at our wedding in St Paul's.'

'Lucky her!'

'Would you like to try it on?'

'May I?'

He advanced towards her and took out the tiara, luminous with the biggest diamonds she'd ever seen. Rosie didn't care much for old jewellery, preferring modern Danish designs in unostentatious silver and semi-precious gems like garnets and moonstones, but this was magnificent: a diadem fit for a queen, emeralds and diamonds glowing in the firelight. Duncan placed it reverently on her head.

'There, you look like even more beautiful now, like one of the princesses from the fairy books.'

The safe lay open. How to get him out of the room? 'I wish I could see myself,' Rosie said. 'Would you be a darling and fetch me a mirror?'

'There's a looking glass on the wall behind you.'

Rosie cursed inwardly. Thinking quickly, she said, 'Shall we play dress up, like we did when we were children? What would your bride wear on her wedding day? I seem to remember being shown your mother's photo album and she had on the most stunning dress. She told me it had been designed by the royal dressmaker, along the lines of the Queen Mother's gown. Does she still have it?'

'You know Mummy, she never throws anything out. There are clothes in her wardrobe that are older than me. I can ring for Baxter to fetch the gown.'

'Oh, I'd hate to put her to any trouble. The servants will be busy with the preparations for the Hogmanay Ball. Besides, wouldn't she tell your mother that you've been showing me the family jewels?'

Duncan blanched and looked around as if someone could see him and was about to reprimand him. 'I hadn't thought about that, I'm not really supposed to get the tiara out.'

Rosie put a hand on his arm. 'Don't worry, I won't say anything. But would you be an absolute darling and fetch me the wedding dress? It'll be our secret.' She lowered her voice, so he had to bend down to hear her. 'I'd hate your mother to find out I was trying on her wedding gown. I'll have to change in here, so promise to turn your back and not to peek.'

Duncan blushed. 'Of course, I would never do anything so ungentlemanly, especially not to you.' His eyes lit up. 'I say, shall I fetch Father's grey top hat and tailcoat so I can be the groom?'

'Splendid idea!' That would mean she would have more time alone with the safe.

'Don't go away,' he said and moved to the door. 'I'll be back as soon as I can, but I'll have to go up to the attic. Will you be all right on your own for a while?' Rosie picked up a *Scottish Field* and showed it to him; he smiled and practically sprinted from the room.

Once she was sure he was at a safe distance, Rosie went over to the safe and took out a bundle of papers. Glancing at the closed door, she looked for a blueprint, but they seemed to be mostly legal documents: wills, deeds and bond certificates. In her haste to put them back they spilled on the floor. Terrified, she started to pick them up only to hear footsteps approaching. She froze, crouched on the floor, but it was a light tread. One of the maids, no doubt. They receded and, her heart pounding, she stuffed the papers back in the safe. Where were the plans? Alex's informant must have been mistaken. Or perhaps they'd been moved. She bit her lip and peered into the safe; it was deeper than she'd thought. Rosie reached inside and felt blindly, and her hand closed around a cardboard tube. She pulled it out and held it in shaking hands. Inside were rolled-up plans on the kind of transparent paper she used to trace sketches onto a canvas. They were covered in detailed diagrams that her mind in its panic couldn't make out. At the top, under Top Secret stamped in red, there were strips of paper with typing on them. She looked closely and saw the words were in code. Underneath, there were some diagrams of buildings and coast lines, and what looked like engines and formulae she couldn't make head nor tail of. Heart hammering against her ribcage, Rosie fumbled in her pocket for the powder compact where she'd hidden the microdot camera and laid out all the plans on the floor, anchoring the curling sheets of paper with books at each corner. Working quickly, her breathing and heart rate now under control, she took photographs of everything. On an impulse, she went over to the desk by the window and found a piece of paper and a pencil. Working quickly, she copied down the lines of code. She could help Alex, who was not a cryptographer, save him time by solving the code. He'd be so pleased that she was using her initiative in the field. The sound of footsteps over the hall flagstones made her roll up the papers and replace them in the tube. Her hands sweating, she shoved it back in the safe and hurried to the sofa. She was just in time. The door handle turned, and Duncan appeared with garment bags over one arm and a hat box slung over the other.

He looked flustered. 'I had to hunt for the blasted thing, searched the attic then remembered Mummy likes to keep everything in her dressing room. Turned out it was in a trunk under a pile of blankets.'

Rosie realised she was still holding the tiny camera and slipped it in her pocket. She unzipped the larger garment bag and shook out the dress. 'Why, look at the dropped waist, and double train! It must have been the height of 1920s fashion when your mother walked down the aisle.' She bent to pick up one of the trains and froze; the books she'd used to weigh down the blueprints were still on the floor.

Duncan followed her gaze and frowned. 'The tweeny has been in here dusting and hasn't put the books back. Most of them are deadly dull, but I'm told they're awfully valuable, collected by generations of Sinclairs. There's a

Shakespeare First Folio somewhere, and some ghastly old Bible from the fifteenth century.'

Rosie helped him put the books on the shelves. Still wearing the tiara, she picked up the dress and held it against herself. 'Moira must have been slim as a toothpick. I suppose it was the fashion then, not to have any breasts, or bind them at least. I'm afraid I'll never fit into this, I'm far too busty.' Duncan went scarlet and Rosie suppressed a smile. 'It's a shame we can't play dress up after all. Tell you what, why don't we put all this away, and look at one of the fairy books together? I've always loved the colour plates.' Duncan nodded and helped her put the dress back in its bag. Just then, a hubbub broke out in the hall as Moira's strident tones bellowed for the dogs. Rosie took off the tiara, wincing as it caught her hair, and thrust it at Duncan. 'The bridge game must have broken up and your mother could come in here any time.'

He quailed, a little boy again. 'Mummy will be furious. The tiara's worth a fortune and not supposed to come out of the safe without a witness in case it's replaced with a fake. I'll put it in the safe while you nip upstairs and put the dress back.' He opened the door a crack. 'I can hear her going into the drawing room. You'll have to be quick.'

Rosie grabbed both garment bags and the hat box, checked the hall was empty and ran past the chatter of voices in the drawing room and up the stairs, her heart beating a wild tattoo. She paused at Moira's bedroom, but

Baxter was inside, laying out an evening dress for her mistress. Rosie made it unseen to her room and stuffed the smaller garment bag with the tails and the larger one bulging with satin, tulle and lace in the bottom drawer of a huge mahogany wardrobe. The hat box went on top of the wardrobe, she was betting the Sinclairs wouldn't miss them, not for a while anyway. Her heart beating wildly, Rosie collapsed on the bed and began to laugh. She was trembling again but this time with excitement rather than fear. Mission accomplished – all that was left now was to slip away from Summer Isle House to meet Alex in the old fisherman's bothy and hand him the film. She removed the tiny spool from its case, wrapped it in tissue and pushed it into a jar of cold cream. The piece of paper with the code, once folded into a small square, easily slipped behind the case of pressed powder in her compact. The Hogmanay Ball would be the perfect opportunity to hand the film to Alex. Then she remembered Simon and his safe cracker skills. A few minutes later she knocked on Ned's door. He was in a corner armchair reading and smiled when he looked up and saw Rosie.

'Just the person I was thinking about,' he said, showing her the cover of *The Goblin and the Princess*. 'I used to read this to you when you were little. This edition is illustrated by your mother's friend, Katharine Mackenzie. She was a sweet little thing but completely obsessed with fairies, and one might say she was away with them too.'

'I remember Aunt Kit and all her stories about the little people; fairies stealing people away to their magical land and brownies creeping into houses to clean and tidy, or spill the milk and break the crockery, depending on their moods.'

Ned closed the book. 'Kit was certainly a woman after George MacDonald's heart. Do you remember the goblins with their tender feet? I know it's a children's story, but it seemed a better way to spend a morning than sitting around a bridge table listening to gossip from the parish pump.' Rosie came and sat on the edge of his bed, smoothing the satin eiderdown while she thought of what to say.

'I skipped out of the card game too and nipped into the library for some peace. Thank goodness that awful Sir Alistair wasn't in there this time.'

'Too busy cheating at cards, no doubt. He's an acquired taste but knows his stuff as an art historian and antiquarian. Clever chap.'

'Perhaps that's why he was taking down the Reynolds over the fireplace yesterday.'

Ned sat up and put the book on the floor. 'He was doing what?'

'I thought it was a bit odd too, and he looked as if I'd caught him doing something he ought not, but once he explained, it all made perfect sense. Apparently, he thinks it's a reproduction and he was taking a closer look at the back.' Ned smoothed his moustache, a sign that he was thinking hard.

'That does make sense yes.' He got up and kissed Rosie on the head. 'Will you excuse me? I need to find Gus and have a quick word about something – shop talk, you know what we dreary old government types are like.'

Rosie followed him out of the room and watched him hurry down the stairs. Ned never hurried as a rule. Rosie smiled. Alex had told her that Ned had been suspicious of Alistair Baird during the war. He would make sure the blueprints were kept out of Baird's hands.

Chapter 22

The next day, the house was full of harried servants carrying enormous vases of flowers and silver vasques bristling with champagne bottles. Rosie, who had been brought tea and toast in bed by Baxter to keep the house guests out of the dining room, stood on the stairs watching footmen bearing heavy trays tinkling with crystal glasses, and village men in shirtsleeves moving furniture and hefting rolled-up rugs.

Moira strode into the hall, calling over her shoulder. 'Not there, it'll get knocked over during the reels.' She stopped when she saw Rosie. 'I don't know how we'll be ready in time for the ball,' she called up to her. 'I've been at it since before dawn, but it's been one cock-up after another.' Rosie came down and put her arm around Moira, who looked her age in the harsh morning light streaming in from the cupola.

'Is there anything I can do? I hope you're not doing everything by yourself. Where are Duncan and Sir Angus?'

'Oh, those two! They were just getting in the way, so I sent them into Inverness for more booze. That idiot of a wine merchant didn't deliver enough, and I just know we'll be drunk dry again this year.' She patted Rosie's arm. 'Thank you for offering to help, dear, but it's all under control. Ned is taking a stroll in the gardens, why don't you join him?' Moira wheeled round and shouted at a man struggling with an enormous Chinese vase: 'No, not there! All we need is for an eightsome reel to get out of hand – and they always do – and some young buck will go crashing into it. Gus will have a fit.' She turned to Rosie confidingly. 'I think it's a frightful thing, would much rather have a nice Staffordshire planter or a pair of those sweet wally dugs you see in Glasgow tea rooms, but Gus says it's from the mink dynasty. Although why a vase should be named after a smelly little stoat, I don't know.'

As Moira strode off to chivvy another helper, Rosie escaped through the French windows and crunched over the snow-covered lawn to look for Ned. Rabbit and what looked like fox tracks crossed the white expanse but there were no footprints. Ned must have taken the gravel drive, now cleared of snow by delivery vans and cars fetching guests from Achnasheen railway station. Rosie spotted someone standing on the loch shore and hurried down, calling, 'Hello, there!' The figure turned to reveal it wasn't Ned but Alistair Baird. It was too late to change course and she braced herself for another brusque encounter. But Baird was all smiles.

'Isn't it a glorious view? Worthy of Whistler or Turner.'

'Or William McTaggart.' Rosie expected him to sneer at her for her parochial loyalty to Scottish artists, but he surprised her.

'You're right, his later works, when he'd given up painting children, and when his fascination with seascapes took over, are astonishing. He painted along the west coast, but also on the east coast, mostly in Crail.' He paused and looked out over the choppy loch. 'Talking of Crail, I believe that's where you met Simon.'

'Yes.'

'At that peculiar Russian language school. I'm afraid it didn't quite take with Simon. He can barely say a word other than *do svidaniya* and *spasibo*, but then he has other talents.' Baird pulled out a silver cigarette case and offered it to Rosie, who shook her head. He busied himself with lighting one, hands cupped against the wind coming off in from the water, and said out of the corner of his mouth, 'There was an old friend of mine from the war at Crail. Alex Kuznetsov. Ever come across him?' Rosie hesitated. She had kept her affair with Alex quiet from the students, but it was a small town – more of a village really – and the camp was full of men living cheek by jowl with nothing better to do than gossip. Word would have got around. There was no point lying.

'Yes, I do know him. Quite well, as a matter of fact.' Baird narrowed his eyes at her through the smoke and looked at her for a long moment.

'Is that right? I wonder, does he share your interest in art? As far as I remember he couldn't tell a Picasso from a Pissarro. A soldier through and through, loves his guns and gadgets, but not a great one for fine art. What on earth did you two talk about? Or perhaps you didn't do much talking?' Ignoring the innuendo, Rosie scuffed her shoe against the sand and bent to pick up a shell, playing for time. But Baird seemed to lose interest in his line of questioning. 'Forgive my curiosity, but I saw you slip into the library with young Sinclair yesterday and wondered if he might have replaced the dashing Kuznetsov in your affections. You were in there for quite a while, and I saw him bringing some clothes for you, garment bags if I'm not mistaken. Were you showing him your gown for the ball? Or perhaps admiring the counterfeit Reynolds you seem so keen on?' He turned to her, his eyes cold. 'Or were you using your feminine wiles on that young fool?' Baird's smooth charm had disappeared. He was a predator sensing a rival for his prey. Not so much as a supercilious cat as a snake, fangs primed with deadly venom. Rosie knew that if he exposed her, she could go to jail for breaching the Official Secrets Act, and the trail would lead to Alex, who could be imprisoned or, God forbid, executed for treason. She made herself take a deep breath and let it out slowly, as Alex had shown her. Baird had his suspicions and was trying to smoke her out; she had to keep calm.

'If you must know, although I don't see how it could possibly interest you, Duncan and I were discussing what I should wear for the ball tonight. He was showing me an evening dress Moira had kindly offered to lend me, but he accidentally brought her wedding gown – you know how some men are so stupid about such things.' She eyed him coolly. 'Although I'm sure you would never make that mistake. Anyway, I could tell right away it wouldn't do. I was only agreeing to see it to spare Moira's feelings, but she was so insistent, even though I'd told her I'd brought my own, picked out by Ned. It only needs taking up a bit. I'm not sure Moira trusted my uncle to find something suitable for a Highland ball, but Ned has impeccable taste, as I'm always telling everyone who cares to listen.' Rosie knew she was babbling and was relieved to hear a shout and see Ned coming over the dunes towards them. 'Here he is now; speak of the devil.'

'A nice little tale you spin, my girl. No wonder Kuznetsov singled you out. You have quite a talent.'

'I have no idea what you're talking about.'

He took a long drag of his cigarette. 'Don't you now? We'll see.'

Ned reached them, shaking the sand from his brogues in disgust. 'There you are, Rosie. I've been wandering lonely as a cloud, but there's only so much of my own company I can stand.' He nodded at the other man. 'Alistair.'

'Edward.'

Ned linked his arm through Rosie's. 'I must steal my niece away, there's pressing business afoot.'

'A problem with a dress I understand. Nothing a needle and thread won't fix.' Baird smiled thinly and walked off along the strand, pausing to pick up a pebble or shell and throw it into the water.

Ned frowned. 'What on earth was all that about? That was odd, even for Baird, who is one of the oddest fish I've come across in a long and chequered life. Never mind him now, let's take a turn around these splendid grounds, as Moira instructed, no doubt to get us out of her hair while she terrorises the staff.' Rosie fell into step beside Ned. She wished she could confide in him, but she had promised Alex that she would keep his secret, even if it meant deceiving her beloved Ned, and worse, betraying the trust of Moira and poor, helpless, hapless Duncan.

That night, the ball was in full swing as Rosie curtseyed to the rising chord that marked the beginning of Machine without Horses, a tricky dance that she'd thankfully learned as a schoolgirl. Rosie patted her side where she'd tied a small cotton bag with the camera film around her waist and under her dress. She smiled at her partner, a red-faced and perspiring Duke of Somewhere who looked as if this dance might be his last. The jigging music started, and the hall sprang into life. The locals all knew the dances, but some of the London set looked a bit lost and got tangled up, slapping their ankles together as if greeting their sergeant major and jumping up and down instead of lightly skipping from one foot to the other for the *pas de bas*. Rosie saw Sir Angus have a word with the band leader and the next dance was a simple but lethal eightsome reel. Duncan appeared in front of her, and she was glad it was him and not some boisterous oaf who would send her spinning down between the two rows like a child's top. Down the line, an over-enthusiastic man was already wheeching and whooping and clapping as some poor woman was whirled and burled to within an inch of her life.

When Duncan came to turn her, he said, 'Shall we sneak away to the stables, like we used to? It's so noisy in here.'

Rosie twirled around, pretending not to hear him, while she thought of an excuse. She desperately wanted to get away to meet Alex but had to wait until the Bells. One of Ned's creaky old friends came to her rescue. The next dance was the Dashing White Sergeant, and he whisked her away. As the trio she was in stamped their greeting at the next three dancers, Rosie suddenly came face to face with Alex. He grinned at her as he clapped his hands and before she could speak to him, he was turning his partner into a figure of eight and had passed on to the next trio. When the music stopped, Rosie found him at the punch table, wincing at the little glass cup in his hand.

'My God, what's in this, petrol?'

'What are you doing here? I thought I was supposed to meet you on the loch shore tonight, after midnight, that's what we agreed.'

He didn't look up from the punch bowl. 'There's been a change of plan, one of my contacts got word to me that Sinclair's suspicions have been aroused.' Rosie felt her face grow hot. She'd let the cat out of the bag trying to deflect attention to Baird, and now Alex had to scramble and change their careful arrangements. He seemed not to notice her agitation. 'We don't have any time to lose; the ball is perfect cover. Nobody knows me here apart from Ned, and he'll just think I've gate crashed to surprise you on New Year's Eve. It's the kind of romantic gesture women adore, apparently.'

'Alistair Baird is here, and he said he knows you and he knows about us. He's here with Simon Fairweather, who will recognise you from Crail. They're after the same thing as you.'

His face darkened. 'I knew I was right to set you after Fairweather. He comes across as a moron, and nearly had you fooled with his golden boy looks and simpleton act. But he isn't as stupid as he looks.' Rosie looked around the milling dancers and finally located Simon and Baird talking to Sir Angus and Lady Moira. Baird suddenly looked up and around him, as if sensing her eyes upon him.

'Quick, before he sees you,' Rosie said, pulling Alex behind a pillar entwined with holly and ivy. She peered round from their hiding place and saw Sir Angus climbing the steps to the wooden stage. He knocked a spoon against his glass and the band fell silent. The guests turned to look at him.

'Friends, family and neighbours, welcome one and all.' A huge cheer prompted the laird to quieten the crowd with a gesture. 'It's been a great year for Summer Isle House and for Poolewe . . .'

Alex whispered, 'Have you got it on you?' She nodded. 'Let's go now, while everyone is listening.'

'But . . .'

'Quickly, no time to lose.'

They slipped out of the great hall, through the drawing room where Alex opened the French windows. A blast of snow hit Rosie in the face, and she shivered, her arms bare and goose pimpled. 'I don't have a coat and you're in black tie, we'll freeze out there. There's a blizzard on its way.'

'You call this a blizzard? In Russia it's a flurry. I thought you were made of sterner stuff.' Alex took off his dinner jacket and wrapped it around her shoulders. 'Come on, let's make a dash for it.'

They ran down the lawn into the teeth of the icy wind, the snow seeping into Rosie's silk dancing slippers within seconds. She slid and stumbled on the steep slope at the bottom of the garden. In the distance she could hear church bells ringing in the New Year and a faint cheer from the house. She glanced back and for a moment thought she saw a figure silhouetted against the French doors, but a gust of snow blew into her eyes and when she could see again nobody was there. Alex helped her to her feet and led her to the stables and into a car she recognised, this time its hood up.

'You brought the Sunbeam all the way here, in this weather?' He shrugged and grinned and reached into the tiny back seat and pulled out a sheepskin.

'Get under this. There's a hip flask of brandy in the glove compartment. I'd take a nip if I were you, it's going to be a long drive.'

'Where are we going?' Instead of answering he revved the gutsy engine, drowning out any further questions, and the little car sped down the driveway, scattering gravel. In a few moments they were on the road, warm air blowing into Rosie's frozen face and melting the ice in her hair. She looked at Alex's profile in the dark as he concentrated on the winding single-track road and found herself exhausted but elated. She had never felt more alive.

Chapter 23

They drove across country through the night. Rosie slept, waking to see the occasional sign lit up in the car headlights for Dingwall, Inverness and Nairn. They stopped briefly at a petrol station in Elgin to fill the tank, the attendant yawning and scratching his head. It was still dark when they drove through Buckie and Banff before reaching the top of a vertiginous cliff. Alex stopped the car, and they got out and Rosie stretched, stiff from the drive. The moon came out from behind a cloud, and she could see a steep path leading down to a narrow ledge with a tiny row of fishing cottages that seemed to be clinging to the very edge of the world, their backs to the cliff and gable ends facing the pewter expanse of the North Sea.

'What time is it?'

Alex looked at the height of the moon. 'Around five. Another three hours before dawn breaks.' He pulled a small knapsack out of the car and shrugged it on. 'Let's go. There are dry clothes, waterproofs and boots at the rendezvous point.' A gust of wind nearly blew Rosie off her feet. She lurched forward, holding onto Alex.

'Where are we?'

'Crovie, a fishing village.'

'And who are we meeting?' But the wind was howling, and he didn't seem to hear her. He set off down the path and after a descent that left Rosie's satin dancing slippers in shreds and her feet bloodied, they reached a narrow, cobbled stretch in front of the row of houses. A stone bank that dipped down to the water was all that separated the cottages from the fierce sea that raged and battered the hamlet, as if it wanted to break down the villagers' doors and drown them in their beds. Spray from the waves shot up into the air as they broke against the barrier and within minutes Rosie was soaked as they ran towards a blue door in a white cottage. Alex took a key out of the knapsack, and they darted in out of the storm. It was the smallest house Rosie had ever seen. There was a room with a scullery off it and steep stairs leading up to an attic, no doubt hung with fishing nets. Alex lit a Tilley lamp that cast a warm kerosene glow over the timbered walls and thrust a coarse towel into her hands before lighting the stove. Rosie was shivering so much her teeth chattered uncontrollably. She towelled her hair and tried to get warm, rubbing her arms and legs to get the circulation going before peeling off her clothes. Alex seemed immune to the cold and fetched her a blanket from a bed in a recess screened off with a curtain.

He rummaged in a sailor's canvas bag leaning against a wall and gave Rosie a blue Guernsey sweater, a checked flannel shirt washed soft over time, a pair of men's trousers, thick socks, and hiking boots.

'Not exactly Paris fashion,' he said.

'I don't care, I'm beginning to feel my fingers and toes again,' she said, tightening the belt around her waist to its last notch before lacing the too-big boots. 'I'll make us some tea.' She stretched her hands over the old-fashioned stove to soak up some of the blessed heat and watched Alex strip down, his flanks pale in the half-dark, his shadow in the glow of the Tilley lamp huge against the wall. Rosie thought of Peter Pan, the lost boy searching for his shadow in the Darlings' nursery. She shook her head to clear it: ridiculous to think of a childhood tale at a time like this. The hot tea warmed her, and they huddled together in the bed under rough blankets.

'Rendezvous is not until tonight. They'll send me a signal,' Alex said. 'I'm going to get some kip, you should too.' He fell asleep almost immediately, but Rosie felt wide awake despite having been up all night. She watched Alex sleep for a while, his features softened in the lamp light. He frowned and muttered; Rosie smoothed his forehead, and he settled again. The sun wouldn't be up until nearly nine, so she had a couple of hours before Alex woke. She slipped out of bed and padded over to a small table in the scullery next door. The slip of paper was still tucked into the back of her compact and she retrieved it now along with the tiny pencil that had come with her dance card. Alex would be pleased, no doubt, if she managed to crack the code before he wakened. It would save him time and make him look even better in the eyes of his superiors. Rosie smoothed out the note's creases and got to work. It had been eleven years since her last decryption. At first, all she could see was a jumble of letters, so she closed her eyes, emptied her mind, slowed her breathing and looked again. At least this message would be in English, not like the German transcriptions of radio messages she'd decoded in the war. Recurring letters settled into a pattern and soon she was absorbed in the task. After an hour, words began to emerge, but concentrating on the letter-by-letter decryption, she didn't take in their meaning until she'd transcribed the entire message. She sat back and read what she'd written down. There were two paragraphs.

Proposed location of United States Navy ballistic missile submarine base: British Royal Navy Submarine Base, Holy Loch, Cowal Peninsula on Firth of Clyde, Argyll and Bute, Scotland.

Sweat broke out under her arms and down her back as the words *nuclear-powered submarine* and *prototype* jumped out at her in the next paragraph. She remembered the mechanical drawings on the blueprints that she'd photographed.

The plans were instructions on how to build the nuclear-powered and armed submarine developed by the Americans. Rosie folded the paper and put it in her pocket along with the lipstick tube in which she had hidden the film. She went next door and sat by Alex's side and waited for him to waken. Outside, the sky began to lighten on this, the first day of 1957. In the grey light, he looked tired and washed out, but still beautiful, still her Alex. There must be some kind of explanation for what she'd discovered. Impatient, now she shook him by the shoulder, and he opened his eyes.

'What is it? Is everything all right?'

'Alex, why are we here?'

'I told you, we had to change plans when we got wind of Sinclair's suspicions.'

'So, we're meeting your people from MI6? Why here? It's hard to get to by road.'

'They're coming by sea.'

'Crazy in this storm.'

'Not if you're in a sub.' He sat up. 'Where's the film? Can you give it to me now?'

Rosie's hand went to her pocket and tightened around the lipstick tube. She tried to see Alex's face, but he was hidden in the shadows. Only his eyes gleamed in the light that crept in through a chink in the curtain.

'Why is a sub coming here?' She waited, watching him, and realised how little she knew about him.

'The waters are deep enough for a sub. We thought it the safest rendezvous point, remote enough to get away from Sinclair and his handlers.' He was a good liar. If she hadn't decoded the message, she would have believed him, just as she'd believed every lie he'd told her since they met. She'd been a fool, worse than a fool.

'The sub, it isn't one of ours, is it?' He didn't reply. 'It's the Soviets who are coming; you're going to hand the film over to them.'

'Nonsense, I'm on your side, Rosie, surely you know that?' There was the tell: *your side* not *our side*. Rosie looked at the man she had fallen in love with so easily. Too easily. She would give him a chance to explain, hoping against hope that he would allay her suspicions. 'There's something else in there, a code, isn't there?' she said. He looked away but she took his chin and forced him to look at her. 'Isn't there?'

Alex took her hand away. 'I'm not who you think I am.'

'I'm beginning to realise that.' Rosie scrambled off the bed and put on a sou'wester hanging on a nail by the door.

'Where do you think you're going? There's a storm coming in over the sea.'

'I don't know, I don't care. I only know that I want to get out of here.'

He leaped up and put his arms around her and nuzzled her ear, and she felt herself leaning into him.

'Rosie, please, don't leave me. I'll tell you everything. It's me, Alex, I love you.' With a sob she turned and buried her head in his shoulder. He took her hand and led her to a small table and chairs near the stove. The only sound was the wind getting up outside and the boom of waves breaking against the barrier. She waited for him to start talking and after a while he did.

'I grew up in England, went to the right school, played rugby and was in the rowing team at Cambridge, everything to make me what is known as the right sort. But I'm Russian, and you can't change your blood.' He traced a whorl in the table as if to gather his thoughts. 'My mother was a loyal Communist Party member and so was my father; like I told you, he was a diplomat in the Embassy of the new Soviet Union in London. I was born in England but when I was six, diplomatic relations were suspended, and they had to go home. I was left behind in boarding school and spent holidays with Uncle Yegor. Turned out he was KGB, but I didn't know that until I was older and he was my handler.' Alex told her how Yegor had trained him in espionage, taught him tradecraft, but more importantly about the cause, that nothing must stand in the way of communism, that capitalism had sown the seeds of its own destruction, and that revolution was inevitable but not easily achieved. It was Alex's duty to be part of the fight to stop the Americans taking over the world, spreading their credo of greed, and exploiting and oppressing poor people wherever they could. Rosie had heard this argument expounded at art school, but she'd never seen anyone do so with such conviction. Alex had been brainwashed as a child. Nothing and nobody would change his mind or be allowed to stand in his way. A serpent of fear uncoiled inside Rosie as she took stock of her situation: she was alone and vulnerable and far from help. She was trapped in this strange village between the sea and the cliffs, the only way out on foot and up a steep path. She would have to play for time, go along with his plans until she could think of how to get away from him.

'So, you're KGB.'

'Yes.'

'All those speeches you made to me about stopping the nuclear arms race, that was all lies?'

'No. I believe that the playing field should be level so one does not have the advantage of the other.'

'What was on those plans that you got me to photograph?'

'The location of the nuclear submarine base.' Rosie waited. 'All right, you deserve to know, there was something else on there.'

'I've already worked it out. There were mechanical drawings and formulae. They're blueprints for a nuclear-powered submarine, the technology used to build the USS *Nautilus*.'

Alex thought for a moment. 'You decoded it. I didn't think you'd have time.'

'You underestimated me.'

'Clearly.' He sounded impressed and Rosie fought a surge of pride. 'How do you know about *Nautilus*?'

'Jim and Ned were talking one night. They said the Soviets didn't have the technology yet, but the British are close. That's what you had me steal. Not to prove Sir Angus is a spy, but to hand over to the Russians.' He didn't say anything, and she pulled away from him and shoved her hands into her pockets. The film was still there, and she curled her fingers around it. 'You're a sleeper agent.' He shrugged. 'All those years at Bletchley Park, your work with Ned on SIGINT. You were the leak, not Baird. Is he even KGB?'

'Yes, but he doesn't know about me. My deep cover has never been broken.'

Rosie felt another stab of fear. 'Until now.'

'Yes.' Alex reached for her, and she flinched. He dropped his hand.

'And I'm part of your mission. I'm just another lie, we're a lie.'

'At first, yes, but not now. Rosie, listen to me.' He took her by the shoulders, and she tried not to move away and reveal her fear. 'I've told you everything to prove that I love you and trust you with my life, that I want to be with you always. I know you're a good person, someone not afraid to act and face danger, and that you hate the thought of war as much as I do. Together we can fight for peace. If both sides have the same firepower, neither will make the first move.' His eyes were pleading; Rosie turned her head so she didn't have to look at him. She wished she could block out his words. 'I'm going back to Russia,' Alex went on. 'I'll be given another identity, and they'll send me elsewhere. I want you to come with me, to fight with me for a fairer and safer world.' Rosie got up and Alex watched her cross to the window. The wind and rain had abated, and the sea was calmer, but black clouds were gathering again on the horizon. She turned back to him, her arms crossed.

'Tell me exactly what is on the film. I need to know everything.'

'You were right. Plans for a new type of sub, a ballistic missile submarine the Americans call Polaris, with sixteen missiles, each one armed with three thermonuclear warheads. We haven't developed our own yet.'

'I take it by we, you mean the Soviets?'

He nodded. 'Our subs are still powered by diesel and electricity, not nuclear-powered. The plans you took from Sir Angus will even out the race, give everyone a fair chance and stop pre-emptive attacks from an American-British base in Scotland. '

'When are your friends coming?'

'Tonight.' The sound of the sea was everywhere. Alex knew there was nowhere she could run to. She was trapped.

'What will we do meanwhile?' Alex didn't smile but she saw his shoulders relax.

'Eat, rest for now, gather our strength. There will be

time later to go over your new identity and cover story.' Rosie turned back to the window and watched a seagull ride a thermal.

'All right.' She heard a movement behind her. Alex wrapped his arms around her. She held back tears as she felt his familiar warmth and solidity.

'*Dusha, dushenka*, I'll never let you go. Together we can make the world a better place.' Outside, the banked clouds split open, and rain fell in dark curtains on the heedless sea. Rosie turned and he held her face in his hands. When they kissed, she felt as if she were sinking through the waves to the darkness below.

Later, after they had slept for hours and eaten from the supplies in the cottage, they went out. The tide was out, and the rain had stopped long enough for Rosie and Alex to walk safely along the path in front of the line of cottages.

'It's such a wild place, but there's beauty in its wildness. I could paint here,' Rosie said as they passed a shuttered cottage. If she could talk about her work, it would help her to keep calm and convince Alex he had turned her.

'You're an artist so that's what you choose to see, but there is suffering and hardship behind those doors.'

Rosie shoved her icy hands in her pockets, checked the tube of film was still there. 'I imagine that's true of any fishing village in Scotland.'

'More so here. Many of the villagers left after a huge

storm in 1953,' Alex said, glancing at the cottage before looking out to sea again. 'But they weren't always fisherfolk; they were forced to come here, cleared from an inland estate and their crofting way of life to make way for sheep. Farmers had to learn how to fish, how to sail, tie nets and find the herring banks. These seas are treacherous, and the living hard. The herring industry went into decline and then the flood washed away most of the cottages.' He raised an arm in greeting at a couple of old men in caps smoking and sitting on herring barrels further along the path. 'Now most of the young people have all gone to look for work and a less gruelling life.'

Rosie concentrated on what she could see around her. *Talk about art, keep away from ideology or you'll betray yourself.* 'I'd still love to paint it. The raging sea, the cottages so near waves that could consume them, and behind and above them the cliffs and the vast, changing sky.'

'It's not the way I think. I'm a pragmatist who sees social problems, injustices and then figures out how they can be righted.'

'Art, the life of the mind and spirit, is important too. Man cannot live by bread alone, after all.'

He raised his eyebrows and laughed. 'Are you quoting the Bible at me, a dyed-in-the-wool atheist?'

Rosie sat on the defence wall and looked down at the rocks. The air was pungent with washed up rotten seaweed. She felt the tube with the film press against her hip. Alex hadn't asked for it again, but he would soon. He stood next to her, scanning the horizon with binoculars. Even with the tide out, Rosie could hear stones rumbling and crashing against each other under the surf, the noise echoing off the cliff face. After a while, she reached for his hand. He helped her to her feet and pulled her in close and she clung to him, tracing the sharp line of his cheekbones with her fingertips, his lips, the stubble on his chin. Later, she would draw him, before the memory of him faded, but she couldn't think about that now. There was still no way she could escape; a couple of old fishermen wouldn't be able to come to her rescue, and most of the cottages looked closed up for the winter. Besides, who would believe her? There was a chance that Alex would let her go. She had to trust her instincts: that under the mask he had had to wear since childhood, there were real feelings and that he did love her. She would have to speak to him soon but not yet; they still had a few hours left before night. The sun was setting, turning the sea into a fiery lake.

'Let's go in. It'll be dark soon,' Rosie said, looking at her watch. 'It's only half past three. The days are so short this far north. Is it the same in Russia?'

'It depends where you are. The sun has the decency to stay in the Leningrad sky until about six at this time of year.' Alex turned her chin up towards him and kissed her. 'Let's take advantage of the early night and try out that peculiar bed. Once they arrive, we won't have the chance to be alone for a while.'

'How long do we have?'

'Long enough.'

He put his arm around her and as they began to walk away, Rosie looked back. The tide was coming in and anything dropped over the sea wall onto the rocks would be washed out to sea.

Chapter 24

Rosie sat by the range, clutching a mug of tea, her head on Alex's shoulder. The wind was howling and screaming down the chimney and rain lashed the window. Outside there was only darkness. She looked up at Alex.

'How long now?'

'Not long.' He went to the window and looked through his binoculars. Rosie went to stand beside him. After a while she felt his shoulders stiffen. 'There, did you see that?' He handed her the binoculars. At first, she could see only blackness, then a glimmer of light on the horizon flashed for a second. More lights revealed the dark mass of a submarine, and a dinghy with men in it motoring towards the bay. She handed the binoculars back and Alex stashed them in the sailor's canvas bag. He pulled on a black waterproof jacket and handed another one to her. 'You'd better wear this.' Rosie held the coat without putting it on. 'Hurry, they'll be here soon.' He held out his hand. 'You'd better give me the film now.' She hugged the coat and shook her head. Alex went still. 'Rosie, give it to me.'

'I don't have it.'

He stared at her. 'What do you mean? You told me you took the photographs, that you had the film safe around your waist in a bag under your dress, and I saw you stash it in your pocket when you changed. You can't have lost it! It'll be here somewhere, just look.' Rosie shook her head again. She crossed her arms and dug her nails into them to stop herself trembling. Alex grabbed her by the shoulders. 'I've had enough of this. Hand it over.' He shook her, hard. 'Now!' Rosie had never seen him angry. His mouth was twisted, his breath coming fast. She tried to pull away from him, but his grip was too strong.

'I told you; I don't have it. I threw it into the sea earlier when the tide was coming in.' Alex let her go and pushed his hands through his hair. His eyes were wild.

'Do you know what you've done, you little fool? This isn't a game. These are dangerous men.' He went to the window; the dinghy with its searchlight trained on the water was now near enough to see without binoculars as it approached the beach where the villagers pulled up their boats. In a matter of moments, the men were clambering over the side and dragging the dinghy up the shingle. Alex bowed his head. Rosie knew she had been right: he would never hurt her, but now a new fear emerged.

'Alex, listen to me, you'll be all right, they're on your side. Just tell them I couldn't get into the safe, that there's no film.'

'I told them you had it. I made a call when we stopped at Elgin and the code word was relayed to them. They'll think I betrayed them, that I'm some kind of double agent.' He stood, thinking, before turning to her. 'Do exactly what I tell you. I'll put out the lamp when I go out that door, and as soon as I'm gone, go upstairs and hide. Don't look out the window and stay there for as long as you can. It's better they don't know you're here. I . . . I'll tell them I got rid of you. That you were a liability.' He couldn't look her in the eyes. 'Here's the car key but wait until the coast is clear before you take it.' She folded her fingers around the metal key, feeling the teeth digging into her palm.

'What about you? What will they do to you?'

'They'll take me back to Moscow and I'll be interrogated by the KGB. I can talk my way out of trouble, and they'll want to keep me, I'm one of their most valuable assets. They've spent years investing in my cover.' His words were reassuring but his eyes kept darting to the door and Alex, who she had never seen look anything but calm and in control of his emotions, was sweating and his hands were shaking.

Rosie pulled at his jacket. 'No, it's too dangerous. We can run. Please, Alex. Come with me. Ned can fix this, you can be a valuable asset to MI6, if you tell them everything you know. We can go out the back way, get out behind the cottages. You said there was another path leading to the next village.'

'It's no good, they'll come hunting for us.' He touched her cheek. 'Goodbye *doushenka,* take care of yourself.' He doused the lamp and before she could stop him, he was out the door. The room was engulfed in darkness and the reek of kerosene pinched her nostrils. She felt her way back to the window and looked out to see him walking towards the shingle beach. The men stood silently by the dinghy. She saw Alex stop and after a few minutes, one of the men raised his weapon. Too late, she realised she had signed Alex's death warrant. The KGB would never forgive him. She knew what happened to traitors in the Soviet Union, but she'd blocked it out of her mind. The men were arguing with Alex now, gesticulating and waving their guns around. Without stopping to think, her only instinct to try and stop what was happening, Rosie wrenched open the door and ran along the path, shouting, but the wind whipped her words out of her mouth and knocked the breath out of her chest. She fought against it, running slowly as if she were in a nightmare, unable to make much headway as the heavens poured down on her. Through the rain she could make out a struggle as some of the men pulled Alex into the dinghy while two of them pushed it down the shingle beach and into the sea. The outboard motor roared, and they sped off. Rosie reached the beach and shouted after them, but the dinghy was nearing the black hulk of the waiting submarine. She heard a shot crack out and saw a flash out at sea. In the distance, she saw a body tumble into the water. Rosie sank to her knees in the surf and bowed her head, oblivious to the water washing over her.

Chapter 25

Rosie wanted to die. She rolled onto her back in the wet shingle. Something snuffled behind her, and a cold, wet nose found her upturned palm.

It whined and came over and settled beside her and started to lick her face. 'Go away,' Rosie tried to say, but a wave rippled over her, and her mouth filled with sea water.

'My darling girl, it's all right, I'm here.'

She felt herself being lifted out of the water. 'I have it, it's in my pocket. I'm sorry.'

'What is the lassie saying? She shouldnae be out here without a jaiket, she's soaked through,' a voice, said, then a clamour: *whit was she thinking . . . a nicht like this . . .* Above the steady in and out breath of the tide, there were faint whistles and shouts. A bright light shone in her face, blinding her.

'She's delirious, she needs to see a doctor,' a man said. A man she knew. But who? Rosie wanted to tell him that it was all right, she was dead, and nothing mattered any more, but it was as if she were asleep and dreaming and couldn't speak. *Maybe this is what it's like to be dead.* Did she say that or think it?

'Bring her in out of the storm, sir. Poor wee soul, she's lucky you found her.' A woman was speaking now. Rosie tried to open her eyes, but her lashes seemed stuck together.

'Thank you. Which one is your cottage?'

'This is ane, with the red door. Put her in the bed and I'll fetch some hot water and dry claes. Are you polis, sir, and is it your men searching the brae and the Rotten Beach? Who is it they're looking for? Is it a convict that's escaped frae Peterheid? Or smugglers?'

'Never mind that now, there's a good woman. Hurry up with the hot water and dry clothes, would you? And no, I'm not with the police, I'm her uncle.'

Rosie's eyes flew open and stared into Ned's worried face. There was a whine, and two paws and a curly black head appeared at the side of the bed. 'Boris! How did you get here, boy? And where's . . .' A wave of pain washed over her. 'Oh God, Alex, my Alex!'

'Hold on, Rosie, my girl, you've a fever. A doctor's on his way, shouldn't be long, meanwhile let's get you out of those wet things.' Her head swirled and she closed one eye to focus.

'I think I'm about to be sick.'

Later.

Darkness.

A bright light, a pencil of light. Someone pulling at her eyelid. Then she remembered.

'Alex! Alex! Come back! Don't shoot! Leave him alone!'

'There, there, don't fret now.' A warm dry hand on her forehead. She was burning hot and slippery with sweat. Now she was shivering, the sweat chilling her skin. She thought of the cold, cold sea and thought she was sinking through the darkness to the bottom, waters closing over her head, and the black shape of a submarine silently moving through the deep. She started to struggle to get out of bed. 'No! No! Leave him alone!' Someone was holding her down, had the men come back for her? Rosie fought the hands that were restraining her. 'What have you done to him? No! Get off me!' Her arm was rubbed with something cold and there was a needle prick. There was another wave, but this time of sleep.

She woke to hear a different voice, soothing, comforting. 'Hush now, dear, this will make you feel better.' A doctor's voice. The gentle hand on her brow was like sinking into a warm bath. Rosie fought against the darkness.

'No, not this! There's still time to save him. Let me go!' Her words were slurred, her tongue thick, her thoughts clouding.

'It's working, she's calmer, her pulse is slowing. That's right, you rest, there's a good girl.'

Rosie was sinking deeper into the black. She could hear the sea moving restlessly outside the window. Rosie saw him, silhouetted against the sun on a beach, his features dark, like the first time she met him. *Alex! I'm coming, wait for me.*

Chapter 26

Rosie had no memory of being taken by stretcher up the vertiginous path to a waiting ambulance or of the drive south to Edinburgh. She woke up in a hospital bed in a private room and wondered where she was and what had happened. Then she remembered and a nurse ran to fill her arm with something that made her sink back into merciful oblivion. When she surfaced from the deep, familiar faces swam before her: Stella's in tears, Jim's a frown of concern. Where was the smile that made creases around his eyes? Her mother whispering endearments, stroking her brow. Ned, dear old Ned, looking older. Monty. Why was Monty here? And where was Valentina? She tried to ask him; did she ask him? Next time she opened her eyes it was dark outside the window, and he was gone. She turned her head and there was Gabriel Paxton. She managed a smile. 'So tired.'

He patted her hand. 'You gave us a fright.'

'I'm not sure if you're a dream. Is this a dream?'

His face blurred and he was saying something, but she couldn't make out the words. It went on like that, faces and voices coming and going as she went in and out of consciousness, succumbing to an overwhelming need to sleep, to forget. As she slowly recovered her strength, the memories of that terrible night invaded her sleep as she fought the sea and, desperate and voiceless, as she tried to reach Alex in a howling vortex. Her waking hours were weighed down by crushing shame: to have been seduced and persuaded to inveigle her way into the Sinclairs' home and betray their trust. Of course, Sir Angus wasn't a traitor, she could see that clearly now. If she hadn't been blinded by her feelings for Alex, she would have seen through his preposterous lies. Awake, she was wretched with self-loathing and cringed at how she had so nearly betrayed the most ultra of secrets, and she raged at Alex's duplicity, his cold-hearted manipulation of her feelings. But in her dreams, he was still her great love, and she mourned him, her anguished cries snatched away by the wind on a beach at the edge of the world.

Rosie thought Alex couldn't hurt her any more than he already had with his lies, until Monty came back to see her. This time she was strong enough to sit up and lucid enough to hear what he had to say. He stood at the end of her bed and spoke carefully.

'A damn shame what happened to Alex, but really it was only a matter of time.'

'What do you mean?'

'We've had our eye on him for a while now. The Soviets were getting their hands on all sorts of classified stuff. If we'd got to him first, he could have been useful. As I say, a damned shame.'

'You're MI6 too.' He shrugged and Rosie closed her eyes. Was nobody what they seemed? 'You were there that night, when they found me. That's why Boris was there. How did you know where we were?'

'Never mind all that now. Rest up now and get your strength back. I'll need to talk to you properly later, when you're discharged.'

Rosie wondered dully what would happen to her. She'd been afraid for Alex, that he'd contravened the Official Secrets Act, but it had been her crime, and she could go to prison for it. The weight on her chest grew heavier and her eyelids drooped; she was suddenly desperately tired. Fighting sleep, she watched Monty walk towards the door. Before he went out, he turned back.

'You do know that Alex was married?'

Rosie's eyes flew open, and she stared at him. 'You're lying.'

'Oh no,' he said, smoothly, 'I never lie about matters of the heart, not like Alex.'

Rosie couldn't take it in. 'He had a wife?'

'Valentina.'

She sat up more in the bed, wide awake now. 'That can't be true. She was with you.'

'God forbid. I don't care for too much drama in my women. There's a reason her KGB code name is Crazy Horse.'

Rosie didn't think she could feel more betrayed, or foolish. All this time, Alex and Valentina had been together, conspiring to trap her. She remembered the whispered conversations in Russian, how Valentina was barely civil to her when they first met, and what she now realised had been an insincere show of friendship. Alex had never loved her; he belonged to Valentina.

Montgomery waited until she was looking at him again. 'It took all her training not to tear your face off when he started in on you. She was used to him seducing women to gain their confidence, but for some reason you really got under her skin.' He opened the door and spoke to someone before turning back to Rosie. 'Valentina's on the run now her cover's been blown. My men are looking for her now, all the ports and airports have been alerted. She's dangerous and might come looking for you. I've put a couple of policemen outside your door, so you should be safe.'

Rosie called out to him. 'Wait, Valentina called him Sasha, but what was Alex's code name?'

'White Raven. That was his KGB code name. Poor bastard.'

* * *

It was a few nights later that Rosie woke with a start. The

hospital room was dark and on a floor that was too high to let any light from streetlamps in to penetrate the blackout curtains left over from the war. She lay still, hardly daring to breathe. There was someone in the room, creeping about. A nurse would have bustled about, too intent on doing her checks to worry about disturbing a patient. An intruder then. Rosie's eyes grew accustomed to the dark and she could make out a shadowy shape over at the small wardrobe, going through her clothes. Rosie took a deep breath and switched on the light next to her bed. The room flooded with yellow light and Valentina stood, frozen with her hand in Rosie's trouser pocket.

'What are you doing here?'

Valentina dropped the trousers and stalked over to the side of the bed, her dark eyes glittering with reflected light. Her hair was a new mousy brown and she was wearing a beige mackintosh over a black poloneck and pedal pushers. Her face was the same deathly pale, but she'd softened her look with pink lipstick, and the dramatic kohl eyeliner and trailing scarves were gone. Valentina raised a hand, the long crimson nails now short and unpainted, and Rosie shrank back involuntarily. Furious at her own reaction and tired of being scared and confused, she said, 'If you come near me, I'll scream for help.' Valentina sat on the edge of the bed and threw one leg over the other and chuckled deep in her throat. She shook back her mane of hair in a gesture Rosie recognised from her persona in Crail.

'How naïve you are. Do you really think anyone is coming to help you? There was a policeman outside your door, but he didn't stand a chance against a KGB officer.' All trace of a Russian accent had gone. She leaned forward and Rosie could smell the stale tobacco on her breath. 'Now, tell me where the film is, and you will live to see the morning, unlike your so-called protection officer.'

Rosie suppressed a gasp. 'You're an animal, no, a cold-blooded reptile. A murderer.'

'I prefer assassin.' Valentina bared her teeth in a smile. 'Are you really so horrified? What do you think Alex was? We trained together in Moscow, and together we've dispatched quite a few people who have got in the way of our mission.' Rosie remembered how Alex could look sometimes, his expression distant and cold. Then another memory: Alex looking at her in the morning light coming in from the attic window in their cottage in Crail, his eyes soft, his mouth tender. Monty's words came back to her. *She was Alex's wife.* Her throat was dry. She coughed and Valentina got up and poured some water into a glass and handed it to her. 'Are you ready to talk?' Rosie took a sip of water and fought to keep it down.

'You're married to him.'

Valentina shrugged. 'Maybe. Sometimes. I forget. It depends on our cover story. Sometimes we are husband and wife, other times brother and sister. In Crail we were neither and that worked until he brought you into the picture.'

'You were jealous because he fell in love with me.'

Valentina laughed but her eyes were cold. 'As if he would have feelings for someone like you, a spoiled Western woman, a decadent artist, unlike our Soviet artists, who paint with purpose.'

'I've seen some of their work, nothing more than paint-by-numbers propaganda.'

Valentina grabbed her shoulder and Rosie winced. 'I'm not here to discuss such trivial matters. Tell me where the film is.' Rosie tried to shake her off, but her grip was like iron.

'I threw it in the sea. That's why they shot Alex.'

'I don't believe you.'

'You don't seem to care that he's dead. I thought you loved him.'

Valentina let go. 'I was trained to control my emotions; they make you weak, it's why you were such an easy target.'

Rosie doubted anyone could completely cut themselves off from their feelings, especially for someone like Alex. She decided to change tack and play for time.

'Why was he called White Raven?'

'Monty told you, huh? Alex and I were the type of agents who use sex. The men are called ravens, and the women sparrows. We were trained to separate our feelings from sex. It's easy after the first hundred or so partners – old men, pimply youngsters barely out of school, women, some ugly, some beautiful like me. You learn to close that bit of your mind off.'

Rosie tried to discern a note of regret, but Valentina seemed indifferent, as if she were explaining something unremarkable. She tried not to think of a young Alex being trained this way in some dingy room. The Russian woman leaned towards her more and Rosie grasped at a way to keep her talking.

'But why a white raven?' Valentina moved back a fraction and Rosie let go a breath she'd been holding.

'In some cultures, a white raven brings death. That is how he was seen by our handlers and appeared to his enemies, but I prefer the other meaning. A white raven can also be a symbol of hope and transformation, that was what he was to me.'

A tear ran down Rosie's cheek. 'For me, too,' she whispered. If she was hoping to appeal to their shared feelings, she was mistaken. Valentina spat on the floor.

'You weep for him, for my Sasha? You think you knew him? Only I knew him, the real man behind all the cover stories. We were the same, more than husband and wife, more than brother and sister. He didn't love you, he only used you.'

'If you know him so well, tell me why a boy brought up in Britain, steeped in our democratic values, would betray this country for a totalitarian regime?'

'He told you what you wanted to hear. Alex was Russian, through and through, and our memories are long. You talk of oppressive regimes, but you have no idea what it was like before the revolution. His mother was only a child when her parents were massacred by the Cossacks at a peaceful demonstration along with thousands of other factory workers. They were taking a petition about their working conditions to the Tsar, to their beloved Little Father, trusting that he would listen to them and help them.'

'But Alex didn't suffer like that, his parents were privileged diplomats.'

'Who abandoned him, went off to a life of luxury in South America, rubbing shoulders with ex-SS officers and their fat wives. It was left to his uncle Yegor, a high-ranking KGB officer, to be his true father.' As Valentina talked about how Alex had been trained by his KGB uncle, she didn't let on she already knew about his past; instead, her hand inched towards the call button. Quick as a striking cobra, Valentina grabbed her wrist and twisted it painfully. 'You think you're a match for me?' She twisted again and Rosie whimpered. Valentina reached into her pocket with her other hand and brought out a syringe.

'I lied to you about killing the policeman outside. I only gave him something to knock him out. But I have a special dose for you that you won't wake up from.' She yanked Rosie's arm towards her; Rosie felt the needle go in and shouted, 'No!' At exactly that moment, the door swung open and a uniformed officer charged in and pulled Valentina off her and onto the floor. The Russian struggled and screamed obscenities, but he was a big man and sat on her until he could get the cuffs on her. Outside the room, a walkie-talkie crackled and the other protection officer, looking dazed, staggered into the room.

'Whit a wild cat,' the first policeman said. 'Sneaky wee besom, too. She managed to knock you out, Sean my lad. Lucky I was away on the tea run or we'd both be out for the count.' He grinned at Rosie. 'Are you all right, Miss?' There was no time to answer. She leaned over the side of the bed and was sick.

Chapter 27

Once Rosie was strong enough, Ned and Lily brought her back to Charlotte Square. The familiar smell of home wrapped itself around her as soon as she walked in. It was all still there, solid and real, welcoming her back as she walked from room to room: the black and white tiles in the hall; the drawing room with its worn tapestry cushions, her mother's sketch books by the fire; Ned's study with its mahogany desk and shelves of law books and slim volumes of poetry; the staircase with its ironwork balustrade; her room with its sash windows overlooking the square's garden. In her studio the smell of rags soaked in turps and linseed oil overlaid with dust made her open a window. There was an unfinished canvas on the easel, a seascape of Crail with large patches of white among the blues, greens and greys. She pulled on one of Ned's old shirts she used for painting, picked up her palette, squeezed out the colours she would need and started mixing. But when she lifted her brush, her hand froze. The waves seemed to pull her towards them, and she thought she could hear the rush of surf on shingle, the haunting cries of gulls riding the thermals. She cleaned her brush and wiped off the palette, took off her painting shirt and locked the door behind her. Up in her room, Rosie kicked off her shoes and crept under the bedcovers fully dressed and sank gratefully into sleep. When she woke, Ned was sitting in the armchair by the window.

'What is it?'

'Cosmo Montgomery is downstairs. He wants to talk to you, about Alex Kuznetsov, and this Valentina Nazarova woman.'

'How much do you know?'

'Enough to know you put yourself in grave danger, but only after you'd betrayed my trust, not to mention that of the Sinclairs. What were you thinking?'

'I didn't know Alex was KGB. Did you?'

Ned shifted uncomfortably. 'Not until Baird approached me at the Sinclairs' party, said he'd seen you both leave, that Alex and you had stolen top secret information. I thought he was making up a cock and bull story until I rang Montgomery. It took me a while to get hold of him, and by that time we'd intercepted Alex's messages about the rendezvous point in Crovie and needing a passport and new identity for a woman in her mid-thirties. Monty didn't want me to come, said he and his men had it under control, but I insisted. When I got there and saw you lying on the beach, I thought . . .' His voice caught and he looked out the window. Rosie saw he had aged in the last few weeks. 'You could have got yourself killed. How could you have let yourself be taken in like this?'

She hid her face in her hands, unable to look at him. 'I'm sorry, I'm so sorry. I didn't mean for anyone to get hurt. I thought I was helping. Alex said Sir Angus was some kind of mole, handing over defence secrets to the Russians, that he needed proof to flush him out.'

'Gus is a friend of mine, one of my closest. I've known him for years. How could you think he was anything less than an honourable, decent man dedicated to the service of his country?'

'But, don't you see, that's what I thought Alex was, and if you're honest, you did too.' Ned sighed and passed his hand over his eyes.

'You're right, I was taken in by him. We all were.' He stood up and held out his hand to help her out of bed. 'Let's go and face the music together.'

Monty was in Ned's study, standing with his back to them, his hands clasped. When he turned round, all traces of the affable clown she'd known in Crail had gone and, in their place, there was the grim expression of a man bent on getting at the truth, and exacting punishment. He glanced at Ned who left the room, and Rosie's stomach plummeted. Monty sat down behind the desk and nodded for her to sit across from him. Rosie knew she was in a world of trouble.

'What did Nazarova tell you?'

'She wanted the film.' He raised his eyebrows. 'I took photographs of the plans in Sir Angus Sinclair's safe.'

'And?'

'I told her I didn't have it. Then she told me that she was working with Alex.' Rosie tried and failed to keep her voice steady. 'You were right about them having been together and that he'd been using me.'

'Did she give you any names?'

'An Uncle Yergev, who trained him as a boy.'

'Yergev Sokolov.' Monty nodded, grim-faced. 'He passes himself off as a Russian businessman. We've had our suspicions, but this confirms them.'

'That's helpful, then?' Rosie said, hopefully.

'You're not off the hook yet, you've created one hell of a mess. I've a good mind to charge you with breaking the Official Secrets Act.' Rosie shrank back. He picked up Ned's Mont Blanc pen and put it down again. 'Look, I know you didn't know who you were dealing with. I take it Alex spun you a tale about saving the world from nuclear destruction, preventing World War Three?'

'How did you know?'

'I've read your file; I know how hard you worked at Bletchley. You wouldn't knowingly betray your country.'

Rosie turned away, undone by his sudden kindness. 'I've been such a fool. And I betrayed the Sinclairs, went to their home under false pretences, used poor Duncan to get into the safe, I don't think I can live with what I've done.' Monty came over to her side of the desk and gave her his handkerchief.

'No need for that kind of talk. While you've made an awful hash of things, you did flush out Alex Kuznetsov, albeit unknowingly. And you forced Baird into the open too.' Monty described how Alistair Baird realised his cover was blown when Rosie alerted Ned that he had been sniffing around the safe; the clincher had been finding Simon Fairweather trying to break into it. 'Not a bad day's work for an amateur. At first, I wondered why Alex got you involved, but he must have seen certain qualities in you. He had a good eye, I'll give that to him, and formidable powers of persuasion.'

'You sound as if you admire him.'

'Gutsy to play both sides against each other and stay hidden for so long. I've only unearthed a couple of sleepers in my career, and he was the best, had us all fooled right through the war. Setting up the anti-Soviet surveillance unit was a genius move. To be completely honest, it wasn't hard to pretend to be his friend.'

'Or mine.'

Monty shrugged. 'All part of the job. We put on different masks, turn on the charm when needed.'

'What a way to live.'

'There are worse ways. The adrenaline keeps you going. Life would have been pretty dull after the war otherwise.'

He smiled at her. 'Admit it, you found the whole thing exciting, and you're not so bad at pulling the wool over everyone's eyes, even people who have known you since you were a child.' Rosie winced but Monty carried on. 'You could be an asset to us, if you really wanted to make amends.'

'What do you mean?'

'Alex has already trained you in some of the Soviet methods – the same basic spy craft we use – and you've proved you can work under pressure, that you may even have acquired a taste for danger, which is essential in our business.'

'You want me to work for MI6?'

'There are consequences for what you did You may not have meant to, but you betrayed your country all the same.' His tone was mild, but she could hear the threat. 'Think about it. But not for too long.' He picked up his coat and Rosie stood to let him pass. 'What did you do with the film? There's stuff on it we don't want the Russians getting their hands on.'

Rosie was careful not to blink. 'I didn't give it to Alex, if that's what you mean. It's probably at the bottom of the sea by now.'

'That explains why they shot him. Bad luck, Alex, old boy.' He handed Rosie his card. 'I'm afraid Valentina gave the local police the slip and we haven't found her yet. If she comes here, ring this number, it goes straight through to me. These are dangerous people you've been dealing with; they may think you still have what they want.'

'Before you go, why was Boris in the cottage when they brought me in from the beach?'

'That bloody dog! Alex left him in my billet. I don't think he ever cared for the poor bugger, probably just a ploy to meet you. Women are soft about strange men with a dog, makes them seem less threatening. Oldest trick in the book.' He stopped at the door. 'I don't suppose you want the mutt?'

Chapter 28

When she heard the front door shut behind Monty, Rosie came out of the study; Ned was waiting for her.

'What did he want?'

Rosie shook her head. 'I can't talk about it now. I'm so tired.'

'Of course,' he said and put out his arm 'Lean on me, you're as white as a sheet. You should have stayed in hospital longer, and I should have kept Montgomery at bay for longer.'

'It's all right, it's better to have heard him out. He tried to recruit me.'

'What?'

'I said I'd think about it.'

They stopped outside her room. 'It's not the life for you, Rosie darling. Tell him no.'

'I'm not sure I have much choice.' She closed the door and got back under the covers. All she seemed to do these days was sleep. What seemed like minutes later, Lily shook her awake.

'What time is it?'

'Nearly seven, you've been asleep for hours. I didn't want to disturb you, but dinner is nearly ready, and it's your favourite. Will you come downstairs?'

'I'm not sure I could eat.'

'Won't you try, for me, and for Ned? He's been so worried about you.'

There seemed to be a black ball on Rosie's chest. With an effort she threw back the covers and went to the mirror to draw a brush through her hair. A pallid boggle stared back at her, purple shadows under the eyes, tiny and red with crying, her mouth pinched and skin paper dry. She looked a sight.

'What does it matter?' Rosie muttered and went back to sit by her mother. She lay her head on Lily's shoulder.

'I know, my darling, it's awful. Ned told me Alex drowned in a terrible accident, and that you were there. I wish I could say something to make it better, but I know it wouldn't help. Nothing ever did when I lost Jack.'

'Oh my God, Jack! I'm sorry, I'd forgotten about his case. How is it going?'

'Jack handed himself in and the army is holding him in the garrison prison in Glasgow until the trial.' Lily's voice shook and Rosie put her arm around her mother. 'The only thing that's keeping me from losing heart is that Ned is defending him.'

'Will the trial be heard in one of the courts?'

'No, in the Maryhill garrison, in front of five regimental officers and a Judge Advocate General. Ned explained it all to me.' Lily rubbed at streaks of blue paint on her hands, something she did when she was worried. 'But it's open to the public, like any civilian court, so I can be there for Jack. He insisted he doesn't want visitors, but Ned said he'd take me to see him soon.'

Rosie took a deep breath and shut out the storm of painful memories that swirled in her head. 'I'll come too.'

'Are you sure? I'm not sure you're strong enough,' but Lily looked hopeful and took her daughter's hand.

'If I weren't well, that bossy nurse wouldn't have let me come home.'

'She was terrifying, wasn't she? Ned was the only one who could get her to crack her face.'

'Imagine taking a broken pay packet home to that one, face like a bulldog chewing a wasp.'

Rosie's heart lifted to see her mother smile. 'Where on earth did you hear expressions like that? You sound just like Jeanie.'

'Moira Sinclair's new maid is from the Gorbals and is teaching her ladyship a new vocabulary.'

Rosie clutched a set of imaginary pearls. 'Thet ghillie is es rough es a bedger's ahse.' She was gratified to see her mother collapse in giggles.

'What's all this hilarity? I can't believe you're leaving me out of the fun, as usual.' Ned was in the doorway. 'Excellent impression of Moira, though. Gus doesn't know where to put himself when she comes out with these gems in front of the minister.'

Still exhausted at dinner, Rosie barely touched her food. The housekeeper tutted when she came in to clear the plates, grumbling about the waste and how Cook would be raging.

'My dear Mrs Jackson, you know we all live in mortal fear of Cookie. Will you be an absolute treasure and hide the scraps?' Ned said with his most charming smile.

'And where am I supposed to hide them, up ma jouk?'

Ned eyed her ample bosom primly encased in black. 'I'm not sure there would be room.'

'Ned!' Lily said, wrapping him on the knuckles with her spoon. 'Don't be a boor. Mrs Jackson, will you please tell Mrs Mulvey that her dinner was as delicious as ever. Rosie, give me your plate, please.' Lily lifted the slices of perfectly pink lamb and a couple of boiled potatoes speckled with mint off it and put them on Ned's plate. 'There, in penance, you can eat them.'

He reluctantly picked up his knife and fork. 'You are a termagant, Lily Crawford, I don't know why I put up with being bullied in my own home.'

'Hush now and eat up.' Mrs Jackson shook her head and left the dining room. Rosie knew Ned and her mother were doing their best to take her mind off Alex. She smiled at Lily, but she was staring at the painting over the mantlepiece with such sadness, Rosie put her hand over her mother's.

'I've never understood how men can romanticise war,' Lily said, looking at the portrait of a soldier on horseback.

Ned looked at the painting too. 'That's easy, it's the thought of escaping the humdrum and everyday, of adventure and the chance to be a hero; it's every young man's dream. That's my grandfather, he was in the 2nd Dragoons, Royal Scots Greys, fought at Waterloo under Wellington where they charged the French. I used to love hearing his war stories, how the men of the 92nd hung onto their stirrups during the charge, and how they captured the eagle of the 45th Régiment de Ligne. All guts and glory. Bit different from what Jack and I went through. Plenty of guts, not much glory.'

Rosie heard her mother make a small noise of distress, and Ned winced. 'Sorry, Lil, clumsy of me with the trial coming up.'

Rosie didn't take her eyes off her mother. 'When's the trial?'

'Couple of months, middle of March,' Ned said.

'Not long, then.'

'Long enough if you're sitting in an army cell. I've hurried it along as much as I could, but the Judge Advocate needs to see all the evidence, and the prosecution have to build their case. I'm ready with my arguments, but then I have the advantage of being close to the accused, and of having been on the spot and in the same regiment as Jack, the Highland Light Infantry, when he went missing.' Lily was folding and refolding her napkin and trying not to cry. Rosie couldn't bear to see her so unhappy, and wondered fleetingly if it would have been better if Jack Petrie had stayed out of her life.

The house at Charlotte Square, once a place that rang with laughter and talk, was quiet now, with Jack gone and Lily frozen in misery. Ned spent hours in his study going over the finer points of Jack's defence and even the normally garrulous Jeanie spoke in hushed tones when she visited, hurrying Lily into her room where the two old friends could speak in private. Meanwhile Rosie was still trying to work out her feelings about Alex, fighting off flashbacks from the night he was killed. Stella tried to comfort her when she came over from Glasgow with her mother one day, but it wasn't in her nature to be sympathetic to someone else's troubles for long. She fidgeted while Rosie raged and wept about Alex and went over and over his lies, weeping hopelessly, helplessly. When she wailed, 'He was my life!' Stella lost patience.

'*Arrête!* He was just a man, a good-looking one, I'll admit, but there are plenty more where he came from, and you're an attractive woman, when you try, that is. It may seem like it just now, but truly it's not the end of the world. And going on and on about it won't do any good.'

Stella glanced at the mirror and smoothed a perfectly shaped eyebrow. 'All this moping about will ruin your looks.'

She picked up a lipstick from Rosie's dressing table and tried it on before making a face and wiping it off with a tissue. Her tone brightened and Rosie knew she was about to change the subject to one closer to her own interests. 'I've been talking to Jim,' Stella said. 'Now there's a handsome man and sexy too with those southern gentleman manners and that heavenly accent. He's set me up with a film studio contact in Hollywood, someone at Columbia, the studio that made *Rock around the Clock* and *Don't Knock the Rock*. They're working on another one, *Let's Rock*, and need a choreographer for the dance scenes.' She picked up Rosie's swan-down powder puff and dusted her perfect little nose. 'I'm sailing for the States next month.'

Rosie sat up straighter, her problems momentarily pushed aside by Stella's news. 'What about the Taylor Girls? And what does Jeanie have to say about it?'

'Oh, I haven't told her. I'll send the old bag a telegram when I get to Los Angeles. Don't worry, she'll be fine.' Stella strolled over to Rosie's wardrobe and pulled out a silk kimono and held it against herself in front of the mirror. 'Can I take this? I think it suits my colouring better than yours.'

'No, put it back, Mother brought it back from Shanghai.

You really ought to tell Jeanie. I know you fight, but she loves you and you love her.'

Stella sighed and dropped the kimono on the floor. 'You don't know what it's like carrying the weight of your mother's dreams on your shoulders, and the jealousy when you do what she couldn't. Your mama has always encouraged your art but in a gentle way, not like mine. She's always been a tyrant, strapping me into pointe shoes at eleven, before the bones of my feet had a chance to develop. It was torture, like Chinese foot binding.' Stella kicked off one of her high-heeled mules and examined a deformed and bunioned foot.

'But you love dancing.'

'I do, well I did, but it's taken its toll. I should have retired years ago, but Mama won't hear of it, says the company needs their star, that I bring in the punters, and to think of the other dancers.' She sat down next to Rosie. 'Hollywood is my chance to get away and start a new career.' Stella's eyes shone and Rosie knew there was no arguing with her. 'Just think, no more freezing my arse off in draughty theatres in nothing but sequins and feathers. I could end up working with a class act like Gene Kelly.'

'I loved *An American in Paris*,' Rosie said.

Stella threw herself onto the bed. 'Tell you what, let's go to the flicks. Take our mind off things. There's a new *St Trinian's* out.'

'Oh God, that reminds me, I really should get back to St

Leo's. The headmistress has been understanding about my needing to recover from pneumonia, but I'm quite well now and the girls' exams are coming up.'

'That's the spirit! Get back to work and you'll feel like your old self. But first, let's call up Jim and get him to take us to the movies.'

'The movies! Get you! You'll be talking about sidewalks and elevators next', Rosie teased. 'All right, but not *St Trinian's*.'

Stella picked up a copy of the evening paper and squinted at it. She'd started to need reading glasses but was too vain to wear them. There's also *'The Bolshoi Ballet* or *The Bridge on the River Kwai*?'

Rosie made a face. 'Neither. You know what, Stell, can we go another time? I'm suddenly really tired.'

Stella sighed in frustration. '*Comme tu veux*. But I'll be back soon with reinforcements – Jim in other words – to get you out of this house of gloom and doom.'

When Stella and Jeanie left, Charlotte Square sank back into silence. Rosie thought she would suffocate under the weight of her own feelings. The molten fury against the man who had used her and lied to her had solidified into a cold lump of depression. The shame of having been duped into nearly betraying her country meant she couldn't even grieve for Alex. To try to quell the maelstrom of anger, loss and excruciating guilt, Rosie made herself get out of the house. She would go and see Margot, who would surely be more sympathetic, and certainly a better listener, than self-centred Stella. The walk to the West End passed in a blur as painful memories assailed her: Alex touching her face in their attic bedroom in Crail, Alex's face darkening into anger then despair as she told him she didn't have the film; the crack of a shot in the dark; the cold rush of seawater soaking her hair as she lay on the pebbled shore. When Margot opened the front door, she took one look at Rosie's stricken face and put her arm around her and led her into the kitchen. As the kettle boiled, she listened as the whole story tumbled out. Rosie could speak freely, knowing that Margot, like her, had signed the Official Secrets Act, and that, unlike Rosie, she would never be fool enough to breach it. The more she talked, the more ashamed she grew, and when she finished speaking, she couldn't look at Margot. When she finally dared raise her eyes, expecting to see the disgust she felt at her own actions, Rosie saw only pity. And with that, she was undone. Margot held her until she stopped sobbing. Rosie took a shuddering breath and stared listlessly at the linoleum.

'I'm so sorry,' she managed to whisper. 'I've been such a fool. And I've lied and tricked my way into someone's home, stolen from them, and given Ned such a fright, running away in the middle of the night. Then Mother has been worried sick while I've been in hospital.' She buried her face in her hands. 'It's such a mess.'

Margot got up to make tea and brought them both a

cup. 'Drink this and you'll feel better. Rosie, it's not as bad as you think. You didn't hand over the blueprints, you destroyed the film, so no harm has been done to our defences.'

'What about Alex? I sent him to his death.'

'He knew the dangers, and it was his own people who did that to him. In the end, you did the right thing, and that's what matters. As time goes by the shame will fade, as will your feelings for Alex. I know it doesn't seem possible now, but this will pass. You can put this whole thing behind you and get on with your life.'

'I wish Cosmo Montgomery thought the same.'

'What do you mean?'

'He says the only way I can make up for what I did, and stay out of jail probably, is to work for him.'

'For MI6? Spy for him?' Rosie nodded miserably.

Margot edged her chair closer. 'Listen to me, Rosie, you are not to do this. Look how cut up you are about lying to the Sinclairs and to Ned, but it would only be the beginning of a life of dissimulation, until lying became second nature and you would be capable of switching off your emotions, doing to someone else what Alex did to you.'

'I don't think I have a choice.'

'There's always a choice, you just have to accept the consequences. It's always better to face the music.'

Rosie nodded. For a moment she felt lighter because

telling Margot everything had been a relief, and her friend had taken some of the burden of shame off her and given her the confidence to act when she felt helplessly trapped. But as she wandered through the West End back to Princes Street and climbed the Playfair Steps to the rackety Old Town, the grief that she'd held in check as she grappled with her guilt shouldered its way in. Every corner held a treacherous memory. Rosie walked down Canongate, her feet taking her towards Arthur's Seat. It was where she had gone most often with Alex, and where he'd persuaded her to join his mission, and, in the end, where he'd tricked her into treason. If she went back there now, perhaps she could lay his ghost to rest on its craggy sides.

A stiff wind was blowing in from the Firth of Forth and Rosie had to lean into it as she toiled up the path leading to the summit. By the time she reached the second pond, she was out of breath, her lungs still weak from pneumonia, and had to sit down on a bench. It was a weekday and the children who were usually there feeding the swans and ducks or fishing for minnows and scooping tadpoles into jars were all in school, and the climb was too steep for the littler ones and the mothers with their unwieldy prams. Above, seagulls circled, their mournful cries reminding her of the old superstition that they were the souls of drowned sailors and fishermen. She saw Alex at Crail harbour, talking urgently about the nuclear threat; Alex in black tie grinning at her as they sped away from

Summer Isle House; Alex cupping her face in his hands the last time they were together, the rain lashing against the fisherman's cottage window. For the first time, she realised she would never see him again, touch him, hear his voice, walk with him, lie in his arms. Rosie stared up at the wheeling seabirds and let the tears come. Frank had hurt her, but she now realised he had only hurt her pride, and it was nothing compared to this pain that made her want to scream and tear at her clothes and hair. Rosie's spirits always used to lift when she watched the soft colours of spring, the pale grey of the sky, the blue haze of the Firth of Forth, and the tender green of the elms pushing out new leaves. But now she felt nothing apart from this leaden pain; she might as well be dead. If only she had died with Alex in the storm rather than being left behind. It would be quick, and the physical pain couldn't be worse than what she was already feeling. Here, where she was now, was a peak with a sheer drop notorious for fatal falls. She could step out into the air, her eyes on Edinburgh and all its beauty and perhaps feel something again, her arms outstretched to welcome oblivion.

Rosie stood up, ready now. She was about to continue up the path when she heard a commotion in the water and turned back to see a rabbit in the pond. It was near enough that she could see the whites of its eyes as it frantically struggled in the water, ears back and head disappearing only to emerge and swim in circles. Rosie didn't know rabbits could swim, and she couldn't imagine how this one had got into the pond and why it couldn't get out. The sides were too slippery, she guessed. Without pausing to think, she pulled off her shoes and socks, rolled up her trouser legs and waded into the water, ignoring the cold mud oozing between her toes. She grabbed the rabbit with both hands, nearly letting it go as it wriggled and fought to be free, and carried it to the side of the pond where she put it down on the grass. The little creature went limp. Rosie took off her scarf and rubbed its sodden fur, talking to it.

'There now, you poor wee thing, what were you doing in the water? Did a fox chase you in? There's no fox, you're all right now, I've got you, you're safe.' The rabbit's nose twitched; it opened its eyes and stood on trembling legs and moved off a little. It stopped to clean its ears with its paws and looked back at her before lolloping away. Rosie held her breath and watched. In the pond, a noisy squabble broke out between two ducks, and the rabbit raced away. Rosie sat back on her haunches, the grass cold under her bare feet, watching it disappear into the bushes. Terrified in the face of almost certain death, it had fought desperately to survive. Who was she to throw away her life? It would be the act of a coward to run from pain only to inflict it on others. She thought of her mother, of Ned, of Jeanie and Stella, of Margot, and what it would do to them. And then there was her pupil, Anne Rankin, who was showing real promise and would need help with her portfolio if she was to get into art school. The sun broke through and gilded the clouds, seeming to make the air shimmer, as if telling her: this world is bigger than your pain. In that moment, Rosie knew that she too wanted to live.

Chapter 29

The elation lasted until she reached the door at Charlotte Square. Inside, it was dark. None of the lights had been switched on and none of the fires had been lit. It was Mrs Jackson's day off, and Lily and Ned were at an opening at the Royal Scottish Academy. Rosie shivered and thought longingly of the Sinclairs' blissful central heating. She kept her coat on as she trailed up the stairs, her fingers skimming the wooden banister. She remembered Alex running up these stairs, pulling her by her hand as she laughed, out of breath. Assailed by a sudden bout of grief, Rosie sat down on a step. The house was empty; she could howl all she liked. After a while, she realised someone was watching her at the top of the stairs. Rosie scrubbed at her face with a crumpled handkerchief and glared at Ned, her face hot with shame.

'I thought you were at the opening.'

He came slowly down the few steps and sat down beside her. 'Couldn't face it.'

'The warm hock.'

'And the cold claret.'

Rosie stuffed the damp handkerchief into her pocket. They sat quietly, his solid presence a comfort. She leaned against his shoulder, feeling his strength through the woollen suit jacket. After a while Ned stood and held out his hand to help her up.

'Why don't we drive to Glasgow tomorrow with your mother? I'm sure Jack could do with a visit.' Rosie knew what he was doing: ever since she was a little girl, he'd told her the way to feel better was to do something for someone else.

The next morning in the Maryhill barracks of the Highland Light Infantry, they were led to a waiting room where they could see Jack through a grubby window sitting at a table with two military policemen standing at ease at his back. Ned and Rosie let Lily in to speak to him first, but she soon came out, red-eyed.

'Jack says he'd like to talk to you,' she said to Rosie.

'Are you sure? Wouldn't he rather speak to Ned?'

'Go on, my girl,' Ned said. 'He must have something important to say to you.'

Rosie took a deep breath before she went in. Jack stood to greet her, shook her hand and politely asked after her health. She had expected to see him bent and diminished, but he stood straighter than she'd ever seen him. He waited until she sat down before he took his seat. They sat in silence for a moment.

'I expect it's kicking in by now, about Alex, I mean.'

Rosie closed her eyes and nodded. 'I want to die,' she whispered.

'I wanted to die too, nearly managed it a few times,' he said and leaned forward. 'I understand. It's only natural what you're feeling. When you love someone beyond all reason, and know you'll never see them again, well, it feels like life has given up on you.'

'So, it's easy to give up on life.'

He nodded. 'But if you can get through this bit, if you can hold your nerve and crawl through the mud and blood and filth, you'll get to the other side. That's if you're brave enough, like Ned and Lily. But I wasn't, I wanted to die that day when I was in No Man's Land. I heard a whizz bang coming and I was glad, after what I'd done to that poor soldier, stealing his name so I could run away. I looked up to the sky and laughed – can you imagine that? Then the explosion came and when I came to, my mind took pity on me, and I lost my memory. I even forgot your mother, my own name. The only thing I could remember was wanting to die and I nearly did in that French hospital. But a woman saved me. She wasn't Lily but her kindness healed what was left of me, and I'll always be grateful to Justine.' He laid his hands flat on the table. 'Rosie, listen to me. Everything seems hopeless now, but trust me: if you just hold on, you'll be all right, eventually. You'll have scars, but then who doesn't? Love is a risk, but it's worth all the pain. I know it's horrible now, and I can't tell you how or when you'll feel better, but when you get through this – and you will – you'll find love again. I was lucky, three times: when I met your mother, when Justine found me in the hospital, and now that I have this chance with Lily, who I thought I'd lost.'

'But you could lose her again. The court martial is coming up. Mother is beside herself with worry about you.'

'And I'm sorry about that, but I'm not worried. If I go to prison, I'll take my punishment and hope Lily will be there when I come out. I was a coward and ran, but don't you run. Stay and fight. And you will because you're strong like your mother.' He smiled at her, and for a second, Rosie could see the man Lily had fallen in love with all those years ago.

'I don't think you're a coward, Jack. I think you're brave, and I'm glad you've come back.'

'Thank you.'

'There is one thing you could do for me, though.'

'What's that?' He looked around at the imposing military policemen. 'I'm a bit tied up at the moment.'

'Tell me about my mother. What was she like when you met her? She never talks about the time before she married my father.'

Jack smiled and began to tell Rosie all about the young woman he'd met on her first day at art school.

'She'd dropped her portfolio all over the front steps and was furious when I tried to help her and started looking through the pieces of her artwork. She was tearing a strip off me, but I didn't hear a word. I was smitten.'

'And Ned, how did you all get together? He won't talk about those days either.'

'Oh, they loathed each other on sight.'

'No! Tell me more . . .'

Chapter 30

Going back to work helped, but the grief kept coming and going like the tide. At the end of the first day, Rosie walked back from school where she had spent the morning catching up with her classes. The girls had stopped chatting and those who had been perched on the attic windowsills of the art room with their friends had jumped down and gone back to their drafting desks. They had looked at her expectantly, pleased to see her back and to get a break from their other subjects. It was spring term and exams were on the horizon, which meant the girls were fizzing with nerves. St Leo's believed in educating women to take up careers and pushed the academically able ones towards university. In Rosie's art class the alliances and rivalries between the girls melted away as even those without any talent could forget being drilled in past exam papers and lose themselves in paint, charcoal and paper, knowing that their teacher would murmur encouragement and help them see the world in shapes, colours and shades, if only for an hour or so.

Rosie had found being back at school calming and she hummed as she strolled up the hill to Charlotte Square, where the garden was an amethyst and gold carpet of crocuses, and the cherry trees had dressed themselves in pink and white. Edinburgh always looked its best at this time of year, she thought, the sky high and blue above the crescents and squares, and the private gardens coming to life behind their iron railings. Rosie pushed open the front door and was nearly knocked off her feet by a streak of black fur.

'Boris! What are you doing here, boy?' She kneeled next to the excited dog and stroked his soft ears. He gazed up at her in adoration and tried to lick her face.

Mrs Jackson came into the hall, wiping her hands on her apron. 'That dug's a menace. It won't take a telling,' but, despite her harsh words, she bent down to pat Boris. 'I couldn't leave it tied to the railing on the steps. Some folk shouldn't be allowed to have an animal.'

'That'll be Monty. He asked me if I wanted the dog but I'm sure I said no. What a nuisance! I'm not sure Ned will be keen on a new member of the household. What do you say, boy?' Boris tilted his head and raised an eyebrow. Rosie laughed. 'You old charmer, I never could resist you. Are you hungry? Of course you are.' She looked up at the housekeeper. 'Can you get Cook to rustle up something? Leftovers will be fine.'

'Waste of good food, if you ask me.' She glared at the dog but when Boris lifted his ears at her, she pursed her lips to stop a smile. 'Come on then, you.' She walked towards the door leading down to the kitchen in the basement, the dog trotting at her heels.

Over the next few days, Rosie was amused to see Mrs Jackson warm to Boris, who followed her as she went about her chores, watching with interest while she cleaned out the grates, scrubbed floors and polished. Best of all was when she hung the laundry in the back garden, meaning he could sniff his way around the shrubs and chase pigeons into a panicked flurry. Pretty soon, Boris had the whole household wrapped around his paws. In the evenings he lay quietly in front of the fire in the study, sighing contentedly while Ned read the London papers and sipped whisky. In the drawing room, the dog liked to put his head in Lily's lap and soon made his way onto the sofa where he slept while she sketched or read. Ned, usually so urbane, betrayed his youth growing up in the country by whistling for Boris when he went out for his daily walk and made it his business to train him to walk to heel, sit and stay like a good dog. But at night, when Rosie gave into her grief and cried over Alex, it was her bed Boris jumped up on so he could sleep at her feet as if protecting her against the image that haunted her dreams: Alex floating under the sea, his skin white as a pearl, his sightless eyes gazing into the black depths.

Strangely, Boris seemed to have taken a dislike to Jim, whom he had always liked for his propensity to throw sticks. Now, when Jim came to see Rosie, the dog tried to sit between them on the sofa.

'That mutt is jealous,' Jim said after Rosie scolded the dog for growling at him. 'He adores you. At least he has good taste.'

'I don't know what's got into him, perhaps it's all the changes. I keep meaning to call Monty to tell him to take him away, but I don't have the heart: he reminds me of Alex.'

Jim was quiet for a moment. He cleared his throat a couple of times before taking her hand. From his banished corner, Boris lifted his head and gave a warning growl.

'It may be too soon, but I'm being posted out of here and if I don't say this now, I'll regret it.'

Rosie's shoulders fell. Stella would be leaving soon for the States and now Jim was going too. She was losing people, one by one.

'What will I do without you? You've become a dear friend.'

He grimaced. 'A friend! That's just what I don't want to be. I didn't have the guts to tell you before. You were with someone else and then, after you lost him, it seemed too soon. I know it still is, but I don't have time to shilly-shally.' He took her other hand in his and kneeled at her feet. 'Darling Rosie, I love you. I think we could be happy together, that I could make you happy.'

Rosie's first reaction was bewilderment. 'But what about Stella? I thought . . .'

'That firecracker has no use for me other than as a one-way ticket to Hollywood.' He smiled. 'I didn't mind calling in a favour from a pal at Columbia, but I knew her fascinating ways were just an act, I've been around enough actresses in my time. I went along with the pretence up to a point, out of pride more than anything. I didn't want you to know my true feelings, not until now anyhow. What do you say, Rosie? Do you think you could give me a chance?'

'Oh, Jim, you're such a kind, sweet man . . .'

'I don't like where this is going.'

'But . . .'

'Yes, but. I've heard that before and it's never good.' He got to his feet and reached for his hat. 'No need to say anything else. Now I've gone and made our friendship all awkward, and for that I'm truly sorry.'

Rosie stood and faced him. 'If things were different, I couldn't think of a better person to give my heart to. I'm sorry, but I don't feel that way about you, even though I do love you dearly as a friend.' She touched him lightly on the arm. 'Please don't say we can't be friends anymore.'

Jim tried to smile. 'We'll always be friends. Who else would put up with my taste in musicals?'

'When do you leave?'

'A few weeks.'

'So soon?'

'I'm not moving to the moon! It's the modern age of transport and it has been known for the odd Brit to make it across the Atlantic. There's always the *Queen Mary*, and BOAC and Pan Am are starting flights to New York from London next year.'

'New York! I've always wanted to go. I'd love to see the MOMA and the Met and go round some of the independent galleries and studios in Greenwich Village.'

'It's a date then. We'll meet in New York, and I'll give you the tour. I'll even take you up the Empire State Building with all the tourists.'

As the days went by, Rosie began to settle back into the routine of her old life. Teaching kept her mind busy during the day, and after school she shut herself away in her studio and gradually began to paint again. She often went to Margot's noisy, messy household, sometimes being persuaded to stay for the children's tea and listen to the boys' stories as they vied for her attention. Alone with Margot, she knew she could talk freely about Alex, but didn't want to wallow and burden her friend. More than Stella, she missed Jim. Even though they had sworn to remain friends, he stayed away, and when she called him, he was always too busy with the handover to his replacement at the base. His theatre project was on hold, the building under lock and key until he decided what to do with it.

Rosie continued to visit Jack and was glad she understood him better, but the court case hung over the house. As the trial date grew nearer, Lily was too distracted and worried to talk, while Ned spent hours in his study making last minute adjustments to his defence. When school broke up for the summer holidays, Rosie found herself at a loose end, having seen her charges safely over the stage to receive their book gifts and the headmistress's words of wisdom at the leavers' ceremony. Restless, she took to the streets of Edinburgh again, seeing everywhere the ghost of the carefree woman she had once been arm in arm with Alex.

On the day of the trial, she was rummaging in her wardrobe for something smart enough to wear in court when Lily came in and sat on her bed. Boris, her ardent admirer, followed and jumped onto an armchair strewn with clothes. Rosie turned from the wardrobe and shook her finger at the dog. 'Boris, you menace! Get down!' He hid his eyes behind his paws and Lily laughed.

'Let him be,' Lily said. 'You need to go shopping anyway, that old fisherman's jersey he's sitting on is more holes than wool.'

Rosie tipped Boris off the chair. 'I don't care, it's my favourite, it's roomy and comfortable. I was wearing it when I met Alex.' A wave of sadness made her sit down heavily, the jersey in her arms.

'It comes and goes, doesn't it?' Lily said.

'When does it get better?'

'It never did for me, not until Jack came back.'

'That's not going to happen for me.'

'No, darling.'

The trees outside her bedroom window were a blur. Rosie buried her face in the jersey. She drew back. 'It smells of dog. Honestly, Boris, you're such a pest.'

Lily got up and took the jersey out of her hands. 'You can't hold onto this scabby old thing forever. If it's a man's sweater you want, Ned's wardrobe is stuffed full of cashmere. He won't even notice if you borrow one.'

Rosie took the jersey back and held it up. 'You're right, it's falling to bits. I suppose I'll have to nip along to Forsyth's at some point. All my skirts are too tight around the waist now. School dinners are ruinous – all those steamed puddings with custard.'

Lily sat down on the bed again and the dog jumped up next to her. 'I wanted to talk to you about the court case. I don't think you should come.'

Rosie frowned. 'Why not? I want to be there for moral support, for you and for Jack. I really like him. I can understand why he means so much to you.'

'I know, and I'm glad of that, but if he's sent to prison, it will be hard, and I don't want you to see me fall apart. You've had enough to deal with, and you need to be quiet and at home, not sitting in a court room in Glasgow for days on end listening to legal briefs and watching over me. And, if Jack does go down, he'll be kept in military prison,

Ned says, until they transfer him to Saughton Prison in Edinburgh, where at least I can visit him every day.' She leaned forward. 'I know you want to help, but Jack and I need to do this on our own. I have to be strong for him, but I can't do that if I'm also worrying about you.' Boris whined and put his head in Lily's lap. She stroked his ears. 'Besides, someone has to be here to look after this good boy.' Rosie watched her mother talk nonsense to the dog. She had aged in the last few months: her skin papery around the eyes, her clothes hanging off her, and she'd gone almost completely grey. Rosie didn't have the heart to argue.

'I'll do whatever you think best.'

'Thank you, darling.'

Rosie went down to the studio and took up her brush. Summer stretched before her, each day emptier than the next.

Ned and Lily had been in Glasgow for a week when Rosie woke up in the middle of the night, knowing something was different. Boris wasn't in his usual place at the bottom of the bed. Downstairs she could hear frantic barking. Switching on her bedside lamp, she pulled on her dressing gown. Mrs Jackson and Mrs Mulvey didn't live in; she was alone in the house. Rosie imagined Valentina, gliding between the shadows, murder in her eyes. The last time Monty had called round, supposedly to check on her, but really to press her to work for him, he said they still hadn't caught Valentina. Trembling, Rosie reached the bottom of the stairs and took up the silver letter opener on the hall table. Boris was whining and scrabbling at the front door as if he wanted to get out. She stood listening in the moonlight streaming in from the astragal, the tiles cold under her feet. Boris moved and she saw a piece of paper lying on the floor. She picked it up: a postcard of Crail harbour. She turned it over and read: *Meet me in our place.* It was Alex's writing. Rosie pulled open the door and ran down the steps. The street was empty.

Chapter 31

Rosie's footsteps rang out as she made her way along George Street, a name sounding in her head to the rhythm of her ragged breath as she ran: *Alex, Alex, Alex*. The Festival hadn't started yet, and Edinburgh was in the lull before, its citizens tucked up in bed apart from the likes of printers, workers at the Ferranti factory and nurses and doctors on night shifts. It was as if she had the city to herself. Turning into a deserted Princes Street, she spotted a policeman and hid in Jenners' doorway until he was out of sight and earshot. Along Calton Road she passed a noisy group of queens heading for Calton Hill and ducked her head when one of them called out to her, 'All right, hen? Business a wee bit slow the night?' She hurried on, leaving their cackles and cat calls behind. By the time she'd reached the crag on Arthur's Seat, it was nearly two in the morning. The wind had picked up as she'd climbed higher and she shivered, wishing she'd grabbed a jacket before rushing out. Below, the lamp posts were like fairy lights strung along the squares and circles of the New Town. The castle rose darkly above the sleeping city, silhouetted against an inky sky. As she waited, Rosie began to wonder if someone had played a cruel trick on her. Perhaps Valentina had written the note. It would have been easy enough to copy Alex's handwriting, luring her into this lonely place to then get rid of her. Every year there were reports of people falling to their death on Arthur's Seat and everyone would know how low she'd been lately. She'd even thought about ending it all, in this very place. What a fool she'd been to raise her hopes like this, as if she hadn't been there when Alex was murdered. Rosie heard movement behind her. This was it; she would die now. She realised she wanted to live, more than anything else. Well, she wouldn't go without a fight. She whipped around, crouched and ready to launch herself at Valentina. A figure loomed out of the darkness, and she snarled like a cornered animal.

'Rosie.'

Her legs gave out and she sank to her knees in the wet grass. As young girls, she and Stella had washed their faces in the morning dew on the first of May, Stella insisting it would make them beautiful. Stupid to be thinking about that now, with Alex standing in front of her, wearing a seaman's cap and peacoat . He kneeled and pulled her onto her feet and into his arms. He smelled of the sea, of salt and tar and seaweed.

Rosie searched his face. 'You're dead. You've come back from the dead.'

'No. I'm very much alive.' Alex cupped her head in his hand and kissed her and Rosie felt she would drown in the warmth of that kiss. She stroked his face in wonder, tracing his features, the hollow at the base of his neck.

'Alex, is it really you?'

He laughed. 'Yes, I'm no ghost.'

'But how? I heard the shot, saw your body being pushed overboard.'

'A shot from my gun and that was one of the idiots who pulled a gun on me in the dinghy. I had to shoot him. I kept my gun pointed at the others and they didn't try anything. It gave me a chance to get on the sub and demand to speak to the KGB officer. He had been one of my trainers, knew I couldn't have betrayed my country.'

Rosie stiffened. 'But you did.'

'What?'

'Betray your country. This is your home, more than Russia. You wanted to tell the enemy our secrets, tell them how to build a nuclear submarine so they could destroy us.'

'No, never that. Only to level the playing field. With both sides equally armed there could be no possibility of all-out war and the end of all of us. You know this, Rosie, we've talked about it. I thought we wanted the same thing, to save countless lives and avoid the end of the world.' He gestured towards the city below. 'If the Americans get ahead in the nuclear race, leaving Russia vulnerable to attack, this could be another Hiroshima and everyone you know will be turned to radioactive ash.'

Rosie buried her head in his chest. 'Stop it! I can't think clearly with you here, I don't know what's right or wrong anymore.'

He tightened his arms around her. 'Then let me think for us both. MI6 haven't got wind that I'm alive yet but it's only a matter of time. I can't stay here; I have to leave, and I can't ever come back.'

Rosie tried to pull away from him, but Alex held her arms fast. She clenched her fists and glared at him. 'I'm going to lose you all over again?'

'Not if you come with me.' He kissed her again and she couldn't help herself, she kissed him back. 'I don't want to lose you. It's why I came back, for you. I know that Jim Harrison is waiting in the wings, desperate to scoop you up.'

She looked at him sharply. 'Have you been spying on me?'

He shrugged. 'It's what I do.' He tightened his grip on her arms but let her go when she grimaced. 'I'm sorry, I can't bear the thought of him touching you. I don't trust him with his affected manners.'

'I don't care about Jim, not in that way. He's a friend, a good friend. If you've been watching me, you know how I've been since that night, when I thought you'd been killed.'

'I do, but when you thought I was dead, surely it must have crossed your mind to find comfort in Jim?'

She shook her head. 'Let's not do this, not now. I don't know what you want from me.'

'There's a Ben Line freight ship, the *Bencruachan*, berthed at Leith's Victoria Dock bound for the Far East. She stops at Rotterdam where we can get off and head for Spain by train. I've bought us both passages and got you a passport in a different name so we can travel as husband and wife, a Serb and a French woman. You speak French, don't you?'

'School French, polished up a bit during a year in Paris after art school.'

'Good enough to get through border checkpoints if you let me do most of the talking. We can make our way down to Spain where I start my new mission – our new mission – to work with the underground resistance against Franco's regime.'

Rosie took a step back from him. 'Alex, wait, slow down, this is too much for me to take in.' But in the back of her mind, she tucked away *Bencruachan* and *Victoria Dock*.

He stepped closer and tucked a strand of hair behind her ear. 'There's nothing to think about. Come with me, *moya dusha*, and what a life we will have together! Just think what it would be to bring down a fascist regime. The West is too complacent; we in the Soviet Union are the only ones left who are willing to take on the Far Right. We can make a difference, fight for freedom and against tyranny. It's a just cause, the noblest there is.'

Rosie's breath quickened and for a moment the adrenaline surged through her and his words swept her back towards adventure and excitement. Then she remembered.

'Is that what you told Valentina?'

'What? What about Valentina?'

'Monty told me about you and her, that you were together, married even. Did you call her *moya dusha* too?'

He dropped his eyes. 'It was nothing. She is nothing. Valentina went rogue and tried to kill you, and that I can never forgive. Moscow is not too happy either. She knows the identity of agents here and could have compromised our whole operation under interrogation. After she escaped, she contacted our handler, and was taken back to Russia to face a trial. It'll be a death sentence, one she deserves.'

'And before that, before she went rogue, did you love her?'

His tone grew bitter. 'We were married in secret, when I was a young fool, just out of Cambridge. She had been sent to pull me deeper into the organisation, to seduce me. Once she was sure I was on board, she made it clear that she didn't love me, that it was all part of the great game. Laughed in my face when I wept and clung to her like a pathetic young fool. It shames me now to think how I begged her. I was heartbroken at first, then angry, but it made me tougher. It's one of their training methods, to cut off your feelings.'

Rosie felt as if a cold hand had plunged into her chest and wrapped itself around her heart. 'That's how you got to me; you seduced me.'

'You were the reason I was sent to Crail. We knew you were there, that you were Ned's niece and had a connection with the Sinclairs, that you could get close to the son and get the plans for us. It was a risk, we didn't know if you'd go for it, so they sent me.'

'The dashing Colonel Kuznetsov. How could I resist? What a fool I've been.' The heat rose in Rosie's face. A cold wind whipped in from the Firth of Forth, but she didn't feel it. 'It was lies, all of it. You used me, and now you want to use me again, as cover no doubt, to get away. And you think I'm so gullible that I'll do anything you say.'

'Rosie, please, listen to me. It's true that I used you, but only at first. I didn't want to fall in love with you, it went against all my training, but I couldn't help myself.' He looked her in the eyes. 'My darling, you are my life, and I need you. I didn't have to come back for you. If what we had means anything to you, you have to believe me. It would have been safer to disappear and let MI6 think I was dead, but I can't live without you. I love you. Can't you see that? Rosie, it's me, Alex, it's us.'

Rosie's head felt heavy. Her shoulders slumped and she swayed. The thought of losing him again, of going through that darkness again, was too much to bear. Alex caught her and pulled her towards him. He whispered into her hair, and she nodded, leaning into him as the sky lightened over Edinburgh.

Alex wanted her to leave with him for Leith there and then, but Rosie insisted on going back to Charlotte Square first.

'I can't come with you now, it's too risky,' he said.

'I'll go alone, then. I want to say goodbye to my home, pack some things and leave a note for my mother and Ned.'

'I'll meet you on Jamaica Street Lane at five this morning. The *Bencruachan* leaves at seven so that should give us just enough time, but you'll have to be quick; we can't miss that ship. It's my only chance.'

Chapter 32

Near Holyrood, Rosie hailed a taxi that was dropping off late night partygoers and asked the driver to take her to Charlotte Square. It wasn't until she unlocked the front door and was met by a bundle of black fur that Rosie remembered about Boris. After an ecstatic greeting and a bout of ferocious tail wagging, he settled down and looked up at her as if to say, *what now?* She ran upstairs and threw some clothes into a small valise. She glanced at herself in the mirror and pulled her fingers through her hair and took a deep breath to steady her nerves. What she was about to do was the hardest thing she'd ever done; she was about to betray Alex, the only man she had ever truly loved.

'Stand firm; this is your chance to redeem yourself,' she said to her reflection. Grabbing the valise, she ran downstairs, scribbled a note and left it on Ned's desk. She picked up the phone in his study and dialled a number. 'That's right, the *Bencruachan*, Victoria Dock at seven this morning.' Outside, it was still dark – the sun wouldn't be up for another hour – but Jamaica Street Lane wasn't far. When she got there, she couldn't see Alex, and for a moment she wondered if he'd guessed her plan. Headlights flashed and she made her way over to a Morris Minor that had been hidden in the shadows. From inside, Alex opened the passenger door for her, and she climbed in.

He grinned. 'Bit of a comedown from the Sunbeam, but it's inconspicuous.' Rosie nodded, unable to return his smile. 'I know it's a wrench leaving your family and home, but you'll see, once we're on the water you'll feel different.'

As the car rumbled over the cobbles, Rosie looked out of the window at the Georgian terraces and their secretive, locked gardens and wondered what it would be like to never see Edinburgh again. The car turned into Leith Walk, leaving the New Town behind as they moved down towards the sea. When they neared the shore, the air grew thick with harbour smells. Alex turned to look at her and put his hand on the back of her neck.

'I knew you'd come. I'm glad.' A horn blast made him take his arm away and he turned the car, parking it on the side of a dock. A freight ship loomed over them. As she got out of the car, Rosie glanced behind her, but they were alone on the dock. The ship's horn sounded again, and she followed Alex to the gangway. In the east, the sun was casting a blood-red path on the waves.

Rosie grabbed his sleeve. 'What's the rush? I thought you said it was leaving at seven.'

'Did I? No, it's leaving now.'

Alex would never get a detail like that wrong. She glanced up at the ship and read the white letters painted on its side.

'This is the *Bencleuch*. You said the *Bencrucchan*. This is the wrong ship, Alex.'

'No, it's the right one. Come on, we'd better be quick, they're getting ready to leave.' Rosie looked around and saw men untying the dock lines. She placed her hand on the gangway rail, slick and salty with condensed seawater but stopped short. Alex was halfway to the deck when he sensed she wasn't behind him. He turned and saw her standing on the wharf. The ship's horn tore through the air; he ran back down to Rosie.

'What is it? What's wrong?'

'I can't, Alex. I can't spend my life waiting for you, and never knowing if this is the night when you'll be caught, when you won't ever be coming home to me.'

'It's the chance I've always taken. You don't need to worry about me. Rosie, we've been over this; the time for talking has gone.'

Rosie shook her head and took a step back. 'No, no. I can't live a life made of lies, hiding, running, not knowing who to trust, wondering if people are who they say they are. I'm not like you.' She straightened her shoulders. 'I love my country. I can't betray everything I believe in and everyone I know.'

In the distance sirens cut through the air and Rosie looked over her shoulder, but the noise faded again.

Alex gripped her by the arms. 'You betrayed me. I didn't think you would, but I don't hold it against you; I know what you went through in the war, how it's hard for you to see clearly. But this country's over, it's not what you fought for. It's rotten here, honest workers are exploited to line the pockets of the rich, women are treated as second-class citizens. Rosie, listen to me, there's still time to change your mind. I told you the wrong departure details out of force of habit. MI6 will be headed to Victoria Dock and the wrong ship in the next hour; this is Western Harbour. We still have time to get away.'

Rosie shook her head and stepped away from him. 'If I went away with you, I could never live with myself. Goodbye, Alex.' She turned away to hide her tears. The ship's horn blasted again, and a crewman shouted down from the deck at them. Alex waved at him. He put his arms around her and held her tight into him, whispering *I love you*. When Rosie turned around, he was gone, and the gangway was being taken away. She waited for Alex to appear on deck as the mooring lines were cleared but there was no sign of him. As the ship began to move away, she sank onto a bollard and hugged herself to try to ease the sandbag of grief on her shoulders, her tears as salty as the haar drifting in from the sea. All the strength she'd summoned to tell him she wouldn't be going with him drained out of her. Alex had been her one great love and she'd thrown away her last chance to be with him. The rest of her life stretched before her: an empty road leading nowhere. The seagulls overhead seemed to mock her, and she thought miserably *what difference would it have made for one woman to have left Scotland, turned a blind eye to what her lover had done?* She covered her ears to block out the seagulls' din. She stayed like that for a while, until an insistent sound penetrated her hands and grew louder: police sirens. The sound abruptly cut off as engines were killed and doors slammed. Shouted orders rang through the air *Spread out! Spread out! Find him!* Rosie stayed where she was, gazing out to sea and willing the ship on the horizon to disappear. *She's here, sir, the Anderson woman.* Hands grabbed her by the arms, dragged her off the bollard, and cuffed her. She kept her eyes on the ground as they pushed her towards an unmarked car. Monty was leaning against it, smoking a cigarette. He signalled the policemen to uncuff her and leave.

'I thought you'd have more sense than to give me duff intel,' he said and threw the cigarette butt on the ground. Rosie lifted her head and stared at him wordlessly. 'I don't have time for this. Where's Kuznetsov?'

'He's gone. He tricked me.'

'I'm finding that hard to believe.'

'I don't care what you believe. I tried to do the right

thing, but he must have smelled a rat and given me the wrong details.'

Monty looked at her for a long moment. Rosie didn't flinch.

'I must say, I was surprised Alex was stupid enough to contact you before he left Scotland.' He lit another cigarette and squinted at her through the smoke. 'He took a hell of a risk to come and see you again, you've obviously got under his skin. No wonder Valentina was spitting blood in Crail. I'd have had you watched if I'd known Alex was still alive, known that he would come back see you. What was it? One last tumble to remember him by, or did he want to recruit you for the KGB?' He studied her face, and she tried to keep it expressionless, suddenly afraid of this man she had once thought so affable and harmless. 'Perhaps you're working for them now. God knows, you've already done enough harm, proved yourself an expert little liar as well as a trollop. The French had the right idea – if it was up to me your head would be shaved and you'd be paraded in the streets. This was our last chance to get the White Raven.'

Rosie looked out to sea. 'I tried to help you, but he outsmarted us all.'

Monty opened the car door. 'Don't think you're off the hook. We'll continue this conversation at the police station.'

Chapter 33

The interrogation went on for hours. Rosie didn't know for how long or whether it was night or day. Monty was relentless, his questions like hammer blows. He wanted to know everything that Alex had told her, where he was going, and what he planned to do next. Was she a KGB agent now? Had anyone else approached her? Who was her handler? And on, and on. Monty, his shirt sleeves rolled up above his elbows, leaning over her, his face inches from hers, like a different man from the one she'd known at Crail. At least Alex had been himself. He had lied to her at first, to get her on board, but she now knew that his feelings for her were not playacting, that what they had had together was real. It helped her stay strong as Monty became more and more aggressive, threatening her with prison, or worse.

'Treason is a capital offence. And, if you think about it, your actions could have endangered the lives of countless submariners, even civilians. If the Soviets had got hold of the blueprints for a nuclear armed sub, we would be toast, all because you couldn't keep your legs closed.'

Rosie was too weary to be outraged. 'I've told you time and again that I never gave Alex any information. I got rid of the film in the sea.'

'But you did worm your way into the Sinclairs' pile, sneaked into the safe and took pictures. Alistair Baird told us everything. He's on our side now, too, even gave up his pretty boy Fairweather, who will be tried not only as a spy but for the crime of homosexuality. You can't trust any of them.'

'Not even you.'

'Oh, especially not me. I'm one of the best in the secret service, could give that phoney James Bond a run for his money any day.' He sat down opposite her and played with a packet of cigarettes, turning it over and over. 'You know, of course, that it's not just you who is in hot water over this unfortunate affair?'

The sweat running down Rosie's spine went cold. 'What do you mean?'

'Well, there's your uncle. Ned's career will be finished once this gets out. Harbouring a Soviet spy in his own home, in his own family?' He tutted.

'But you were all taken in by Alex.'

He shrugged. 'Doesn't matter, still looks bad for Ned. Questions are already being asked about shielding his old friend, Jack Petrie, a deserter. I believe the military trial is not going well. I might even have a word in the judge's ear; we went to the same school.'

Rosie sat up straight. 'Ned had nothing to do with any of this. He didn't know Alex was working for the Soviets; he'd known him since the war, trusted him implicitly, so did Churchill.'

'The fact remains that you knew about Alex, yet you didn't inform the authorities, not until it was too late, and with the wrong information.'

'No, you're twisting everything!' She banged her fists on the metal table and glared at Monty who only raised his eyebrows. Rosie's head dropped onto her arms. It was no use; he would never let her go. Her life was over. She didn't hear Monty leave the room until the door closed behind him. Tiredness took hold of her, and she tried to shut out the thoughts crowding her mind. Even if he was bluffing about Ned, if she were to be hanged for treason, what would it do to him and her mother? The room grew colder and still no one came. No doubt Monty was leaving her to stew about all the threats he'd made. Isn't that what interrogators did, let your worst fears play on your mind? She would think about something else, about her latest painting, about trying to capture the light on the sea at Crail, the way it shone through a wave as it was about to break. No, not that. She couldn't think about the place that was filled with memories of Alex. Rosie raked her fingers through her hair and stared at the obscenities scratched on the metal table, trying to empty her mind and concentrate on any patterns she could see. The lock turned and someone came into the room. She braced herself for another onslaught and jumped when a hand landed on her shoulder.

'Rosie, it's all right, it's me, Jim.' She spun round to see her friend's kind face creased with concern. 'Come on, I'm getting you out of here.'

Chapter 34

Jim drove her to Charlotte Square and insisted on taking her arm to get up the front stairs. Rosie tried to bat him away but clung to the railings when she realised her legs weren't working as they should.

'Darn it, I've never met such an ornery woman in all my days,' he said, as he helped her to the front door. It was opened by a flustered Mrs Jackson and an excited Boris who jumped up and pawed at Rosie's front, but she was too weary to make a fuss over him.

'There you are! I was worried when I let myself in this morning and the dug was on its own, following me from room to room, whining and carrying on worse than a bairn. And then I couldn't find you in your bedroom or anywhere in the house. You've had me worried sick.'

Jim kneeled and tousled Boris's ears to be met with a growl and a baring of teeth. Instead of backing away he offered the back of his hand for Boris to sniff. 'Good boy, don't you remember your old pal? What about all the times

I've thrown a stick for you when we've been out for walks with Rosie?' The dog's ears perked up at his favourite two words and he put his head down and shuffled nearer to Jim, who laughed. 'That's better. Now, go to your bed.' Rosie and Mrs Jackson looked on in amazement as the dog trotted off obediently towards the kitchen.

'I don't know how you did that,' Rosie said. 'He's the most unbiddable creature. He usually only listens to Ned, and then not always.'

'I grew up with American foxhounds, good hunting dogs, friendly and easy going, but stubborn and strong-willed. Just when you think they're behaving, they scent a squirrel or a possum and are off like a shot. Boris is a piece of cake in comparison.' He saw Rosie swaying, caught her and lifted her to carry her up the stairs.

Rosie scrabbled back onto her feet. 'Honestly, Jim, this is not *Gone with the Wind*, and I'm no Scarlett O'Hara.'

He grinned at her. 'Scarlett wouldn't be caught dead in trousers and a raggedy old fisherman's jersey. If you won't let me help you, will you at least allow Mrs Jackson to see you safely to your bed? I'll wait for you down here until you're rested and sample some of Ned's excellent Scotch. We need to talk about what happened today.'

When Rosie woke, it was dark outside, and a branch was being hurled against her window by an unseasonable squall. She listened to the rain and the wind and wondered if Alex's ship had met the storm at sea, if it had safely docked at Rotterdam. In her mind's eye she saw him slip down the gangplank, his cap low over his eyes, and disappear in a crowd. She saw him make his way to the railway station where he could catch a train that would take him on his way south. Rosie knew he was all right, that he'd evaded capture, otherwise Monty wouldn't have held her so long and persisted with all those questions. They couldn't catch the White Raven; they never would, he was too clever for them, braver than anyone she knew and more determined. She no longer believed in his cause but she did know he was sincere, that in his eyes he was fighting for equality and peace. It was true what Monty had said: he had lied and manipulated his way into the highest reaches of the British intelligence service, even convincing Ned, who was nobody's fool, and drawing her into his dark world. But she also now knew that he loved her.

Rosie stretched her limbs. The desk sergeant had signed her out without a word, and only now did it sink in that she had been spared a horrible fate. She'd have a long soak in the bath, wash the stink of the interrogation room out of her hair, put on clean clothes. The bath did the trick; the hot water was soothing, and when she wiped the condensation off the bathroom mirror, the grey, pinched face she'd seen earlier that day was now a healthier colour. By the time she came downstairs she was feeling strong enough to talk to Jim and answer his questions. After all, he was the military, and no doubt wouldn't look kindly on her helping America's sworn enemies, even if she had been tricked into it.

He was sitting with Boris's head on his lap, reading one of Ned's books and smiled up at her. 'I took the liberty of lighting the fire. I thought you might need it.' Rosie sat down on the sofa opposite him and patted the seat next to her for Boris to come over. The dog only closed his eyes and sighed from his perch next to Jim. 'It's my southern charm, either that or Mrs Jackson's shortbread that I've been feeding him.'

Rosie grabbed a cushion instead and hugged it. 'How did you get me out?'

'Let me get you a Scotch first, it'll do you good.'

'No, no whisky. I want to know what you said. Monty was going to feed me to the wolves before you turned up. How did you know I was there?'

Jim leaned forward, elbows on his knees, and this time Boris shifted with a sigh. 'I work for the American government.'

'Yes, I know, you're in the American Air Force.'

'Yes, but I'm also an intelligence officer.'

Rosie rubbed her forehead. 'You mean you're another bloody spy.'

'No, I work in intelligence, there's a difference. I don't go around pretending to be someone I'm not. I keep an eye on things here, make sure Britain isn't harbouring another

Kim Philby. My guys were beyond furious when that all blew up, following the fiasco of the Manhattan Project being leaked to the Reds. Bottom line, we don't trust the Brits to keep our nuclear secrets safe, and on the evidence of this latest debacle, we're right. I threw the book at Monty, pulled rank on him. We call the shots in the so-called Special Relationship. What is it the French say? *En amour, il y a toujours celui qui donne les baisers et celui qui tend la joue*, that there's always one who loves and the one who is loved in any affair. We're the latter by a long way.'

He sat back and stroked the dog's ears, and Boris settled back down with a sigh. 'I've been tracking Alex for the last couple of years. I have a high-level informant in the KGB who would like to spend his retirement sunning his ample form on Palm Beach instead of freezing in a dacha in the outer reaches of the Soviet empire. He has an expensive mistress who is desperate for the trappings of capitalism, and I traded safe passage to Florida and all the Cuba Libres he can drink for information on Alex's mission, which incidentally he called Ring of Roses in your honour; isn't that just darling?'

Rosie felt a pain in her side and had to take a deep breath. 'You still haven't told me what you said to Monty, how you got me out of there.'

'I told him the truth. That you were no threat to security. I confirmed you'd thrown the film with the blueprints into the sea at Crovie, that you met Alex on Arthur's Seat.'

'How did you know all that?'

'I had you followed, from the moment you met him. Gabriel Paxton was seconded to my team. I sent him to look after you and report back to me.'

Rosie stared into the fire and let her hands dangle between her knees. Another person who wasn't who he said he was. 'I thought Gabriel was my friend.'

'He is. He kept you safe.'

'I still don't understand how you know I threw the film into the sea. It's a tiny place and I didn't see Gabriel there; he's not exactly hard to miss.'

'Remember the fisherman sitting at the other end of the bay? One of our best men. He's a former actor, learned to disguise himself as anyone – even a loud-mouthed queen.'

'The one who talked to me on the way to see Alex on Arthur's Seat?'

'He was one of a chain of people who kept an eye on you. The next intel I got was a call from my opposite number in MI6 telling me the White Raven was about to be arrested as he boarded the *Bencruachan* on Victoria Dock. But my man had already followed you to Western Harbour and watched Alex get on the *Bencleuch*.'

'You let him go. You could have stopped him, why didn't you?'

'We know his plans now. Franco's no friend of ours, and Alex is his problem now. Besides, we have people in the underground movement in Madrid. They'll keep me informed.'

'You told Monty all this?'

Jim grimaced. 'No, I wouldn't trust him to stay off Alex's tail; he's got a real bee in his bonnet about him. I read the riot act, told Monty I'd never seen such incompetence, trying to pin everything on a woman whose only crime was being taken in by the KGB's best agent, that Ned Raeside would hear of his bungling and would not be best pleased that his niece was being bullied and threatened. Englishmen like Monty may boast about having a stiff upper lip, but they hate to be embarrassed, and like all bullies, he backed down pretty quick.' Jim's voice softened. 'I'd have dragged him in front of the head honcho at 54 Broadway if he'd laid so much as a finger on you.'

'And Alex? Will he be safe now?'

Jim shook his head. 'After everything he's done, all the lies he's told you, you still want to know if he's safe?'

'There's another French saying, from George Sand I believe, *Il n'y a qu'un bonheur dans la vie, c'est d'aimer et d'être aimé.* There is only one happiness in life, and that is to love and to be loved.'

'And look where that got poor old George Sand, stuck on a damp island she hated looking after a sickly Chopin. Just another doomed relationship.'

Rosie waited.

'Yes, Alex will be safe, as long as he never comes back to Britain.'

'I still don't understand why you stuck your neck out to save me.' A log fell with a crack in the fire. Jim looked at Rosie.

'Don't you?'

Chapter 35

Rosie was working on a portrait of her mother when Ned came back from Glasgow. She pulled him into the studio and sat down with him on the threadbare chaise longue where she posed models. He sat with his hands between his knees for a while before looking up at her with tears in his eyes.

Rosie's hand flew to her mouth. 'You lost the case. Poor Mother, she must be heartbroken.'

'No, we won, if you can call it that.'

'But that's wonderful news! Tell me what happened, and don't leave anything out.'

'Jack pled guilty. The judge was a dry old stick and had been badly wounded in the first war. He'd lost four brothers at the Somme, so I knew he wouldn't look kindly on Jack, no matter how much I argued that he'd had amnesia when he was found and couldn't tell anyone who he was or where he was. When I said he'd suffered from shell shock, do you know what he said? *Who didn't? An officer pulls himself together and carries on for the sake of his men.'*

Rosie shook her head. 'You'd think he'd have more fellow feeling.'

'It gets worse. The prosecution brought up the death of a young private who was killed bringing what he thought was Jack's body back from No Man's Land. His family were in the gallery and Jack kept turning round to look at them. At one point he actually cried out *I'm so sorry* when a relative started sobbing into her handkerchief. The judge banged his gavel at that, I can tell you. Turned an interesting shade of puce.'

'Jack was badly wounded and lost his memory, surely that's not a crime?'

Ned was grim. 'Desertion is a crime and he's lucky he didn't get caught during the war as he'd have been executed after only the most cursory court martial. Luckily the death penalty for desertion was abolished in 1930, but Jack was still looking at a stretch in prison. The worst moment was when the prosecution called Jack to the witness box and asked him how his dog tags and jacket came to be on the mutilated body that was brought back by his men.'

'Poor Jack, he must have been terrified.'

'I've never seen him calmer. You must remember he's carried this weight of guilt for more than forty years. He was finally able to make a clean breast of it, and he did. Jack looked straight at the private's family and said he saw his men's faces every night and often talked to them, asking their forgiveness for leaving them.'

'Oh no, after that I'd have thought the judge would come down on him like a ton of bricks.'

'You'd think so, but Jack's honesty and his contrition got to him. The army hates people who lie and try to worm their way out of trouble. They'll forgive the most heinous mistake if a man owns up to it. But Jack wasn't out of the woods yet.' He leaned back against the wall and tucked his thumbs into his waistcoat, savouring the moment.

'Come on, you old show off, what did you do?'

'I pulled the plumpest rabbit out of my hat. You see, the army also hates its records being mucked about. Once you're recorded dead in law, you're dead, and Jack's dog tags on the body meant he was dead in the army and the law's eyes. Even though the prosecutor argued the fake death was part of the desertion, as Jack was presumed dead, he was not recorded as a deserter. I also argued in mitigation that Jack had until then a sterling war record, he'd risked his life over and again to save his men and been awarded the Victoria Cross. The day in question, he'd volunteered to go out to scope out the enemy position to spare any of his men being killed. I based my plea for mitigation on the fact he handed himself in.'

'And that was enough to convince the court?'

'Not quite. I called as a witness, the brother of the private who had been killed rescuing what was thought to be Jack's body. He told the court his family held no grudge against Jack, that his brother Charlie had written home saying the lads had the best officer in the British Army, that Jack had done everything in his power to keep them safe, and had put the youngest men, like him at the back when they were going over the top. He'd also thrown himself over Charlie and another soldier when a grenade was lobbed into the trench. His testimony clinched it for Jack. He was admonished and spared a penal sentence.'

'So, is Jack home?'

'Yes, with your mother, who is like a young girl again. I haven't seen her so carefree in years. She's even taken to singing, more's the pity. They are sickeningly happy.' But Ned was smiling as he said this.

A thought occurred to Rosie. 'But what about the press? Was Frank there?'

'He was.'

'Oh no, he'll ruin your reputation, and Mother's, and Jack will be in disgrace.'

'Not at all. Charlie's brother's testimony killed the negative story, turned Jack from a coward to a hero. And as for him ruining my reputation for, in his words, harbouring a deserter, that didn't even come up. You should have seen Galbraith's face when we left the court; he was glaring at us like a cat who has caught a bird that has been taken away from it.'

'What if he still writes the story?'

'I tipped off a reporter from the rival paper and Jack gave him an interview. I also lined up Charlie's family who had nothing but praise for Jack. The brother who stood up in court was at Ypres and knows only too well what it was like in the trenches. Jack will be shown in a good light. And if Galbraith tries to put a stain on my reputation in print, I told him I won't hesitate to sue.'

'Jack must be so relieved.'

'Actually, I don't think he is. He wanted to be punished. You should have seen his anguish when he was talking to Charlie's brother after the trial. I'm helping him set up a charitable trust in the boy's name, to award scholarships to help the children of war veterans and their families and set up a place where injured soldiers can go to recover.'

'So, he'll stay in Scotland, working on that?'

'No, I'm sorry, Rosie, they've both decided to move to France. Your mother wants to meet Jack's children, and I can think of no more perfect setting for Lily than a hilltop village in Provence.'

Ned put a gentle hand on her shoulder and Rosie buried her head in his chest. The smell of sandalwood and Turkish cigarettes took her back to being six, when Ned had taken her on his knee and asked her if she wanted to live in a big house in Edinburgh with him and her mother. He'd been her anchor since then, helping fill the gap left by the death of her father.

'France isn't so far away,' he said. 'Once they're settled, we'll motor down to Calais and take the ferry over. Alfa Romeo have a new sports car, a Giulietta Spider, just the ticket for sauntering through country roads with the sun in our faces. It'll take your mind off poor old Alex. I know he turned out to be a bad 'un, but I was fond of him nonetheless.'

'About that. You're not the only one who has a story to tell.'

'Let's go and see Lily and Jack first. I've put some bubbly on ice to toast the love birds. You can tell us all what's been happening while we've been away.'

Chapter 36

It was August and the Festival was in full swing, the perfect time for opening night at the Phoenix. Missing Edinburgh and his theatre, Jim had resigned his commission and as soon as he was back from the States, had thrown himself into giving the old girl a new lease of life. All that summer he'd been overseeing the work, auditioning actors for his repertory company and directing rehearsals in a church hall across the road while the theatre was being readied. With school over, Rosie had been helping Jim, painting flats and designing costumes, just as she had at Crail. Coming home at night, she was so exhausted she barely had the energy for a bath to wash off the dust, but the hard physical work, the mental absorption and being surrounded by hammering and sawing and attending read throughs with a bunch of cheerful actors helped her push Alex to the back of her mind. That is, until she got into bed, when Boris would push open her door with his nose and jump up to lick the tears from her face.

Now, finally, the theatre was ready, and it was first night. The actors fizzing with nerves behind the stage, and the front of house packed and humming with chatter. Rosie spotted Jim doing the rounds and when he looked up, she waved. He came over with the stage manager, a capable young woman from the Western Isles whose soft, lilting accent belied a steely determination to Get Things Done and Bang Heads Together. When Jim had returned, Rosie feared being around him might be awkward, but he had fallen hard for Catriona Munro, who had listened to him pour his heart out about Rosie for a while before taking his head in her hands and kissing him so efficiently and telling him to *wheesht, man* that he now only had eyes for his Highland lass. Catriona had also been shrewd enough to befriend Rosie, smoothing the way for Jim and her to be close friends once more. Pushing her way through the crowd, she reached Rosie and kissed her on both cheeks. When Rosie looked surprised, Catriona laughed.

'I know, not very Scottish of me, but everyone does it in the theatre, and everyone calls you darling; I love it!'

'That's only because actors can never remember anyone's name,' Jim said, coming up to the women and greeting Rosie with two extravagant kisses.

Rosie squeezed his arm. 'Are you nervous?'

'As a kitten.'

'What about you, Catriona?'

'Och, no. Everything's under control, I made sure of that.'

Jim enveloped her in a bear hug. 'My little tyrant. What would I do without you?' Catriona pushed him away but the blush in her pale skin betrayed how tickled she was by his show of affection. The bell rang for people to take their seats and Jim rushed off without saying goodbye, but Catriona took her time.

'Are you all right?' she asked Rosie.

'Yes. Well, I'm getting there, I think.'

Catriona gave her a hug. 'You're strong, you'll be fine.'

'I hope so.'

'Aye, you will.' The bell rang again, and Catriona looked towards the curtain, which twitched as Jim's head peered out. 'I'd better go and sort him out before he climbs those curtains.'

The play was well written and thought provoking and the players were given a rapturous standing ovation. Afterwards in the crush bar, Jim and the actors were surrounded by well-wishers. Rosie stood for a moment on her own, suddenly feeling lonely and wishing Margot had been able to get away from the children.

'Well, don't you brush up nicely.'

Rosie whirled round to see Gabriel Paxton. He winked at her almost imperceptibly and took her arm. 'I'm going to steal you away from this rabble and have a nice long gossip.'

'Gabriel! I haven't seen you since Crail. I hear you were well named – my guardian angel.'

'That's what I wanted to talk to you about.'

But just then Lily rushed over. 'Guess who's here? All the way from Hollywood!' She moved aside and there was Stella, swathed in white Siberian fox fur. With her dark eyes and hair and powder-pale skin, bare shoulders and diamonds, she looked every inch the film star.

Stella flung open her arms. 'Darling! I thought I'd nip back across the pond to see you.' Clutching Rosie in a scented embrace, she whispered: 'And that sweet Jim paid for us to fly back first-class. He wanted to show off his theatre to me, as long as I promised to bring along my new beau and get him to star in the next production.' She beckoned to an extraordinarily good-looking young man who was standing at the bar trying to order drinks.

'Troy, darling, come over here. I want you to meet my oldest friend, Rosie.' The Californian Adonis, in an open-neck white shirt that displayed an even, caramel tan and a muscular but slender physique, sauntered over and flashed blue eyes and a sleepy, sexy, blindingly white smile at Rosie. For a moment she thought she knew him, then remembered the last time she'd seen his perfect features, on a billboard advertising a film in which he played the troubled romantic lead. With a flick of his angelic eyes, he dismissed Rosie and gazed at Gabriel, murmuring *Pleased to meet you.*

Gabriel took his hand and held it a shade too long. 'The pleasure is all mine; I can assure you.'

Stella took a firm grip of Troy's arm as if he were about to escape at any minute and turned to Rosie. 'I want you to be the first to know, darling, we're going to be married, aren't we, my sweet?' Stella went to kiss him, but Troy turned his head, so her lips only grazed his cheek, leaving a scarlet imprint. The age difference between them was so marked that Rosie was left speechless.

Gabriel put his arm around Troy's shoulder. 'Shall we rustle up some fizz while the girls catch up?' Stella watched them walk away, her mouth set. But when she turned back to Rosie her stage face was back on, her eyes sparkling and wearing a smile that had once melted hearts in theatres all over Europe.

'Isn't Troy an absolute doll?' Rosie could only smile and was about to congratulate her friend – what else could she do? – when Jeanie came bustling over and grabbed her daughter by the elbow.

'What are you playing at, carrying on with a boy half your age?'

Stella shook her off. 'You can talk. I've had to dry the tears of plenty of stagehands and sparkies when you were in your prime. You're just jealous because you're past it.' Jeanie put her hands on her hips and Rosie took a step backward. She knew that stance all too well. She drew in her breath, waiting for the outburst, but Jeanie only narrowed her eyes.

'That laddie isnae interested in an auld hoofer like you, no matter how many layers of muck you wear, or how many operations you have to lift your face.'

'How dare you! I've never been near a plastic surgeon. I'm following a special diet by LA's leading nutritionist.'

'Are you, aye?' Jeanie scoffed. 'Well, he's awfie handy with a scalpel, that's all I can say.'

Stella dropped her head and hissed, 'If you must know I went to the same man who did Marilyn Monroe's nose and chin; he's the best in Hollywood. But lower your voice, Mother, I have a reputation you know.'

Jeanie rolled her eyes at Rosie, who didn't dare return her look; she knew better than to get embroiled in a spat between these two.

'I don't even want to think about how much that cost,' Jeanie said. 'Or how you could afford it. If you're such a big cheese, how come you've hightailed it back to Scotland so soon? Bit trickier out there, I suppose, with all the young competition, even with plastic surgery. And that one.' She tilted her chin at Troy, deep in conversation with Jim and Gabriel, who was resting his hand lightly on the small of the American actor's back. 'He plays for the other team, definitely.' Lily put a restraining hand on Jeanie's arm, but she carried on while Stella glared at her. 'And you know it fine well. You've been around enough dancers and actors all your bloody life.'

'I'm not listening to this rubbish for a second longer,'

Stella said and gathered up her fur coat and turned on her heel. 'Troy! We're leaving!'

Rosie saw Jim press his card into the young man's hand as he turned towards Stella. 'I'll drop the script off at the North British Hotel and call you tomorrow afternoon,' he called after him. 'The part was made for you!'

Jeanie and Stella were now facing each other like two warring cats: if they'd had tails, they would be puffed up like bottle brushes. Lily took Jeanie's arm and pulled her away and waved off Stella, who stalked away towards Troy.

Lily shook her head at her old friend. 'You know you only antagonise Stella, going at her like that. How many times have I told you? Honey catches more flies than vinegar.'

'Aye, it's all very well for you to say that, with a biddable china doll of a daughter. My lass has too much spirit, no offence by the way, Rosie hen.'

Lily, always taller than her friend, seemed to grow taller. 'Jean Margaret Taylor! You watch what you're saying. I'll not have you lashing out at Rosie. She may not go around flouncing out of rooms and shouting the odds, but she's the strongest one of us all.'

Embarrassed, Rosie looked around for escape and saw Gabriel making his way towards her. 'It's all right, Mother, I know she doesn't mean it.'

Jeanie looked contrite. 'No, I don't. I'm sorry, I shouldn't have taken it out on you. Stella always manages to get my goat.'

'You're too similar – a couple of firebrands,' Lily said.

'All right. But I'll break that cut-price James Dean's fancy American teeth if he makes a fool out of my Stella.'

'Come and say hello to Jack,' Lily said, soothingly. 'He's with Ned at the bar. We can all go out to dinner together.'

The two women made their way to the bar, arm in arm, where Ned and Jack were deep in lively conversation. Jack had been a changed man since the court martial and Rosie would be sorry to see him go to France. She didn't want to think about Lily leaving and smiled at Gabriel.

'Now, I really must insist on our little tête-à-tête.' He held up a bottle of champagne and two glasses. 'Look what I've snaffled for us; it's the good stuff. I know a quiet corner where we can have a nice long gossip, just like old times at the dear old JSSL.'

When they were alone in an unused dressing room, the door locked, Rosie turned to him. 'I know you're one of them.'

He raised an eyebrow. 'I've never hidden it, my dear. Everyone knows I'm queer. Apart from my mother, of course, it would kill her. She's still holding out for a big fancy wedding. I daren't let her meet you – she'd have us picking out china patterns before you could say Peter Jones.'

'No, I don't mean that. You work for intelligence, MI6, or the CIA, or MI5 – one of that lot – and you've been watching me since I went to Crail. I thought you were my friend, not a minder.'

He eyed her for a moment. 'I suppose Jim told you. But that doesn't change anything. Of course we're friends, both artists, both fiendishly fond of silly chats about nothing, how could I not adore you?' But Rosie refused to be placated until he grew serious. 'You're right, I took on a bit of freelance work for the Americans, but I've a new client now.' He glanced at the door. 'I have news about Alex if you'd care to hear it. But you mustn't say anything, not to Jim now that he's handed in his papers, or to your uncle, and certainly not to that shark Monty. I'm taking an enormous risk telling you.'

Rosie's legs threatened to give out and she put a hand on his arm to steady herself. 'What's happened? Did he get out all right?' She searched his face. 'Or did they catch him?' When Gabriel looked away, it was as if a cloud of black flies swarmed in front of her, and she put a hand on the back of a chair to steady herself. 'Gabriel? If he's dead, I'd rather know.'

'Don't worry, he's alive.'

Rosie let out a long breath. She sat down heavily and looked up at Gabriel.

'Is he all right?'

'As rain. He's working with the Spanish Republic's government in exile in Paris. They think he's a Yugoslavian, which is quite a clever wheeze. You know how the Balkan states despise Francoist Spain. But he'll be on the move soon, assume another alias and sneak over the border from France to join the Spanish guerrillas. He's a trained commando so the separatists will welcome him with open arms. There are all sorts of anarchists among them, and they love the Reds, all that rubbish about dying on your feet rather than living on your knees.'

'Is he safe?'

'For now, but the KGB are a suspicious lot. They're still a bit miffed about their best agent not handing in a film with our nuclear sub secrets after his girlfriend got cold feet and chucked it in the sea. It took Alex all his not inconsiderable powers of persuasion to get off the hook, but one or two of the Russian top brass are still not sure about him and are pushing for a shot in the back of his handsome head.' Rosie shuddered and Gabriel smiled at her.

Rosie was suddenly filled with fury. 'I'm sick of everyone spinning lies. Get to the point – what do you want from me?'

Gabriel hunkered down in front of her. 'To do your duty, by your country.'

'Here we go again. How do you think Alex hooked me in the first place?'

'Ah, but this time, you really would be working for the good guys, as the Americans put it. We want you to go out to Spain and deploy your not inconsiderable charms to get back in with Alex, and report back. The bonus for me is a nice long holiday on the Costa Brava – I'd be your handler and regular contact – and you'd get to cuddle up to your handsome rogue and get your own back on him. Think of the fun we could have together; we could share a studio; it would be excellent cover and a lark. And you'd be doing the government a huge favour. We need to keep Alex in our sights in case he wants to take care of unfinished business in Scotland and interfere with the nuclear sub programme.'

Rosie looked up sharply. 'That's progressing, then?'

'Holy Loch should be up and running in the next five years, when the Yanks' spanking new Polaris nuclear subs will be silently patrolling waters within firing range of the Soviet Union.'

'Why are you telling me all this? What happened to *loose lips sink ships*?'

'Superseded in this case by *need-to-know basis*. And you need to know because you're in it up to your neck, darling girl. I've been reporting back first to the Yanks and now to our lot that you're a valuable asset, and one we don't want to lose.'

Rosie stared at him. 'You can't be serious.'

'Deadly. And the grown-ups think you'd be just the ticket. They think you can be trusted, despite the recent debacle, which we'll put down to temporary insanity brought on by Alex's magnetic effect on women.' He lit a cigarette and regarded her through the smoke.

'I'd have to deal with that brute Monty, and I've already turned down his so-called offer.'

'I'm sorry he gave you a rough time. Those old Etonian bruisers can cut up rough, but he's had strips torn off him. You needn't worry about him anymore; he'll be kept on a tight leash. Jim sent a blistering report back to his opposite number and MI6 don't want to get on the wrong side of the Americans, not after that mess with Philby, Burgess and Maclean. Monty's team redeemed themselves by scooping up Alistair Baird, but they wouldn't have found him out if it hadn't been for you and Alex's Highland caper.'

Rosie's looked steadily at Gabriel. 'Does Jim know what you're doing?'

'Of course not, he's well out of it.'

Rosie thought about the last time she'd seen Alex, how she'd nearly run up the gangplank after him at the last moment, and what it would be like to see him again, to hear his voice, to live with him. Gabriel was watching her carefully.

'What's it to be, Rosie darling? Sun and sangria and a spot of light spying, or another winter in Edinburgh teaching schoolgirls how to draw?'

'What would I have to do?'

'Follow Alex to Spain, say you've had a change of heart, that you can't live without him, pile on the waterworks, get the violin out. Join him in his mission and report back to us.' He spread out his hands. 'Couldn't be simpler. A sweet little deal, in my view.'

'I'd be reporting to you?'

He tried to look bashful. 'My youth belies the responsibility they've put on my shoulders. But yes, I'd be your handler. There will be a secret location in Barcelona where you can send and pick up signals, and I always like a stroll along the Ramblas and a glass or two of *fino*.'

'And I'd be doing this, leaving my job and my home, for Queen and Country? I've heard that one before.'

Gabriel leaned against a dressing table strewn with make-up pots and brushes. 'If you like, or for the sheer bloody fun of it. That's why most of us do it, not for lofty ideals, even Alex, if he were honest.'

'Honesty doesn't seem to figure much in your game.'

'A much over-rated quality and quite superfluous to requirements.' He stubbed out his cigarette in an open jar of cold cream. 'Well?'

Rosie stood up. 'Are you going to threaten me if I don't? That's what Monty did. Because if you are, I'm not afraid of any of you. The worst thing that could ever happen to me already has.'

'What an idea! Rosie, it's me, your pal, Gabriel. I'm an artist like you, not one of Monty's thugs. Think of the fun we'll have – go on, say yes, for me.'

'No.'

'You won't even think about it?'

She didn't say anything, and Gabriel put up his hands. 'Well, you can't blame me for trying. I'd have loved a Spanish jaunt with you, all expenses paid, but I guess it's back to my little studio in Chelsea. Don't suppose you'd like to set up shop with me there? We could work together and even have a lavender marriage. Mother would be over the moon.'

'Gabriel . . .'

'All right, I'm leaving.' He winked at her and a moment later he'd gone. Rosie sat for a while, probing how she felt. She had turned down a second chance to be with Alex, but she knew that she had made the right decision. She opened the door and switched off the light. Along the corridor came the sound of laughter. Her family and friends were waiting for her, and she would never have to lie to any of them again.

Chapter 37

Rosie was helping her mother pack for France. They had put her favourite brushes, pencils and sketch books at the bottom of the trunk and were contemplating the pile of clothes they'd emptied out of the wardrobe onto her bed. Boris was watching them mournfully having unsuccessfully tried to get into a suitcase.

'Look at these tweeds and woollen jumpers and what about the evening dresses?' Lily said. 'I can't imagine I'll need them in France. I'll never fit it all in and Jack said not to take too much stuff, he only has a small place.'

'Leave most of it here, you know Ned will want you to come back and visit, and you'll need your heavy coats and jumpers when you and Jack come back for Christmas.'

Lily sat down next to a pile of clothes and smoothed a cashmere cardigan.

'Ned hasn't told you then?'

'Told me what?'

'He's selling the house and moving to London. Whitehall want him down there to sort out the mess Anthony Eden left behind for the new PM.'

Rosie sat down next to her mother. 'This has been my home for as long as I remember.'

'I know, darling, but with your salary from the school, you can afford a little flat, maybe somewhere in the West End, near Margot and your work?'

Rosie looked up at the corniced ceiling, at the centre rose with its chandelier. The sash window was open, and she could hear birds singing in the garden, a car rumbling over the cobbles, and in the distance the bells of St Mary's Episcopal Cathedral rang out for evensong. It felt like the end of everything.

Lily took her hand. 'I don't like to think of you alone in Edinburgh.'

'I have my work, and Margot is only round the corner, while Stella and Jeanie are only a short train ride away.'

Her mother made a face. 'Those two have been squabbling more than ever since that young man went back to Hollywood, leaving Stella in the lurch. Jeanie was never one to hold back on *I told you so*.' Lily picked up a silk scarf and folded it into a neat square. 'What about Jim?'

Rosie shook her head and smiled. 'He has Catriona. Besides, even if she weren't on the scene, we would never have worked. He's a good friend.'

'Friends are all very well, but won't you be lonely? I

know what you had with Alex was passionate and exciting, but you need a man who will support your dreams and who lets you be you. That's why I was so keen on Jim. I was never sure about your Russian. I recognised the same zeal in him your father had, and men like that are not easy to live with. They're always looking for the next adventure dressed up as a noble cause; the everydayness of family life bores them. They need the highs and lows, but they can be exhausting, especially once you have children. Alex is gone; don't waste your life mourning a dream. I did for years and I'm afraid you paid the price. I was a ghost for most of your childhood, one foot always in the past.'

'You're the best mother I could hope for, and now you have Jack, who is far too cheerful nowadays to be a ghost.'

Lily's smile was bright but there were tears in her eyes. 'It's like a miracle, that he came back to life, to me.' She put her arms around her daughter. 'I know you're strong and you don't need just any old man to come along and save you, like some wilting heroine, but I hope someday . . .'

'I'm all right. You don't have to worry about me. I'll be forty in a few years.'

Lily shook her head. 'I'm your mother. I'll always worry about you.'

* * *

After they had seen Lily and Jack off at Waverley for their train to London to catch the ferry to Calais, Rosie and Ned walked back to Charlotte Square, pushing their way through Festival crowds and Princes Street shoppers. Ned took her arm and put it through his, patting her gloved hand with his.

'I'm sorry about selling up.'

'It's your house.'

'I know, but I don't want to throw you out. What would you say to coming to London with me? I've bought a lovely place in Pimlico, handy for Westminster and Whitehall. There's room for a bedroom for you and a studio.'

'That's the second offer I've had to move to London.'

'Really? Who from? What's his name? I hope some cad isn't trying to take advantage of you being on your own.'

Rosie put her head on her uncle's shoulder. 'You're such an old pasha. Another artist, but I turned him down.'

'Hmm. So, what's it to be? Stay on at the school?'

'I don't think I'm much of a teacher, and there are so few pupils interested in art, it's far too impractical for most parents. I'm not sure I'll go back to St Leo's.'

'Well, if there's anything I can do to help.'

'I know.'

Ned stopped at a tobacco shop and Rosie waited outside

for him in the sunshine. She watched a young couple walk past, the woman heavily pregnant, laughing at something the man had said, and suddenly felt a wave of grief. She hid her eyes behind her hand.

'Are you all right, Miss Anderson?' She looked up. It was one of her pupils from St Leo's, her star pupil.

'Anne, how are you?'

'I'm very well. Would you like me to fetch you a glass of water? Woolies is just there.'

'No, I'm fine. I felt a bit dizzy, but it's passed now.' She smiled warmly at Anne. 'Tell me what you're up to now you've left school. I know your father was keen for you to study law.'

'He was but guess what? I got into art school! I start at Edinburgh College of Art next month.'

'No! That's wonderful!' Rosie took the girl's hands in hers and held her out to admire her. 'I'm not at all surprised, your portfolio was exceptional. I couldn't be more pleased.'

'It's all thanks to you, Miss, to your example, how you encouraged me and taught me to see like an artist.'

'You did it all yourself, you have a gift and I'm glad you're going to use it. I expect an invitation to your end of year show.'

'Would you really come? Where will I send it?'

'To St Leo's. I've decided I rather like being a teacher.'

When Ned came out of the tobacconist's he raised his

eyebrows. 'Glad to see you've cheered up.'

Rosie looked up at the Edinburgh skyline, at the castle and down to the North British clock tower and the Scott monument. She sighed happily. 'Let's go home. We've got a dog to walk.'

Epilogue

Present day

Rosie had been dozing on the sofa when she woke with a start. Through the picture window she could see the sun was setting over the hills dipping them in gold. On her lap was a scrapbook filled with yellowed newspaper cuttings. Here was the opening night of the Phoenix Theatre that showed a striking woman with dark hair piled on her head in white fur and with diamonds, her beauty evident despite the grainy black and white image. Next to her, a younger woman with short, fair hair was half-turned away from the camera as if looking for someone.

She closed the album, careful not to dislodge the tickets for exhibitions and the fliers for dance and theatre shows, the photographs taken at Greenham Common and CND rallies, and, decades later, at the peace camp at Faslane Naval Base. Rosie put the album under a glass-topped coffee table. A little dizzy from bending so far, she sat for a moment. After a while she reached for a small, carved wooden box inlaid with mother-of-pearl that sat on top of the coffee table. Inside there was a cutting from the *International Herald Tribune* dated July 1960 with the headline: **Prominent Yugoslav businessman killed in terrorist car bomb** next to a photograph of a mangled car and a grainy head and shoulders of a man frowning at the camera. The ink on Gabriel's writing was fading but she could still read: *Sorry, darling, but thought you'd want to know.* Underneath the cutting there was a tiny roll of film and a pebble from a beach. She put it to her nose and thought she could still detect a faint smell of the sea.

Rosie put everything back in the box and went into her studio, passing a framed poster for one of Anne Rankin's solo exhibitions. The walls of the studio were crammed with her own paintings: a few self-portraits of her as a young woman, then as she grew older and thicker around the waist. There were many portraits of a golden-haired child, as a baby and at different stages as she grew up into a slender adolescent and a radiant young woman. Rosie kissed her fingers and pressed them against one of the paintings of her daughter. She would be here soon, and Rosie would ask her about her day as head of the art department at a city school, and they would talk about the arrangements for getting to the Glasgow Girls exhibition in Kirkcudbright. It was harder to travel now with the pain in her joints. She caught sight of her reflection and for a moment didn't recognise the old woman looking back at her. She touched her face, felt the paper-thin skin, the lines from a life, a long life well lived. Rosie reached the carton where she kept her drawings and, with one last look at the Russian spy who had been her lover, she put the charcoal sketch away.

Author's Note

The inspiration for this book was a meeting with 91-year-old Moira Beaty, one of the artists known as the Glasgow Girls. She told me about her astonishing early life as a code breaker at Bletchley Park – and her love affair with a handsome and talented British linguist who spoke Russian and worked for British Intelligence in Russia. Moira's adventurous youth, sharp wits and boldness are shared by my main character, Rosie Anderson, who is also an artist and former decoder with a Russian lover, but there the similarities end; the rest is fiction.

Rosie meets Alex Kuznetsov in the peaceful fishing village of Crail, in the East Neuk of Fife, where there was a Russian language school for National Servicemen in the 1950s. The JSSL – the Cold War Joint Services School for Linguistics – put Britain's best and brightest young men through intensive training to turn out spies, translators and interrogators.

Famous graduates include writer Michael Frayn, writer

and actor Alan Bennett, dramatist Dennis Potter, the former Royal National Theatre director Sir Peter Hall, and the former governor of the Bank of England Eddie George. They were put through their paces by eccentric White Russian émigrés and Soviet defectors. The convicted Soviet spy Geoffrey Prime was also one of the 6,000 alumni from the various JSSLs. The Crail school was the last and closed in 1960 with the ending of conscription, but you can still see the abandoned buildings on the former RNAS Crail (HMS Jackdaw) camp a few miles outside the village.

The title of the book, White Raven, refers to male spies called ravens trained by the KGB to use their powers of seduction. In some cultures, white ravens are the harbingers of misfortune, while in others they are a symbol of hope, transformation and spiritual awakening. The reader can decide which interpretation has the most meaning for Rosie.

Acknowledgements

I would like to thank the people who helped me while I was writing White Raven. They include my agent Jenny Brown, and Jean Fraser and her team at Scotland Street Press. I'm also grateful for Duncan Henderson's generous military legal advice – any errors are mine. Thanks to Fiona McGrady who told me about the abandoned Russian language school outside Crail, and to Glasgow Girl artist Moira Beaty, and to her generous daughter Ann for showing me her mother's wonderful paintings and memorabilia. Thanks to Lisa Highton and Sally Magnusson for their valuable suggestions when the novel was still only an idea. And, as always, thanks to my husband Michael and son Adam.